Courage Times Three. A Novel

Brenda Brown Elliott

Copyright © 2013 Brenda Brown Elliott

All rights reserved.

ISBN-13: 9781492188964
ISBN-10: 1492188964

DEDICATION

Courage Times Three. A Novel
is
Dedicated to my loving mother
Lorraine Warren Shields.
My love, admiration and respect
Overflow for you.
Happy 82nd Birthday
Dearest Momma!

Table of Contents

Chapter One 1
Chapter Two 4
Chapter Three 11
Chapter Four 26
Chapter Five 39
Chapter Six 45
Chapter Seven 53
Chapter Eight 62
Chapter Nine 70
Chapter Ten 81
Chapter Eleven 86
Chapter Twelve 101
Chapter Thirteen 108
Chapter Fourteen 112
Chapter Fifteen 116
Chapter Sixteen 122
Chapter Seventeen 132
Chapter Eighteen 143
Chapter Nineteen 152
Chapter Twenty 160
Chapter Twenty-One... 170
Chapter Twenty-Two 173
Chapter Twenty-Three 186
Chapter Twenty-Four 202
Chapter Twenty-Five 212
Chapter Twenty-Six 222
About The Author 226

ACKNOWLEDGMENTS

I would like to acknowledge a few other people who have had a huge impact on my life, which reflects some of this novel's content.

A big thank you to my husband, Alan, for loving me regardless of my illness. Your Christianity speaks volumes and your light always shines brightly.

A special recognition for my four children, Melanie Hascall, Shantell Browning, Fame Lusti, and Tia Armstrong along with their spouses, Brian, Jeffers, Nicole, and David.

I will be celebrating the birth of my twelfth grandchild in a couple of months. Thank you for all of them.

Another big thanks to my sisters, Barb & Craig Mason, Robin & Frank Fondurulia, Rhonda & Ponch Dobak, and my niece Charity Mason.

Not to leave out my cousin Pamela Turner, friends, Patty and Ken Carter, Jim Thuringer, Madeleine and Howard Emery, Shelby and Dave Stickney and never to be forgotten, Barb and Butch Pariseau.

You have all made a difference in my life for the better and I am proud to call you family and friends.

Chapter One

Third born into a family of nine near Krakow, Poland, Valentin grew up in a poor peasant family, as most had during that era in Europe. Following WW1 Poland struggled to keep its independence. By the late 1930's Valentin had reached the age of sixteen. Germany moved her troops into southern Poland in 1939, invading homes and businesses, declaring the south of Poland German territory. Following the Nazi takeover Russian troops invaded the north, declaring it Russian soil. Word was spreading that Adolf Hitler, ruthless dictator of Germany, was forcing all Polish men to fight against Jewish friends and neighbors. Any refusal to fight resulted in eventual death most often. Germany would wreak havoc on country after country across Europe, killing anyone or anything standing in its way. Once again, millions would be deprived of their livelihood, home, food, even their very lives. Only twenty years earlier they'd had to begin rebuilding their broken lives, leaving WWI behind, four mind-boggling years of suffering lasting from 1914 – 1918. Many had never regained much economically or otherwise. In time, all would come to fear the entire destruction of mankind on earth, much to their disbelief.

Although the Baranowsky's were not of Jewish faith, Catholics, protestants and Jews lived alongside one another for quite some time in southern Poland. How often had they pulled one or the other out of a difficult situation? Sharing bread, just to sustain themselves when times were gruelingly tough was commonplace along with sharing well water and outdoor facilities between three families. Hardworking, headstrong men and women worked from morning until night, never having a moment of idle time for relaxation or pleasure. They'd shared violin music and dancing, stories of past lives, and outdoor games for the children on Sundays, just to awaken early Monday morning to begin another grueling six days of backbreaking work. This was everyday life for the poor peasants. Yet, an undiminished faith in God remained steadfast in most households. Prayer was their strongest tool.

Despite religious differences, continued kindness and generosity was the key to loving thy neighbor, which most religious teachings emphasized. It was what their Heavenly Father directed them to do above all else.

German troops forcefully marched their way into Poland. Valentin's mother insisted he leave the country to create a new life for himself in France. Perhaps, there, he would remain safe. Unbeknownst to them and countless others, a second World War lie dead ahead, a war that would alter the lives of millions throughout the world.

Dodging the Nazis in homes of families or friends, in ravines, or beneath the cover of trees, Valentin often survived for numerous days and nights without food or water. Filthy, tattered remnants of clothing hung limply upon his torso. Valentin had often known the pains and pangs of hunger in his lifetime, however, endless weeks of grueling physical punishment through unmanned mountainous terrain, forced him to search desperately deep, enabling him to continue onward. Satan's temptations overwhelmed him at times, driving him unceasingly to giving up, to end it all, until hearing his dear mother's voice encouraging him to push onward. Depending on nothing more than the Lord's good grace, he thankfully acknowledged God's directions, guiding him to his destination in France. Forging his way through Czechoslovakia, Austria and Switzerland, over several weeks' time, he, at last, reached Strasbourg, seated on the northeastern border of France.

Not a single soul could envision the brutality Hitler would inflict upon millions. A cold-blooded persecutor, he ruled an army of merciless, malicious men with an iron fist. Years of suffering, throughout the world, would pass before final defeat.

Europe was at war for the second time in a few short decades. Valentin narrowly escaped death, time and again, until ultimately reaching his destiny in France. This is when and where he would adopt an entire new identity, perhaps never returning to his humble beginnings. How long would the revolting war continue? Would he ever learn of his family's fate? He could only pray God would grant him that pleasure once again.

Taking some time to locate the residence of a shirt-tail relative, Valentin eventually and quite accidentally came upon their home. There, he remained hidden underground for nearly two years along with a few Jewish boys.

The beginning of WWII marked a time in European history that would live on in infamy. The phony war of 1939 ended with the German army sweeping through Belgium. British and French armies were isolated at Dunkirk – on the shores of the Baltic Sea, where they were rescued in the famous evacuation off the beaches. Millions of refugees from the Nord/Pas-de-Calais fled south, fearing a repetition of the brutal German occupation of the 1914 - 18 War.

So long as the war continued, German powers intended to use French resources and manpower to gain a victory. It was at this time Valentin made the difficult choice to emerge from hiding, fighting for France. Germany must be stopped at all costs.

In the long term, Germany planned to use France as the market garden and playground of Europe. As the Nazi's launch pad for attacking Britain, north France was littered with military bases, airfields and later rocket launch pads. Meanwhile over a third of French production was forcibly given to Germany, paid for by taxes on the French as *"occupation costs"*. Using fake documents, Valentin was able to pass as a French citizen, wearing his uniform with dignity and pride, fearlessly fighting with the resistance groups. His new identity became Valentin Augustus DuBois.

Next to follow would be the renowned French Resistance. Charles de Gaulle issued a *"call to arms"* to loyal Frenchmen from London: "France has lost the battle, but France has not lost the war," words that echoed throughout western Europe. Resistance Fighters published a secret newsletter named the "Voix du Nord", later becoming the region's leading newspaper, with offices in the Grand Place in Lille. This is where Valentin would first set eyes on the beautiful, charming and mysterious Lilly May DeMornais.

Chapter Two

Born into an affluent family, residing near the city of Reims, Lilly had lived a life of privilege, with a renowned figure of a father owning vast acreage filled with France's finest vineyards.

Much like Valentin, she emerged from hiding underground to work in the highly secret newsletter office. At the tender and fragile age of 16, she feared little more than her capture and persecution by the Nazis. With a German mother, of Jewish faith, and a French, Catholic father, she lived in constant fear of being discovered. The Gestapo would stop at nothing to see her life mercilessly ended along with the persecution of others, like her own mother. Yet, her obligatory duty to furnish crucial information to her fellow Frenchmen overrode her fears.

Valentin's friendship with Lilly proved to be a treasured reward. Not only was she educating him in ways and traditions of France and its history, she was providing him the pleasurable company of her beauty and kindly attention.

Over two years of living Hell passed while in hiding. Valentin had grown from a boy into an extremely handsome man. Lilly, as well, had blossomed from a young teen-aged girl into a fully developed woman, albeit a very thin woman. The war had taken its toll on all, still, the courageous youngsters had the stamina and perseverance to push forward. It was apparent, from early on, Lilly had eyes for Valentin just as he had for her.

As a Resistance Fighter, Valentin, along with a handful of others, was assigned guard duty over the area immediately surrounding the underground newspaper. One of his duties was to escort couriers from the edge of the city, surreptitiously guiding them to the offices where up-to-date knowledge of the Allies was revealed. It was of dire importance for correspondence to be delivered, keeping them abreast of the current situation near the border. Resistance groups were actively sabotaging the German war effort, continually feeding information to the Allies.

With family so often in the forefront of his mind, Valentin experienced frequent heartache. Were his parents and siblings still alive, he wondered? Should he have stayed to protect his own family instead of fighting for France? Could he have done anything different to prevent his younger brother's death? Regardless of how many times he questioned himself, the fact remained. He couldn't change the past. He absolutely must look ahead to the future.

The city of Lille was often the recipient of numerous bombing raids by the Allies. The Germans had entirely taken over the city, using it to reach Great Britain with their bombing raids. Lilly and Valentin could not have been in more dangerous territory. Valentin remained within close proximity of the Voix-du-Nord newspaper office, keeping a constant vigil over the headquarters. While in eminent danger of incoming bombs, engaging thoughts of the courageous young woman frequently captured his thoughts. Most often their communications were of a business nature. Yet, from time to time, they would speak on a more personal level.

Lilly graciously began teaching Valentin to speak fluent French. At times, they'd exchange words about their respective families. Lilly would listen, with an open heart, to Valentin's boyhood times with siblings, parents and neighbors. It pleased her to know he had dear friends of the Jewish religion.

She couldn't imagine living her young life as a poor peasant, much as Valentin had. Appreciation for all she had been provided, in her younger years, was growing immeasurably throughout her time underground.

Longingly sharing her own childhood memories, Valentin listened intently to her loving descriptions of the home she had been raised in. Lilly had a flare for describing the exact scenario when speaking of those times. How people looked, what places looked like, even the scents and aromas that wafted through the air. Valentin's attention couldn't possibly have been distracted while she spoke of her life.

Their individual lifestyles stretched from one end of the spectrum to the other. A Polish peasant boy and a highly privileged

French girl. Regardless of their social status', they'd both been raised with much love. They understood the true meaning of family. Lilly had often yearned for a sibling, but her mother was unable to conceive again due to complications in Lilly's delivery. Hence, they showered unlimited love and attention on their only child.

Lilly was born in 1925 in Reims, France, which was situated just northeast of Paris. She'd been blessed with a lavish and comfortable lifestyle, afforded them by the vast vineyards handed down from generation to generation in her family.

Her mother, Madeleine, was a citizen of Germany until the age of ten years old. She was taken in by her Great Aunt in France following her parents' illnesses and eventual deaths. Anything money could buy was provided her. Madeleine moved in the highest of crowds wanting for nothing more than to meet and marry her prince. Her utmost desire was to have a family to bestow all of life's privileges upon.

A raving beauty, she was endowed with soft, dainty facial features. Deep brown eyes and a full mane of rich mahogany hair, flowing over an intricate frame, attracted Madeleine to numerous eligible gentlemen.

Her stunning beauty and social graces provided her the ability to capture the heart of her Prince Charming. His name was Masseur Jon Paul DeMornais.

The first World War stripped France of one tenth of its assets. Still, Jon Paul and Madeleine continued living in the fashion they were accustomed. As a child, Lilly received the best education money could buy. Her skills at the piano were none less than Bach himself, or so her parents believed.

All vineyards in the north of France were overtaken in the early stages of World War II. At that time, Lilly's parents, fearing she would likely be killed by the Nazis due to her Jewish heritage, sent their adoring Lilly, their only child, underground.

Endless months of enduring squalid living conditions with few reading materials, no bathing and minimal lighting, Lilly, at times, wished for death to take her. Yet, something deep within kept her going. She knew of Hitler's hate toward the Jews. He wouldn't stop until every last one of them were gone. Never would she allow that to happen. She believed, with constant and fervent prayer, that God would not forsake her. As long as she had a breath in her body, she would do all she possibly could to remain alive.

A kind and loving Christian couple kept Lilly and two young teenage boys hidden from the Nazis in unknown basement quarters. There, with little more than a rolled up mattress to lie upon and a woolen blanket filled with holes, Lilly survived. Merely existed really.

Only small rations of food could be spared them daily, if they were lucky. A small basin of water with a bar of soap would be slid into their quarters from time to time. A bucket was used to relieve themselves, which was emptied on a daily basis. Often Nazi soldiers tore open the basement door searching for hidden Jews. They knew what the consequences would be if discovered. Not only would they lose their own lives, the torment and death of the elderly couple would be carried out as well.

It abhorred them as they listened to the cruel, ruthless soldiers abusing the couple who so graciously protected them. They even shared what meager edibles they had. Tables, chairs and furnishings were tossed about like trash. Each time the Nazi's entered the basement, their candles were quickly snuffed out and silence was of the utmost importance. Barely did they dare breathe. On one occasion, the younger boy, Lucas, nearly let out a sneeze. Lilly caught him, covering his head with her blanket just in time.

All three had fallen into severe depression. No sunlight or even daylight reached them over countless months of time. Being small framed from the start, the little weight they carried on their bodies diminished to no more than skin and bone. Their clothing hung on them as if belonging to somebody twice their size. Rotting teeth and hair loss began to occur. Without the benefit of daylight their skin was ghostly white, as pale as the ashes of the wood stove. Each developed scurvy, causing itchy skin, loose teeth and bleeding into the skin and mucous membranes, from a lack of Vitamin C. Still, they persevered.

The wood burning stove protected them from freezing on bitter cold days and nights throughout the winter months. For this they were especially grateful. It also provided a glimmer of light cast upon them from the fire burning within.

Lilly never ceased praying, knowing God was always with her. With parents of immense faith she was raised to keep Him strong in her heart. These three desolate souls formed a bond that would remain with them throughout eternity. If they survived this hellhole, they'd survive anything, with the Lord at their side.

Just as she, once again, felt herself hitting rock bottom the homeowner approached Lilly with news that the Voix-du-Nord was in need of an assistant to coordinate the printing and processing of the underground newsletter. Lilly could not believe her good fortune. Knowing she possessed the education and knowledge to assist in this project assured her of some freedom.

The opportunity to live again, to use her mind, to carry on intelligent conversations, to gain insight into the happenings of the war, would give her renewed faith. Yes, she faced the possibility of being discovered and killed. However, she must escape her present circumstances before losing her mind. Or ... before she rotted to death.

Lilly spent two years, three months and 12 days in that hole. Now, by the grace of God, she may have an opportunity to eat better, regaining her strength once again. Perhaps she would even be able to gain information regarding her parents' whereabouts. Life may still hold a place for her after all. *Oh, could this truly be possible? Could I actually be leaving this hell hole?* she cautiously questioned.

*****

Lilly gathered her blanket along with a few personal belongings she had pocketed when her parents sent her into hiding. Small photographs of her dear mother, Madeleine, and her strong handsome father, Jon Paul, were enclosed in a locket purchased prior to their separation. *Fear not my love!* her father whispered as they embraced one another. *Be safe my baby. Be strong so that we will once again see each other,* were her mother's parting words as they bid their final farewell.

How many times had she looked at those photographs with tears streaming down her face? Would she ever see them again? Each time her strength weakened, fearing the only way out was death, Lucas or Jerome would embrace her, preventing her frail, withered body from shuddering in fear ... shuttering in loss ... shuttering in utter deprivation.

Courage Times Three. A Novel

She thanked the Lord for her dear friends, Lucas and Jerome. They had become so much more than friends. They were truly brothers in God. She prayed constantly for the boys and for the Pariseaus, the elderly couple who had kept her safe in hiding. Now, moving on to the newsletter office, she wondered if she would ever see them again. Should the day arrive when they would once again be free, she would immediately seek them out. Tears were shed upon their separation. Still, Lilly knew her life was about to improve due to where she was going.

As the fortunes of war turned against the Nazis, they massed thousands of slave laborers to build massive defenses. While behind the lines, the Resistance Fighters launched the clandestine newspaper, organized sabotage, and fed information to the Allies. Next to follow was D-Day and Liberation.

Pockets of German resistance along the coast were by-passed to be dealt with later, as the main advance thrust into Germany. Dunkirk, very near Lille, was the last to be liberated, only days before the end of the European war in 1945.

WWII was much more destructive to France than the first world war. The nation had lost over a quarter of its wealth to war damage and German requisitioning. Again the damage was particularly severe in the north. Battles had been fought through Nord/Pas-de-Calais, the area where Lille was located, in 1940 and again in 1944 - 45, with heavy bombing raids in between. Transport was left badly disrupted. As in the rest of war-torn Europe, there was a serious shortage of basic necessities.

News spread swiftly of the war's ending. Throughout Europe word of the mindless deaths, the cruel slaughtering of innocent men, women and children, echoed across the lands. Valentin found himself, along with masses of others, completely at a loss as to what would become of his life.

At last, word reached Valentin's unit that the war was over. His initial response was to share the much overdue news with Lilly. Without hesitation he swiftly found his way to her side. His voice boomeranged off the walls of the newsletter office as he shouted out the words of freedom.

At first, Lilly stood frozen in utter silence. Never in her short life had a few simple words been more gripping. Cupping her hands around her face in disbelief, Lilly's knees caved in, dropping her to the floor in uncontrollable sobs. Tenderly easing her to her feet, Valentin wrapped her in his arms. Holding each other close, feeling their hearts recklessly beat against each other's chests, neither wanted to let go. Not for a single moment.

Tears of relief, combined with cheers of joy, consumed them both. Following several minutes of sheer ecstasy, Valentin held Lilly's face in his hands, kissing every inch of it ever so softly.

So enthralled in her joy and feeling recklessly daring, Lilly kissed Valentin back with a passion unlike anything either had ever experienced. Had these feelings for each other been there all along? Was this the man Lilly would cherish for a lifetime? Neither of them knew that for sure. But what did it matter at this point? Nothing felt better than being in each other's arms, rejoicing the end of the long cold war.

Lilly's coworkers applauded with joyful tears, not only for the new love found that might now have a future, but for their own freedom as well. Valentin may not know exactly what his future entailed, but one thing he did know, wherever he went and whatever he did, it would be in the company of Lilly DeMornais for the remainder of his life

Chapter Three

The North of France, having been hardest hit, having been raped of their every possession, leaned heavily on the French government to assist them in their needs. This was the part of France Hitler had charged *"Occupation Costs"* leaving them with little more than the clothes on their backs.

Lilly knew her first destination would be the home of the Pariseaus. Cautiously stumbling their way through the war torn streets of Lille, the horror of what had taken place hit Lilly with a force not unlike that of hurricane strength winds. Never had she imagined the destruction that lay before her eyes. When she had been moved to the newsletter office it was in the dead of night. She had had no idea where she was going or where she was at, say nothing of her weakened, frail body and frame of mind at the time. Fortunately, one thing she did have was the address of the Pariseaus.

Debris was scattered everywhere making it impossible to recognize street names and addresses. Opportunely, Valentin had gained much familiarity with the city while serving as a Resistance Fighter. It wasn't long before they located the residence, though portions of the home had been hit by bombshell. Heavy raids, brought on by the Allies, caused more than a significant amount of damage.

Lilly and Valentin fiercely pounded upon the door of the shattered home, fearing the death of those within. Cautiously, Mr. Pariseau opened it expecting to see Nazi soldiers once again. Astonishment and confusion overcame him when he recognized Miss DeMornais standing there with a handsome young man in a French uniform.

Lilly and Valentin immediately realized that without their having any method of communications available to them, they were unaware of the ecstatic news. The war was over? The lengthy and crippling five-year war had really ended? Jubilant shouts and tearful cries of joy bellowed from the Pariseaus! *Thank the Lord! Thank the Lord!*

Without hesitation, Lilly inquired about the Jewish boys, Lucas and Jerome. Yes, they were still in hiding. As swiftly as her legs could carry her Lilly raced down the steep dark staircase, with burning candle in hand, yelling *It's over! The war is over! We are free! e Nazi's have been overtaken and have surrendered.* Again, tears streamed down the faces of these wretched and weary souls.

As Masseur Pariseau and Valentin removed the barriers placed in front of the small narrow entrance to the room, they could hear the faint, barely audible voices, *Lilly? Is that you Lilly?*

Between sobbing jags, her arms wrapped tightly around dear Mrs. Pariseau, Lilly hastily instructed Valentin to widen the opening faster. At last, he was able to access the room, only to find the young men in such a weakened state of existence, it was necessary to drag their lifeless bodies out along the floor.

Immediately they were taken upstairs. The daylight hitting their eyes was so painful, Lilly found it necessary to cover them, then closing the curtains until they could, once again, adjust. It was apparent they were desperately and crucially in need of medical care, food, water and bathing, if they were to survive at all.

The aging Pariseaus were malnourished and immensely weak from lack of necessities as well. Lilly and Valentin remained there for several days, nurturing and aiding them while finding food, supplies and medical attention.

Once confident of her dear friends' survival, they parted ways, vowing to meet again under improved conditions. Then Lilly, accompanied by Valentin, set off on foot through the ravaged, war-torn countryside of France in search of Lilly's family.

Beginning their trek, they knew what few possessions they had would not suffice for long. How would they eat? Where would they sleep? With France reeling from its destruction the only way to get around was on foot. Before leaving Lille, Mr. Pariseau shared the address of his younger brother, Jacque, in Calais. It would likely take two to three days to reach their destination. That is where they would eventually catch the train.

Each day they trudged forward with headstrong determination. On occasion, they would stop at a house looking for a kind handout of bread or anything edible that could be spared. Before dusk, they would seek out a place where they would be under cover for the night. From dawn until dusk they wearily moved forward until reaching the city of Calais.

Once there, they inquired at a shop for directions to the Jacque Pariseau residence. The shop owner spoke of the massive destruction throughout the city, not knowing if their home had even survived the bombing raids. However, they must attempt to find out, not only for themselves but also to deliver a letter to Jacque from his older brother. Before continuing on, Lilly and Valentin took the time to pray, hoping, against all odds, that this family remained alive and well.

Upon reaching their destination they discovered the home was mostly intact except for one corner with minimal damage. A quick knock upon the door brought a short man, balding, slight in size, in response.

Valentin pulled the letter he had promised to deliver out of his jacket pocket, handing it to the man. While doing so, he introduced Lilly and himself. Immediately recognizing the insignia on Valentin's uniform, identifying him as a Resistance Fighter, Jacque welcomed them with open arms. Never had he been more pleased than to learn of his brother's survival.

Jacque's wife, Delores, welcomed them in, introducing their three children to the strangers. Jacque quickly read the note from his dearest brother. Praising the Lord, he generously offered what little they had to the weary travelers. Valentin and Lilly were provided a roof over their heads, once again, and food for nourishment. Lilly continually prayed, reminding Valentin of God's plan for them. They had been saved for a reason. He would not let them down now.

So blessed to be alive, most of the French citizens were thanking God for sparing them from torture and/or death. The churches, what few had not been desecrated by the bombings, filled with flocks of people needing to fellowship with their brothers and sisters in Christ.

Throughout the days of prayer, in the churches and in the streets, crowds of people collaborated together actively setting plans in motion to move forward. Where a church was found in good repair, the French government immediately set up payment centers, handing out stipends to those who had so bravely fought for their country.

Immediately upon receiving their Francs, Valentin and Jacque, along with a handful of other Resistance Fighters, pooled together some of their money to begin repairing homes, churches and buildings, although lumber was scarce. Neighbors, fortunate enough to have their homes intact, offered what they had to those less fortunate. It was a time to love thy neighbor with all their hearts and souls.

Valentin's Polish family was weighing heavily on his mind. He must find a way to learn of their plight. The news he was hearing was that the south of Poland had been bombed as severely as the north of France. After speaking with a fellow French soldier, assigned to the guarding of the church where the payment center was located, Valentin learned that he could try sending a message to his family home. He had no idea as to whether or not they would receive it, nor did he know if any of his five sisters or parents had survived the horrendous casualties of war. He could only pray they had.

Lilly, as well, was anxious to hear news of her parents' whereabouts. She knew they had possibly traveled to the south of France, placing distance between themselves and the Nazis, as they had spoken of prior to their separation. After addressing the envelope, she kissed the note and slipped it inside, with a prayer that her parents would somehow receive it. She could only hope they would learn of her survival, secure in the knowledge that she was safely on her way to join them. They would be extremely pleased that she had been escorted by a French soldier as well. What she wasn't sure of, was whether or not her father would accept the fact that she had deeply fallen in love with him.

With continued prayer and hope; with the unending faith she had in her dear heavenly Father, Lilly believed, with all her heart and soul, that her parents would be alive and well.

The war created massive damage worldwide. It took millions of lives, destroyed unprecedented amounts of properties and left millions of others homeless. Nations from around the world tried to move on after this devastating event, but despite their efforts, their recovery was hampered by many factors.

Courage Times Three. A Novel

France's aim toward economic recovery became almost stagnant due to reasons beyond its control. Among the contributors to its worsened economic condition were its low production rate and the rapid inflation that was brought about by excess in money.

In their struggle to locate building supplies, seeds for planting crops, necessary equipment to remove the masses of debris that were strewn about everywhere, seemingly every inch of the earth, they also faced the daily struggle of mere survival. Government trucks eventually began delivering loads of necessary staples for the citizens, however, not nearly what was needed. The government then allotted land to be used for planting crops.

Humanitarian acts of selfless love, caring and sharing, shone through abundantly. Lilly spent her days gathering children together forming a temporary school, in which she taught the basics. This not only kept the children busy, who were too young to donate their time and labor to the clean up and rebuilding, it also kept Lilly busy, alienating the steady thoughts of her parents' well being, while she awaited news from them.

Three months passed as both Valentin and Lilly worked to save small bits of Francs for their futures. Neither of them had received return word from their respective families.

Understandably they became restless, as the one thing they sorely wanted, as much as being alive, was to marry, becoming husband and wife. All too often the nights would be longer than either of them could bear as they longed to be in each other's arms throughout the night.

Lilly would think about the day when she would be a beautiful bride, dressed in white, saying her "I DO's" to this handsome, strong, God-loving man. But she couldn't bear the thought of marrying without having her parents at her side. Her father must give her away. She couldn't imagine marrying without them sharing in her joy.

Coming from a family of some wealth, she knew they would be somewhat disappointed in her marrying a man of little worth. Yet, she also knew they would love him as she did, for caring for her, protecting her and keeping her happy throughout much of her underground life. So they continued to remain stoic in their efforts until the day arrived when they could marry.

Meanwhile, until she received word from her parents, Lilly shared a bed with the Pariseau's two young daughters, while Valentin shared their one son's bed. With long and strenuous days there was little time for pleasure. Occasionally, following a meal which consisted of little more than potato and onion soup along with a chunk of bread, they would gather together in the candlelight while Jacque or Lilly read from a few books they had managed to keep hidden from the Nazis. Most often scriptures were read from the Bible, placing a sense of calm in everyone.

Valentin, having grown up in Poland with little to no skills, knew next to nothing about the carpentry trade. Jacque, on the other hand, was very skilled in that respect. As the rebuilding slowly increased in Calais, Jacque brought Valentin to work as his assistant. That is when Valentin learned the trade that would earn him enough Francs to move onward from Calais to Reims, Lilly's hometown. This was also the trade that would remain his livelihood for years to come.

Having received no response from their families, Valentin and Lilly finally decided to take the train to Reims, in search of her parents. Somebody must know something of their whereabouts. Friends, neighbors or even church members might possibly have a bit of information to share.

Standing at the train depot, awaiting the train that would return her to her home, Lilly was saddened to leave the second Pariseau family behind. How they had grown together. All they had endured in the difficult days following the end of the war burned a memory in her mind that would remain forever.

With Jacque and Delores being approximately 10 years the elder of Valentin and Lilly, they sometimes felt like parents to the younger, unwed couple. Lilly had also developed a close attachment to the girls, whose bed they had so unselfishly shared throughout those few months. She envisioned Valentin and herself having wonderful children like the Pariseaus.

One day they would look back at these times with a clearer perspective about what life taught them here. If there was one thing Lilly and Valentin were both passionately aware of, it was God's ability to teach them many important lessons in life, most obviously, trusting in Him and doing for others.

Regardless of life's difficulties, hanging on to the belief that He was always there to protect them, to guide them down the right paths, and to encourage them to move forward, He would have an emphatic impact on them forever.

Amidst tears, hugs and kisses they bid farewell. As the train slowly began to turn her wheels, she sounded her lonesome whistle. The Pariseaus remained in place waving, until the train pulled out of sight. Life would be different without the endearing couple in their home. One day they knew, they too, would meet again.

While traveling the train to Reims, Valentin made the acquaintance of a Polish gentleman who had been forced to fight for the Nazis. He learned that all men in Poland refusing to fight, were still being tortured and killed. This news brought enormous sorrow and concern to Valentin. Although those in his family who had remained behind were all sisters, his mother and father had remained as well.

Prayer, faith and hope were the strongest tools to use on their behalf. If it was His will for other members of his family to join Him in heaven, there was nothing Valentin could do to change that. However, the power of positive thinking was also a tool to be used in remaining strong. He must never lose sight of that. After all, he was now responsible for the care of his dear Lilly May.

His thoughts turned to his brother's tragic death as the two of them dodged being captured or killed after leaving Poland. Catching his boot string on barbed wire, with Valentin a good distance ahead of him, Hugo struggled to free himself from the wire. Finding themselves in the worst of predicaments with steady bombings, they moved as fast as their legs could carry them.

Had Valentin been allowed the time to backtrack, freeing his brother, neither of their lives would have been spared. Looking back, the bomb hit precisely where Hugo was hung up, causing Valentin to freeze in his tracks. He remembered little from those torturous moments. Blood curdling screams echoed throughout the valleys as He begged God to stop the insanity of it all. For months to come Valentin hated the Germans with a vengeance.

The sight of his brother's horrific death would haunt him endlessly. He lay crippled for an unknown amount of time. Immovable. Broken. Unable to carry on. Valentin cried himself to sleep until the first light of dawn, never feeling more destitute or alone.

Upon awakening, an overwhelming sensation arose within him. It was as though God was speaking directly to him, instructing him to pick up his broken, lifeless body and move on. Remaining stunned for a few minutes, his mind tried to absorb yesterday's atrocious events.

Hugo had paid the ultimate price of war at the tender age of fourteen. Had he not promised his parents that he would take care of him? Hadn't he now failed in doing so? He would never stop asking for his brother's forgiveness.

At the time, however, he must grieve his loss and let go to regain his energy and perspective, re-engaging with life in a vital manner. He was grateful that his parents were unaware of his brother's demise. Nor were they aware of their oldest son's survival. Unless somehow, someway, the note he'd sent had possibly reached them.

Recognizing familiar sites, Lilly's excitement intensified as they drew nearer her hometown of Reims. Valentin had seen beautiful terrain traveling through the Alps of Austria and Switzerland. Yet, it didn't have the effect on him that it would have, had he been in the proper frame of mind to appreciate its beauty. Now, as he listened to Lilly's endless chatter about her homeland, he soaked in the scenery through the train's small windows while passing through beautiful terrain. France was a country of much wealth and beauty in comparison to Poland. If this is where he would spend his future he knew it would be an improvement over his life in Poland.

On the inside, Valentin held much skepticism regarding Lilly's parents' approval of him. Would they absolutely refuse to allow their one and only daughter, a daughter of grace and high social status, to marry a poor uneducated Polish man? He wasn't sure if he could bare the loss of this ever-so-precious woman.

As history often revealed the ugly truth associated with foreign soldiers abandoning the women they impregnated while serving in the wars, it was understood why the fathers and mothers of these girls refused to allow their daughters to date or bring home a soldier. Hadn't he done all he possibly could in returning Lilly to her home?

Never was there a man who loved a woman more than Valentin loved Lilly. He simply could not imagine anyone loving a woman to the degree that he loved her. He was quite undoubtedly sure that Lilly reciprocated his love wholeheartedly. There was nothing either of them wanted more than to be husband and wife. This now weighed very heavily on his mind.

Informing him that Reims was right around the corner, Valentin promptly took Lilly into his embrace. His arms, wrapped around her small frame, made her feel as though nothing in the world could do her harm. Nothing in life could keep them from spending eternity together. He had been a means of encouragement and support for her throughout much of what had been the worst nightmare of her life. And she for him.

Fiercely, he would fight for her hand in marriage. He would protect her, provide her with a good living and a warm home. He would be an upstanding father to the children they would one day have, raising them in God's word. All this he promised to his precious Lilly.

With great pride, Lilly familiarized Valentin with the customs and habits of the French. Patiently, she continued to teach him to speak the French language more fluently. What knowledge she had regarding the functioning of her father's vineyards, she shared with him. Had she been born a son rather than a daughter, her father would have started instructing her in the workings of the vineyards by the age of fourteen, her age when sent underground. It was the vineyards which had been handed down through generations that provided the DeMornais' their affluent lifestyle.

Valentin knew the steady chatter tumbling from Lilly's mouth was her way of dealing with the raw nerves exposed from the fear of what she might find in Reims. He would silently pray for her. Pray that Jon Paul and Madeleine DeMornais had survived the brutality of the lengthy and cruel war. Soon they would have news of their fate.

Sounding as though exhausted from its heavy workload, the train came to a stop in the city of Reims. As Lilly and Valentin disembarked, they exchanged pleasantries with those they had become acquainted with on board.

It was a warm and sultry summer day in Reims. Immediately, Lilly's eyes moistened with tears as she began witnessing the devastation created by the bombings. Only small patches of greenery were exposed, trying to survive here and there. Endless blocks of gray, grimy dirt and dust lay before them.

The beautiful community was in vast disarray with completely downed buildings, war torn streets and remnants of buildings barely hanging on, as if they hoped to one day have life within them again. Gone were the colorful flower boxes that had adorned the storefronts, lining the cobblestone streets and walkways. Nowhere in sight was the proud flag of France displayed, waving at residents and tourists alike, from the summery aromatic breezes that frequented the quaint little town. It was all quite disillusioning to dear, young Lilly DeMornais. With little transportation available yet, they wearily picked up their baggage, consisting of a few basic necessities. Namely, one set of clothing along with a few toiletries and personal items.

Reims was a small city. It wouldn't take them long to reach her family home. She prayed it would remain standing. As they proceeded through the nightmarish scenery they were forced to wait as one weary farmer moved his small family of goats right through the streets of the city.

This was not common practice prior to the war. However, with the destruction of homes and businesses throughout the north, life as she had known it, would never be the same. Where the market once stood, now merely a couple of partial walls limply remained, enclosing massive litter and debris, while rats and mice scurried about. The school Lilly had once attended lay in heaps of bricks. Her favorite apparel shop, frequented often by her mother and herself, lay in ruin.

Those heart wrenching sights made Lilly shudder once again. She must not allow her disillusioned response to damper her excitement in finding her parents. How she had longed for her mother and father to hold her once again.

She had matured from a girl into a woman in the time they had been separated. Instead of wearing her beautiful raven black hair down, she now wore it up in a wrap behind her head. Replacing her fashionable attire was a worn, graying excuse of a dress which hung on her tiny, frail frame. Although she had regained some color within the past few months in Calais, she still lacked in her healthy appearance, as most did. She had gained a few pounds, yet additional weight was still needed. A spark had returned to her eyes, however, that anyone could see was from being in love. Moving onward she thought *soon, very soon*. She was nearly there. With every step Lilly's excitement grew in intensity.

Scattered throughout the neighborhoods were homes which remained intact, as if they had never experienced the war, while others were entirely demolished. Valentin stopped her for a few moments. *Lilly my love, please be prepared for what you may find.* With this statement, Lilly's heart stopped beating momentarily.

No, I mustn't think negatively, was her response. But no sooner had those words left her mouth when she saw what remained of her family home. GONE! It appeared to her that a bomb had landed square in the middle of it.

Oh no, this couldn't be! Mama! Papa! she screamed in terror. *Mama! Papa! You cannot be gone*! Lilly's heart was breaking in a way that she could not comprehend.

Through her screams, Valentin stood helplessly as she searched through the debris for some sign of life. Frantically she picked up bits and pieces of her past. Broken, charred mementos of a life no longer in existence. Valentin's heart broke for his beautiful Lilly.

He approached her as she dropped to her knees in tears. Holding her, Valentin brought her to her feet as his heart and mind searched for the right words to ease her pain. *Oh, my dearest Lilly ... How can life be so unfair to such a wonderful young woman as yourself?*

As he was about to speak again the voice of a woman echoed from across the road. *Lilly??? Lilly, is that you my dear? It cannot be! My eyes must be deceiving me,* cried the woman. Abruptly turning toward the woman, she seemed to shake herself back into reality.

Chantelle? Chantelle ... As the two reached each other's arms tears of joy and total exuberance overwhelmed them. It was Lilly's Aunt Chantelle, her father's sister, who had lived across the road from them throughout her entire childhood.

But where were her parents? Lilly could not speak the words quickly enough ... *Tante Chantelle, where are Mama and Papa?* Lilly and Chantelle spoke so rapidly in their excitement Valentin had difficulty understanding their words. Lilly's expression told Valentin that the news was not good as she hung her head, tears dropping to the ground.

All the while Chantelle continued speaking rapidly in French. Some of it could now be understood by Valentin. As she held the hands of her dear Aunt, Lilly abruptly looked up with a glimmer of hope. *Where?* she pleaded. *Where is she?*

It appeared to Valentin that her father, Jon Paul, had passed on. Her mother, Madeleine, however, was still living in Paris with her Great Aunt Melanie who had taken her in, at the age of ten, following her parents' untimely death in Germany. Lilly turned to Valentin as tears of joy and sadness tore at her heart. For a brief moment they stood silently trying to absorb the news.

Their silence was broken by Chantelle's inquiry as to the identity of the handsome gentleman wearing a French uniform. Taking Valentin's hand into her own, Lilly gazed into his eyes with a look of love, loss, happiness and confusion mixed all into one.

Gently smiling she introduced Valentin as she turned toward her Tante Chantelle. *This man is the love of my life. This is my one and only Valentin Augustus DuBois. He is the man I am to marry.*

Chantelle graciously held out her arms to embrace Valentin, thanking him repeatedly for returning her dearest Lilly. They then entered Chantelle's warm and inviting home.

Just as her father had, Lilly's Aunt lived a comfortable lifestyle, mostly due to the vineyards that remained in the family throughout the years. She had once been married to an extremely handsome and debonair man, Masseur Jeffrey Lane Boudine, who was killed in the first world war. Jeffrey took to spoiling Lilly at every opportunity. She had missed her uncle for many years following his death. Only one child had been born to the young couple before he was called to war. Unfortunately, their newborn infant died within a month of his birth. Chantelle never remarried following his horrendous death.

Now, of course, Chantelle's northern vineyards were dying off, following the damage they had sustained from the air raids. Still, she had managed to keep the majority of her furnishings and belongings. The Germans had no interest in an old French woman living alone. What relics and jewels she had had were taken to Paris when she moved in with Madeleine's Aunt Melanie.

Leaving Reims well before Jon Paul and Madeleine, she had escaped the torture and harassment from the Nazi's that so many others had suffered. Upon her return, after spending a year in Paris, it immediately became apparent that the soldiers had rummaged through her entire home, taking whatever they had thought was of value.

Thick layers of dust and dirt covered every inch of the home. Windows had been shattered throughout its entirety. The exquisitely designed stained-glass faces of the built-in dining room cabinetry had been intentionally smashed to access some of her china. The contents of the cabinets were kept under lock and key to avoid thievery. Little remained in them, however, as she had been wise enough to take them with her to Paris.

Chantelle had spent endless hours, with the assistance of friends and family, restoring the home back to its original state. Never did a single day pass without warm memories tugging at her heart strings of her dear Jeffrey, still bringing stinging pain from the void in her life that could never be replaced. But she was a sentimental woman and would remain in the home the two of them had spent their wondrous years together in.

Nothing could have pleased her more than the safe return of her dearest Lilly. Chantelle was fortunate to be afforded cold running water. They promptly began the task of warming the water for a long, luxurious bath. A longtime friend had recently delivered goods to her from Paris for meals and such. She had yards of beautiful material that had been purchased in Paris. Once they had time to catch their breath she would embark on a project sewing a few new dresses for Lilly.

With the tea set to brewing, Chantelle led Lilly and Valentin to their own separate bedrooms. Lilly was the first to lay her weary bones into the warm fragrant water, luxuriating in the French bath beads Chantelle had provided. Words simply could not express the tremendous pleasure she received from the warm aromatic bath.

Washing her hair, more than once, returned its natural glowing radiance to the warm mahogany brown she recalled from childhood. She likely would have fallen asleep right where she laid had it not been for the rapidly cooling water and Valentin's need for the same. Tiptoeing to her own private quarters, Lilly wrapped herself in a fluffy soft bathrobe that was laid upon her bed by dear sweet Chantelle.

Valentin immediately replaced the bath water for his own pleasure, basking in the warmth, cleansing himself repeatedly. Afterward, he skillfully removed the three inch growth from his face with a straight edged razor, leaving him clean shaven and looking much younger than he had just minutes beforehand.

Only a short time was spent in conversation before both youngsters began to repeatedly yawn. A hot cup of chamomile tea followed by a warm bath were the perfect ingredients necessary to send both into deep sleep. Disturbing thoughts of her father's demise overtook her mind now and then, but she must set those thoughts aside until tomorrow. Warm embraces and heartfelt words were shared among the three of them. The darkness invited them, this time, into a warm and comfortable bed of peace and tranquility.

Once they had retired for the night Chantelle whipped out a few bolts of material she was sure were favorites of Lilly's. Immediately, she set herself in motion selecting a few patterns, then started to sew. Working feverishly throughout the night Chantelle's eyes would occasionally glaze over with tears.

She recalled the pain she had caused Lilly as she was forced to explain the untimely death of Lilly's papa. It wasn't a bomb or Nazis that had directly killed Jon Paul. He had died of a heart attack, which Chantelle explained was likely caused by the demands and difficulties of life during the war, as well as the emptiness in their lives without their adoring Lilly.

Jon Paul and Madeleine had traveled to the south of France, where they'd remained for three years. By the time they'd sent Lilly underground the Germans were already invading the north of France. They knew they would likely be stopped and interrogated by the Nazi militia while trying to escape to the South. With Madeleine of Jewish descent, they undoubtedly knew mother and daughter would be put to death and he would be forced to fight for the Nazis.

Therefore, Jon Paul made the most painstaking decision he'd ever had to make, sending Lilly underground instead of risking her life by taking her along. Madeleine had desperately urged her husband to re-consider his decision time and again. Jon Paul, being the man of the house, insisted they protect Lilly's life at all costs. They may never know if the decision they were making would prove to be the right one or the wrong one.

Prior to leaving the South of France, to return to their homeland of Reims, Jon Paul suffered a massive heart attack, taking his life instantly. Madeleine fell into a deep depression following the loss of her dear Jon Paul. She moved to Paris to be cared for by her Aunt Melanie, living an extremely reclusive life. With no knowledge of Lilly's whereabouts, and communications having come to a halt under German rule, it was still impossible to gain knowledge.

Feeling well rested once again, satiated with much needed nourishment and wearing newly sewn clothes, preparations to meet the train were nearly complete. Chantelle was pleased with the fresh, clean appearance of the young couple, their attire disguising strikingly-slender frames. Sending them along with warm blessings, a small money bag found its way into Lilly's handbag. Chantelle was sure to include gold and silver pieces in the possible anticipation of paper Francs failing to hold value.

Chapter Four

    A renewed outlook on life accompanied Valentin and Lilly while traveling south to Paris. Learning of her father's death was grievously heartbreaking, yet Lilly clung to the joyous knowledge that her mother remained alive. How anxious she was to see her beautiful face once again. Her concern for her mother's state of mind troubled her immensely however. Would seeing Lilly alive and well enable Madeleine to pull herself out of her deep depression? Information shared with Lilly of her frail mother's state-of-mind prepared her, somewhat, for facing a mother influenced quite heavily by mind altering medications. Did she fear the very sight of her loving mama? Could she live with how the war had broken her? Would her mother recognize Lilly?

    Experience taught them just how overwhelming life could be. If anybody could bring her back to reality, it was Lilly. Madeleine surely would be pleased and proud of her newfound love in Valentin. Prayers that her father in heaven looked down on them favorably were often sent up above. He undoubtedly knew of Valentin's heart of gold, how he would provide for her always. Maybe God and Jon Paul had sent Valentin to her side while she worked at the newspaper. Lilly believed, wholeheartedly, that he was, indeed, heaven sent.

    This time the young couple kept to themselves throughout the train ride to Paris. Lilly shared her sense of loss regarding her father. Valentin noted just how willfully she attained the same abundant strength to overcome life's difficulties as Chantelle had done, more than once, in the face of adversity. Pointing that out gave her a renewed sense of personal defeat against the enemy, the depression that she could so easily slip back into. She knew she could not afford to let that happen. Her mother's life and well being would depend on her strength.

Both spoke of the pleasures they'd experienced that first night in Reims as the guests of Chantelle Bourdin. The cup of chamomile tea tasted better than anything she'd ever had, she stated. Robust laughter overtook them as Lilly searched for the right words to describe the wonder of that warm, fragrant bath. *Why Lilly, I have never before known you to be stuck for words when describing anything. Are you sure the cat hasn't gotten your tongue?* Lilly pretended to gear up for a good punch in the arm, a fun-loving reaction to his teasing.

More than once he witnessed her pouting behavior as her bottom lip would begin to protrude significantly, followed with crisscrossing of arms against her bosom. Hearty laughter erupted from deep within, witnessing her foot stomping tantrums on occasion. How he loved to tease her about it, finding it forever endearing. He delighted in the pure innocence of the young lady, the childlike behavior genuinely pleasing to a young man in love. In moments, her naughty disposition would fade into the clouds.

Tell me dear one, did you pout that way when you were made to eat your escargot? Or was it mostly when you had to practice your piano lessons daily? Laughter abounded from Valentin as his arms wrapped snuggly around her. He occasionally envisioned her being a spitting image of her mother, Madeleine. Faith and hope remained steadfast in the hope mother and daughter would have the opportunity to closely bond again.

Reminiscing about the months spent in Calais with the Pariseaus, the young couple paused in prayer for plentiful employment, food for all, and much needed rain for sustaining gardens. Both Lille and Calais residents depended enormously on canned food from summer gardens, especially with a lack of funds to purchase other necessities. Their prayers extended out to all family, friends and acquaintances. Plea's for new opportunities to present themselves, serving them well in the massive task ahead of rebuilding their lives from scratch. It would be years before most would be capable of letting go of the looming death and destruction, the stench, filth, hunger and poverty imposed upon all, hanging in the forefront of their minds, within their very souls. Their faith continued to carry them through however. Those who tossed God's ever loving goodness to the side would suffer more deeply than the ever faithful. He would provide opportunities for a brighter future. Lilly's dependence on Jesus never waned. Her quest to find her endearing mother, Madeleine De Mornais, was about to become a reality. Lilly found it incredible that in a few short minutes she would see her mother in the flesh once again.

Memories flooded her mind with the times her mother brushed her beautiful long hair or sang her to sleep. Cherished thoughts of horseback riding together, the crisp morning air brushing gently against her soft pale skin. Afternoon piano recitals, given exclusively for her father, flashed through her mind, painting a smile across her face. She could hear the gentle applause of her mother, but mostly her father's loud clapping. Always a hearty *"Bravo! Excellent my dear child!"* was her plentiful reward from her dearest papa.

It pleased her so, to have his approval in all she attempted to do. She would deeply miss him. If only she'd had an opportunity to see him before his death. To tell him how very much she loved and needed him. She thanked God that she now had Valentin to carry her through.

Approaching the doorway to Aunt Melanie's home, the palms of Lilly's hands perspired with nervous anxiety. Fearing she could frighten her mother if approaching too hastily, she asked Valentin to sound the knocker.

Melanie's home rested upon a vast piece of beautifully landscaped property in a prime area of Paris. The height of the double doors spoke a warm welcome to visitors. Each door was adorned with a lion's head, used as the knocker. The massive three story mansion attractively displayed enormous French-style windows, encased in elegant Chantilly lace curtains. A meticulously manicured yard painted a picture of delicate flowers in colors of fuchsia, pink and baby blue, set before a grand entrance wrapped in stately pillars. Never had Valentin seen such an exquisite home. The grandeur of it all surpassed anything he had ever imagined.

He was beginning to get an idea of who and what Lilly had been born into. This proved to be somewhat intimidating to Valentin. When Lilly requested him to sound the knocker, he paused in trepidation.

Sensing his hesitancy, she, herself, stepped forward to knock with Valentin at her side. Giving him a nervous smile while squeezing his hand, she impatiently awaited a response. A tall gangly figure of a man opened the door, attired fully in black and white. His nameplate read Oscar. He informed the young couple that he was the butler. *Who may I ask is calling?* he inquired. Lilly unabashedly inquired whether or not her Aunt Melanie was in. *Please tell her that her niece, Lilly, is calling.*

Closing the door, Oscar requested the couple please wait in place while he informed Ms. Rouleau of their arrival. Overwhelming anxiety announced its choking frenzy, creeping up Lilly's body to the top of her neck. Flailing arms, swinging to and fro, accompanied shallow breathing, causing a powerful sense of lightheadedness.

Valentin could see he must bring her back to a sense of calm. *Breathe slowly my dear. Look into my eyes. Breathe very slowly and deeply.* In just a few moments a sense of calm replaced her profound anxiety, preventing any further episodes, like fainting.

Just then both front doors flew wide open. Aunt Melanie stood awestruck at the sight of her beautiful young niece. Throwing herself around Lilly's frail body, holding her firmly to her breast, Melanie praised God for bringing their one and only Lilly May back to them.

I have prayed every morning and every night that our dear Lord would bring you back to us safe and sound. Continued faith has rewarded us once again. And who may I ask is this fine young gentleman?

Proudly, adoringly, Lilly once again placed her dainty hand within the strong but jittery hand of her incredible Valentin, just as she had at Aunt Chantelle's home. With skittish anticipation, Lilly immediately announced her wishes to marry the fine gentleman standing beside her. With tears of joy for grateful blessings this family would once again share in each other's lives. It was likely this magnificent home that would house and protect them for an unknown period of time. Only God knew what their future would bring.

Lilly wasted no time inquiring impatiently of her mother's whereabouts. Aunt Melanie explained how she most often spent her time simply vegetating in her room. Never did she entertain, nor did she join in with Aunt Melanie's guests when she, herself, entertained.

She warned Lilly that she didn't look like the mother she remembered from five years ago. Her worries and losses had stripped her of her youthful look. She ate little, causing severe weight loss. Her pasty white skin lacked vibrancy and color from lack of sunshine. On very rare occasions Madeleine would spend time in the flower gardens with a straw hat covering her face. Lilly had flashbacks of her own days living in a basement without daylight or sunshine. This was not the time or the place to go back, however.

In anticipation, Lilly paced outside her mother's bedroom door as Aunt Melanie informed Madeleine of her guest. As usual, she refused to receive any guests, quietly requesting her Aunt send them away.

However, this time Aunt Melanie wouldn't take no for an answer, demanding Madeleine see this guest and to be prepared for a pleasant surprise. Not being the sort to argue with Aunt Melanie, or anyone else for that matter, Madeleine reached for her bathrobe, ran the brush through her limp, lifeless hair and slid into her slippers. She proceeded to follow her Aunt through the bedroom door into the adjoining reading room.

The initial sight of Madeleine took Lilly's breath away. Then, instantly, their eyes locked. Madeleine gasped for air. At first sight of her daughter, Madeleine thought she was simply a figment of her imagination. But Lilly could no more wait to jump into her mother's arms than she could fly to the moon.

She alarmingly cried out, *Mama!* As she did something clicked in Madeleine's mind, registering the fact this was indeed her long lost daughter, the love of her life, her ever-precious Lilly May.

Through hugs, tears and kisses, Lilly gently and endearingly held her mother's face in her hands, gazing deeply into her eyes with intense love and affection. Madeleine repeatedly ran her fingers through her daughter's hair, touching her face, her arms, trying to absorb the truth of what her eyes were undeniably telling her. Her baby was back ... her baby was alive and well. Occasionally she would look to Aunt Melanie for confirmation. With tears gently rolling down Melanie's face, a slight nod of the head reaffirmed the reality staring them in the face, words unable to find a way to her mouth. *"Papa"* was all Madeleine was able to sound out of her mouth before Lilly interrupted, sorrowfully replying, *Yes Mama, I know.*

All of life momentarily stood solemnly still as their thoughts raced through time. The deeply mournful loss, excruciating pain, hollow emptiness and fearful loneliness silently screamed out their names. So much to wrap their heads around in just a few moments.

At last, Madeleine and Lilly, mother and daughter, were reunited. It would be countless years before they would ever let each other out of one another's sight again. *God is a good God after all!* whispered Madeleine.

* * * * *

Valentin nervously paced the floor of the dining area where he had been served tea while awaiting Lilly's return. Twenty minutes had passed since she'd ascended the grand staircase to her mother's bedroom. As he stood admiring a full bodied oil painting of the family patriarch, Andre Alexander Beauchamp, hanging at the foot of a richly engrained maple-wood dining table, his thoughts bounced about like a jumping bean, incapable of remaining still.

While Lilly had received sad news of her father's death, she had now, at least, found her mother alive. What anguish he began to feel regarding his own parents. What would the news bring of his own family? Valentin thought there was no time better than the present to get down on his knees in prayer for positive news to come his way. He understood that no word would come until the Pariseaus received the post card they had sent with Aunt Melanie's address in France. Some word of assurance, some news that his family had survived the war, was all he wanted. Valentin pleaded with his Almighty God to have at least spared them some of the anguish and agonizing pain brought on by the war.

With head remaining bowed in silence, Lilly entered the room. He had spared her the added strain of dealing with his own pain. She had been through too much herself. He couldn't unload his own agonizing sense of loss on her.

Lilly had come to learn Valentin's facial expressions quite well by now. Sharing a smile that registered joy within her, she could also see how troubled he was. *What is it Valentin? Are you worried about how Mama will receive you?* Lilly left Aunt Melanie to inform Madeleine of the details regarding Valentin, while she prepared to make her presentable before escorting her downstairs.

Valentin softly spoke his own thoughts regarding his family and what their situation might be. *Of course! How could I be so insensitive?* After all, Valentin had set aside all of his own personal needs to aid Lilly in her quest to find her family first.

She assured him how they would discuss the matter with Aunt Melanie immediately. She explained her Aunt's affiliation with people in high places, likely expediting the process to gain news of his Polish family. These were words of great encouragement to Valentin. Perhaps he would learn something sooner than later.

Together they stopped to give thanks to the Lord for guiding them to this place ... this place they would call home for now. And for the patience they would need to receive word, any word, of his beleaguered family.

Madeleine listened carefully as Melanie described the courageous young Polish man who had devoted himself to her beautiful Lilly May. In first hearing of his Polish descent, Madeleine became recklessly defensive. It wasn't long lived, however, as Aunt Melanie shared the details of how he had become registered as a French citizen, taking on a French name, protecting not only her own daughter but their country as well, serving as a Resistance Fighter. She spoke most highly of his undying commitment to Lilly. How he had delivered her, safely and soundly, through the war torn countryside to their very doorstep. A smile emerged from Madeleine's face as she became familiarized with the facts. Indeed, he sounded like the type of man she would highly approve of for her only precious daughter.

Slowly descending the staircase, the ladies joined together with Lilly and Valentin in the dining room. Madeleine immediately stood at Lilly's side, all the while admiring the strong, handsome figure of a man standing before them.

Upon Lilly's introduction, Valentin gently took Madeleine's hand into his own, respectfully placing a gentleman's kiss upon her. *Bon jour, Madam DeMornais!* was all he said, nervously replacing her hand at her side. At that moment, Madeleine reached up to give him a welcoming hug. *Without your brave assistance and the protection of my beautiful Lilly we may never have had this opportunity to re-unite,* stated Madeleine.

So very pleased with Madeleine's response, Lilly beamed with pride at her honorable and brave husband-to-be, Valentin DuBois.

Valentin and Aunt Melanie smiled at one another with enormous relief. Hours upon hours were spent filling each other in on the sordid details of their lives within those past five years.

Madeleine asked Lilly to share some of those times with them. Lilly was unable to respond to her mother. She couldn't risk sending her into a frenzy, learning of all Lilly had been subjected to. Even more importantly, she couldn't risk going back to that place in time herself. The horrifying truth was it was just too excruciating an experience.

So, Lilly refrained from sharing the extreme difficulties of her underground life with her mother until she was sure she could handle it emotionally. She may never reveal some of the ugliness that personally plagued her throughout those years, as God had seemingly given her the ability to live in the present, leaving those most trying times behind her. As the saying goes, leave the past behind, {not forgetting the lessons learned } live for today, and don't worry about tomorrow.

To Aunt Melanie's amazement and delight, Madeleine had come to life almost instantly after seeing Lilly. Not another pill was taken once her daughter had returned to her. With a renewed vigor for life, her eating habits quickly improved, adding the necessary pounds that filled in her body once again.

Up with the light of dawn, prepping herself for another wonderful day with her daughter, Madeleine found reason to live life once more. She hadn't spoken this much since before the war began. Each time Madeleine looked at her beloved daughter, her eyes lit up like a Christmas tree. Why God had spared them from death, they did not know. Regardless, they were here and alive and it was time to move forward, starting their lives over once again.

She wasn't the only one who came back to life, physically anyway. Lilly managed to gain a good solid twenty five pounds. A glow returned to her filled-in face where once little more than cheek and bone existed. Her rich mahogany hair took on renewed life. She was treated to a full body massage, a pedicure, manicure and a fun, bouncy new hairdo. Valentin barely recognized the Lilly he had fallen in love with. In her place stood a woman of stunning beauty, full of the same zest and vigor she'd had prior to the war.

Valentin, too, managed to add much needed weight to his good sized frame. His face took on the distinguished look of a man, giving him renewed confidence and pride in his adulthood. He'd even decided to sport a fancy mustache, curling it upward at the ends.

Melanie had immediately contacted a French diplomat, a legislator of sorts, belonging to the Conseil des Etats, persuading him to do all he could in gaining knowledge of Valentin's family.

With his recently-acquired carpentry skills it took little time for Valentin to find work in the grand city of Paris. For Lilly, the first and most important event to begin planning was her wedding.

Paris had intentionally been avoided regarding air raids by the Germans. Herr Hitler had hoped to include this city of high fashion, an economic leader in newer industrial breakthroughs in Europe at the time, as his playground. Though no bombings affected this city overall, the war stifled growth immensely. Four years of destruction had a major impact on all across Europe and beyond.

The wedding would be elegant yet simple. Madeleine wished to provide her daughter with the best of everything. She knew, if this was her mother's desire, she should abide by her request. Yet Lilly and Valentin's patience had outgrown itself.

When sharing with Madeleine their wishes to wed sooner, it was decided they would marry late in the following month. It was August and a September wedding in Paris would be lovely. Aunt Melanie's breathtaking courtyard would provide the most exquisite grounds for an outdoor wedding. Some of Paris' most influential aristocrats would be included as guests from Melanie's social club. The wedding would serve as one of the first celebrations in Paris following the recent war.

Bottles of the best French wine, still remaining in the wine cellar, would accompany an impressive menu of gourmet delicacies. Lilly would wear a gown designed by top fashion experts in all of France. A gown, elegantly displaying endless yards of satin and lace, would be the envy of Paris' high society women.

For five weeks life was as chaotic as one could imagine. What an exciting time for all. After so much pain and sorrow in their lives, these Europeans finally had reason for a grand celebration. The three women assembled lists from flower arrangements to the menu, from wine lists to guest lists.

Valentin would awaken early each morning and following a man-sized breakfast catch a bus to his place of employment. As a man, he was more than happy to steer clear of the wedding plans and the flurry of excitement created by the women.

He had never seen Lilly happier. Life had amazingly turned a leaf in a very short period of time. Father Mignon from St. Lucias Church was requested to perform the ceremony on the twenty-fifth day of September at 2 o'clock pm.

Two weeks following their arrival in Paris scant, but positive news, arrived through French diplomats regarding Valentin's family. It appeared two of his sisters had been living in Switzerland throughout the war. The Swiss had remained neutral throughout both WWI and WWII, which attracted many Europeans to the country. Once war had ended, however, most transients returned to their homeland. They would hopefully receive further word of his family as more was unveiled. It pleased Valentin greatly to know at least two of his sisters were alive and well.

Keeping in mind some of the transportation and communication was not back to normal throughout Europe, they realized all was being done that could be at the time. Two weeks later, one week before the wedding was scheduled to be performed, Valentin was delivered the tragic news that his parents had not survived. His three younger sisters had been stashed aboard an ocean freighter, carrying them across the Baltic Sea to the island of Bornholm, which belonged to Denmark.

On August 22, 1943, a rocket, most likely launched by the Germans, crashed on Bornholm. It was assumed the Germans were testing the distance their live bombs would carry while doing their best to capture the British Isles, as the contents of the warhead was no more than cement, a dummy bomb. The Nazis had captured control of Bornholm relatively early in the second war, using it as a lookout post and listening station throughout much of the war.

The Soviets heavily bombarded Bornholm in 1945, returning the island to Denmark. No news of their sisters' survival caused much agonizing pain for Valentin. Soon, however, news was received of his older sisters having escaped into Switzerland before being captured or killed. The women then had made it their mission to enter France, seeking some sort of information regarding their long lost brothers, Hugo and Valentin. Valentin realized the odds of their finding him were slim to none with having changed his surname to Dubois.

Valentin's news was difficult to absorb. Not knowing of his younger sisters' fate gave him great cause for heartache and concern. He must continue to lean on God's never ending love, keeping the faith as the ladies of the house encouraged him to do. Although word of his younger sisters surely troubled him and the tragic deaths of his loving parents left a gaping hole within, he certainly had great reason to keep his head above water regarding his older sisters' survival. If they could possibly be located in France, would there, perhaps, be hope that they, too, could be present for his wedding? Sensing it was an unlikely possibility, Valentin still sent daily prayers up above to the only One who could make far reaching dreams a reality. In this, he firmly believed.

Immediately the name of his mother's sister-in-law in the north of France was shared with Aunt Melanie's source, who was tracking them. This is where Valentin had hidden underground for two years prior to enlisting with the Resistance Fighters. His sisters would likely travel there, first, in search of him.

Lilly's excitement grew with each day as Valentin's did. How anxious she was to have two sisters-in-law after living without a single sibling throughout her life. It was a dream come true. Despite spending endless hours scurrying about with the final details of the wedding, she frequently found time to pump Valentin about his sisters. What did they look like? How old were they? Would they know how to speak French? Did they know how to ride? Valentin laughed at the giddiness and excitement that overtook Lilly when discussing his family.

Madeleine's love for Lilly had no boundaries. How she enjoyed hearing Lilly's voice each and every day. Her daughter had grown into a beautiful woman throughout their separation. More than five years had passed. Lilly was about to turn 20 years of age just two weeks after her September 25th wedding date, on October 5th. How proud she was of her daughter. Lilly had learned not only how to survive the vicious perils of war but also how to be an extremely responsible, intelligent woman, never losing the endearing warmth radiating from within. Jon Paul would be so very proud of his darling daughter. She knew, with every breath she took, he was watching over them now and forever.

Three days prior to the wedding a telegram arrived for Valentin Augustus DuBois. As the butler handed Lilly the telegram, she knew, without a doubt, it must have been sent by his sisters or somebody who had been in contact with them. Valentin would not return from his busy workday for another four hours. Lilly was beside herself with curiosity. Dare she open it? Being a telegram there was no way for her to decipher whether it was from a man or a woman, as it was typewritten.

Just as she was about to open it, curiosity getting the better of her, in walked Madeleine. With a stern look and firm hand, Lilly's mother shook her finger at her daughter. Lilly had always been taught to respect the privacy of others and this was no exception. She must wait until Valentin walked in the door before learning the content of the note. Madeleine pointed out how Lilly had much to do yet before Valentin returned. With a pout and a stomp she ran off busying herself with dress adjustments and flower arrangement finalities. Madeleine thought back to the early days when she and her dear husband hid their smiles at their beautiful daughter's dismay when disciplined.

Four hours later Madeleine found Lilly upstairs in her bedroom. The word of Valentin's return had not even fully left Madeleine's mouth before Lilly tore out of the room to the top of the staircase. Rather than trying to get quickly down the steps, Lilly jumped on the winding banister, sliding all the way to the first floor, nearly falling to her face at the end. There, to her delight, stood Valentin, still dirty from his days work.

Holding out the telegram, her hand began to tremble. Even though Valentin, himself, was excited to read the telegram, he couldn't help but roar at the girlish behavior of his soon-to-be-wife. Lilly again spoke so rapidly in her excitement, he could barely comprehend her words. Tearing open the telegram, the look on Valentin's face was worth a thousand words. Sheer excitement overtook him as he read aloud the message:

Dearest brother Valentin.
Received word of your whereabouts.
Taking train tomorrow to Paris.
Will arrive in time for wedding
With Love Greta & Emma

Lilly screeched with exhilaration. Not only would she be Mrs. Valentin DuBois in just a few days, she would also have two new sisters there for the wedding. With great jubilation Lilly found herself swinging around repeatedly in her most wonderful husband-to-be arms. What more could they have to rejoice about? Most sensational news for these two young lovebirds indeed.

Valentin read and re-read the note, his wet eyes no longer able to hold back the tears rolling down his unshaven face. Aunt Melanie and Madeleine applauded with the heartwarming news. Alas, Valentin would once again see his family. He knew, with every breath taken, God could and did perform miracles, namely, this miracle. *Oh, my precious Lilly, there isn't anything our Holy Father cannot accomplish in our world or in the heavens above?*

Just as the excitement began to calm another telegram arrived at their door. This time from Aunt Chantelle notifying them of her arrival the following morning. The time to celebrate had arrived. Lilly knew in her heart of hearts, from that moment on, life would be better than she had ever imagined possible.

Chapter Five

Morning could not arrive soon enough for all. Aunt Melanie would send her driver to pick up Tante Chantelle from the train depot at 12:30 pm. Crews hustled to set up the courtyard with necessary seating arrangements and decorations.

Although Valentin had been told it wasn't necessary to find employment until after the wedding he had been taught to always carry his own weight. Never would he live on the generosity of another.

Lilly felt proud that her Valentin was a man of good conscience and high moral standing. Madeleine was also pleased with his sense of responsibility. The way Valentin viewed it at the present time, it gave him an opportunity to get out the women's way, while at the same time keeping his mind occupied regarding his sisters' arrival. How eager he was to once again see Greta and Emma. So much had occurred in all their lives over these past years. Now, with both of them being older in age than himself, they would be in their mid twenties.

As life reveals, numerous physical and emotional changes take place when developing from a teen into an adult. Meeting together for the first time as adults would reveal two grown women, which felt somewhat odd to Valentin. Who had they become? How had the world shaped them into being who they now were?

Extreme life challenges, such as war, have a way of bringing out the strength of those who sometimes struggle to find it. It can give people a renewed sense of confidence, or perhaps, a confidence they have never known. Valentin simply hoped the war had not made his sisters bitter toward the world. Toward life itself. If that was to be the case he would need to do all he could to bolster their confidence, regaining their resilience. That would mean re-igniting their faith in their Holy Father.

Soon Melanie's driver arrived with Aunt Chantelle. They, too, had been alienated from each other during the past four years. Chantelle had left her home in Reims for that first year during the initial start of the war, living under the roof of Aunt Melanie. Although she was the sister of Jon Paul, Madeleine's Aunt Melanie had taken a great fancy to her. They viewed one another more as sisters. The last time they had spent time together had been under difficult circumstances with the war. This visit gave reason for great celebration.

Precious time was set aside to catch up on each other's lives. Filling them in on the present status of northern France dominated the conversation. Progress was slow, yet Chantelle had seen a few necessary accomplishments come to completion. The cleanup of filthy debris was mostly behind them, but the rebuilding was moving at a snail's pace.

When the Allies attacked the Nazi camps a part of their attack was directed at the borders. Lilly and Valentin had spent over two years right on the border in Lille, viewing their survival as truly unbelievable. Together these strong souls held hands giving praise and thanks often. A constant vigil, of divine nature, had been kept over them day and night.

As Lilly vaguely recounted the days of her underground life, it astonished her how slowly the time had passed back then. Now, since arriving in Paris, joining her mother, once again, and planning for the wedding, she could not believe they had already reached the date of the wedding.

Valentin had taken this one last day off from his work to prepare for the wedding himself. The women, of course, dealt with all of the frivolities, still Valentin had to be sure the tuxedo he wore would fit appropriately. He needed a haircut along with a good clean shave.

Today his sisters would be arriving in Paris. In fact, it would be only an hour before they would walk in the door of Aunt Melanie's home. A stately home with seven bedrooms provided traveling guests a room for boarding right there with the family, allowing plenty of opportunities to converse, sharing an abundance of hugs. This included Greta and Emma Baranowsky as well. How eagerly Valentin waited to embrace the girls.

Courage Times Three. A Novel

* * * * *

Amid tears of joy and relief, Valentin & Lilly greeted his sisters with open arms. Once again, they found it necessary to touch one another repeatedly, assuring themselves it was not a dream, much as Madeleine and Lilly had experienced just a few weeks earlier.

The moment was bittersweet for all. The ugliness of the war had given grief to so very many innocent people. All would set aside time later to do their grieving. Right now was a time for celebrating and rejoicing.

As Valentin introduced his sisters to Lilly and the others he took great pride in seeing what beautiful women they had become. This was the first time he seriously faced the reality of who he truly was and where he had come from. The nostalgia surrounding him was thick and somewhat intense.

He desperately wished he could identify himself as Valentin Baranowsky to all. However, he must remain anonymous, protecting himself against the mindless slaughtering of Polish men still being carried out by the Nazis after the war. For the time being, he must continue on as Valentin Du Bois.

It was of utmost importance his sisters remain vigilant in keeping this secret. They must continue protecting him as was fully agreed by all. Only within the privacy of their own space could they speak in their native tongues. It was suggested by Melanie and Madeleine, however, that no usage of the Polish language should be used until all wedding celebrations expired. Truthfully, they didn't care what language was used as long as they were together.

Swiss citizens predominantly spoke the German language but the family who had used them in Switzerland spoke mostly French, which was the second highest spoken language in Switzerland. To their benefit, all were able to communicate in French, eliminating any speculative questions from Aunt Melanie's guests. It was agreed upon that the girls share the same French surname as their brother during their stay in France, for his continued protection.

What were the odds of these siblings finding each other within this period of time following the war? Surely Jesus had His hand in it, as they knew it could not be simple coincidence. What if Greta and Emma had already visited and departed the home where

Valentin had been hidden underground? Before having received word of his whereabouts in Paris? After all, it had now been several months since the war ended. They never would have received the message he was living under a false name in Paris. What if they had decided to return to Poland in search of their immediate family members? They mentioned how that very thought had entered their minds more than once. In fact, it was a tough decision as to where they should begin their search.

That evening, at the dinner table, Aunt Melanie led in a prayer of thanks for the joyous occasion, celebrating not only the wedding, but the re-uniting of these family members once again. She thanked God for bringing her empty and lifeless home back to life. Endless chatter ensued throughout the dinner hour.

One would never know of the broken state of mind Madeleine had merely existed in during the recent past. Each individual had their own tragic story locked away in their minds, preferring to keep those thoughts under lock and key for now, or perhaps, forever.

* * * * *

Awakening to a somewhat blustery day was not what Lilly had envisioned for her outdoor wedding. Aunt Melanie, however, being prepared for inclement weather, had a crew ready to erect a large tent cover to protect them from the rain. Oftentimes clouds would move on by mid morning leaving them with sunny skies and seasonably cool, enjoyable afternoons and evenings at this time of year.

Lilly kept a close watch on the weather. As the sky began to open up with its brilliance of blue, its abundant sunshine, she knew her wedding would be as perfect as her Valentin. Keeping with tradition, the lovebirds kept a close watch to avoid running into each other before the ceremony. With his sisters holding him hostage and Madeleine following suit with Lilly, they pulled it off without a hitch.

Father Mignon arrived an hour early spending a few moments with the bride and groom. Both bride and groom, having been raised in Catholicism, embraced their vows with full vigor. Throughout the ceremony they recognized God's handiwork in each of their lives, bringing them together here on this special day. How they looked forward to their upcoming lives together!

With the ceremony ending the couple turned to the small group of attendees to begin their walk through the gardens as Mr. and Mrs. Valentin DuBois.

The scene was as picturesque as anyone might imagine. Huge sprays of stunning, colorful flowers adorned every area throughout the gardens and home. Statues of lovely maidens were strategically placed throughout the gardens, some spouting water from the vases they held, streaming into miniature ponds with lily pads in bloom.

Aunt Melanie's rose gardens were the envy of many Parisians prior to the war. They were just now coming back to life with constant nurturing from Melanie and Madeleine.

Everyone knew who the true connoisseur was when it came to growing the very best roses, however. It was Aunt Chantelle, without a doubt. She had the envied ability to communicate with her roses in a fashion causing them to display brilliant colorful shows twice yearly, even drawing neighborhood crowds in the city of Reims. Here, much was to be admired also, in the natural beauty of the gardens and those who nurtured them.

Following an entertaining afternoon of gaiety, with a lively quartet of musicians and light-footed dancers throughout the gala event, a lovely day was had by all.

The joyous couple wouldn't consider leaving their long lost house guests for a honeymoon at this time. That would come later. For now, knowing they could share a bed with each other sufficed just fine.

At the end of a long and pleasant day all retired to their bedrooms for a good night's sleep. Greta and Emma, having traveled some distance on the train just that day, were most eager to rest their travel-weary bodies. Lilly and Valentin repeatedly spoke of the precise timing enabling his sisters to join in the wedding festivities.

The following day, endless hours were spent catching up on each other's pasts. Though difficult to hear, Valentin must know the details of his parents' deaths. Equally hard for Greta and Emma to share the news, they managed to muddle their way through the tears as the story unfolded. Understanding he must put closure to that part of his life, this would place finality on it. Greta also shared the news of their younger female siblings being stowed away on the ship carrying them to Bornholm. That was all they knew, other than what Valentin had learned from Melanie's diplomat friend. To their knowledge, the three younger sisters remained on the island to this day.

They were knowledgeable of the German's takeover of Bornholm however. Word had it the Russians had liberated them, returning the island back to the Danish. Extensive bombings had taken place in order to free them from the Germans. Perhaps they had been relocated to a safer location at some point before the bombings. Once communications improved they hoped to learn more of their sisters' current whereabouts. Negative thoughts of their possible demise were swiftly erased from the minds of all.

Chapter Six

With France having lost so much of its wealth the climb back to what it had previously been grew painstakingly slow. Valentin was offered a position as chief overseer of Aunt Melanie's grape vineyards one day. A willingness to learn all that was necessary to cultivate the fields, to produce some of France's most desirable wine, would guarantee great wealth and good fortune.

As he considered this opportunity, Lilly applied herself in studies that would enable a teaching career. The time she'd spent teaching the children in Calais following the war's end, gave her a sense of great pride and pleasure. She knew from that point forward, given the opportunity to further educate herself, she would embrace it with vigor.

The time had indeed arrived. She pursued her interests with much enthusiasm. It was not common for women to become educated at this time in France or to take on a position teaching high school students, which was her desire.

Madeleine, having simply been the adored and pampered wife of a prominent wine producer, had little to no skills when it came to providing a living for herself. She did begin to receive a very comfortable monthly income from Jon Paul's inheritance however.

Up to this point Aunt Melanie remained financially secure, with her late husband having invested money into other means of securing a profit. She was more than happy to provide others with all she'd been blessed with. Thus, Madeleine, Valentin and Lilly remained living in the comfort of her home for some time.

Greta and Emma also remained with them for several months until they could provide for themselves. Following several months of employment, they'd saved a tidy bit of Francs, enough to provide housing & furnishings for themselves.

Greta lacked the attractive features Emma had received. She, however, was fiercely independent, as the oldest in the family. Much had been expected of her in a family of nine. That determination helped to land her a comfortable position in the fashion retail business. With Emma's striking looks and Greta's driven desire to achieve great financial success, it wasn't long before each had found suitable partners. Both married within a year of their newfound independence, even starting families shortly afterward.

Lilly and Valentin wanted nothing more than to begin a family of their own as well. Using discretion, however, they felt it wise to wait until their feet were planted firmly on the ground. As tempting as the offer was from Aunt Melanie to oversee the vineyards, Valentin had come to love the carpentry trade he'd prided himself on. He felt creating great things with wood was the gift God had so graciously given him.

Lilly admitted, only to herself, she was somewhat disappointed with his decision, yet supported him fully. She would soon reach the end of her schooling and knew, she too, would contribute financially to their nest egg.

The Baranowsky's came to learn more about their younger sisters. Germany had taken control of the island early on in the second war. Evidently they had been moved to the shores of Sweden in the dead of night with others, escaping the wicked hand of the Nazis.

An endless search for the girls remained futile. They continued their search in vain, but nowhere were there any records of their whereabouts. For years they searched tirelessly for the girls. The thoughts they had all insisted on avoiding, admitting they had likely been lost to the war, were slowly becoming a reality.

Suffice it to say most Europeans, most of the world, had survived a cruel and ugly war. Some countries began seeing massive growth in industry, farming, manufacturing, communications and transportation unlike anything they had ever imagined. The word in Europe was that the United States had opportunities including, but not limited to, masses upon masses of land to be purchased.

Had Valentin made the decision to accept Melanie's offer to oversee the vineyards, it would have inevitably been handed down to them following Aunt Melanie's death. He often wondered if he had made the wrong choice, made a mistake in turning down the generous offer, realizing he'd thought more of himself than Lilly when he had made the decision. It was too late to turn back now. He couldn't change the past, so he must look ahead to another dream.

One evening, feeling rather melancholy due to his own selfishness, he admitted to Lilly he may have made a mistake. A selfish mistake that grieved him often. Lilly shared her own misgivings over his decision to refuse the offer. He wondered why she had never spoken to him about it. Lilly explained she had been taught to respect the husband's final decisions on important matters without question. She assured him of the countless opportunities ahead, waiting for them to grasp. He appreciatively thanked his wife for her unending love and devotion.

Together they could dream big. Nothing prevented them from purchasing other lands and developing it themselves if they did so choose. Lilly was proud of the impressive carpentry skills Valentin had developed. She knew well that making a living doing what entirely pleased oneself, was being one step ahead of the game in life. Valentin loved creating products with wood and his hands. She would never dream of denying him that pleasure.

* * * * *

Although the United States had also suffered through The Great Depression, the freedoms and opportunities it offered were difficult to resist. It was gaining the name of the Melting Pot of the World, making available countless opportunities for all who ventured there.

After several lengthy discussions the decision to relocate to the United States of America was made. It meant leaving behind those loved ones who meant so much to them. Leaving behind bittersweet memories to move into a foreign land where they must learn to speak another language, live according to new customs and learn to live side by side with others from many countries throughout the world.

Although Europe consisted of a vast hodgepodge of countries, each with their own spoken languages, travel from country to country wasn't commonplace.

Universally, people have blended in or merged together from place to place since the beginning of time. A move to America would mean embracing lifestyles of people from throughout the world. It would mean leaving Aunts Chantelle and Melanie behind. Leaving both of Valentin's sisters behind. They questioned whether or not a move of that distance would be a reckless decision on their part. So, no rocks were left unturned prior to their final decision to relocate.

Relocating meant a new, fresh start for the young couple. Valentin wished for acres of land where he could raise his family. He and Lilly both agreed they enjoyed challenges. Challenges stimulated their minds unlike anything else. They looked forward to change. Change was refreshing and inviting. They liked setting high goals for themselves. This seemed fearful to many, but to them it wasn't in the least. It was a great opportunity they looked forward to pursuing.

All wouldn't be left behind however. Madeleine would accompany them on this exciting adventure to the land of milk and honey, where she would remain living with them for several years.

The train tickets were purchased that would carry them to the shores of the Atlantic. Soon, they would spend five days crossing the mighty Atlantic to America. Mixed feelings tugged at their heartstrings. But Valentin and Lilly chose to leave the horrors of the war and all of its ugly memories behind.

Madeleine agreed it was best to move forward as well. Deep down she knew she would miss much of what she had embraced in France. More importantly, she would never allow any distance to keep her precious daughter and herself apart in this life again.

They were blessed to be leaving with a tidy amount of Francs, affording them better cabin accommodations and amenities than most. Also, it would give them an excellent start in the new homeland, the United States of America.

The train ride to the Atlantic carried them to the port city of Bordeaux. It was there, after a two night stay, they would embark on the longest and most intriguing voyage they would ever experience in life.

Their last night in Bordeaux offered them a fine departing meal consisting of excellent French cuisine. June on the coast offered warm ocean breezes accompanied by sweet aromatic fragrances of jasmine and lavender. This would leave a most extraordinary lasting impression upon them.

The smell of the sea water initially reminded Lilly and Valentin of their stay in Calais on the shores of the Baltic Sea where they'd spent three months with the Jacque Pariseau family. Several communications had taken place between them over their two year stay in Paris. Just prior to leaving the city, they again sent word, notifying the Pariseau's of their move to America. The likelihood of seeing each other again might now be no more than a dream. Yet, if anybody knew how to dream and to continue carrying hope within them it would be the DuBois'. After all, hadn't they survived the atrocities of the Holocaust? WWII? Even WWI for that matter? Yes, they certainly had. They would continue to hope, just as they always had, which is precisely what their heavenly Father repeatedly encouraged them to do. Tomorrow they would board the massive ocean vessel carrying them to parts unknown.

The sun peaked over the horizon much too soon for Lilly's liking that morning. Excitement had cheated her out of a restful night's sleep. Madeleine, on the other hand, was an early riser as she had been throughout her younger parenting years. Morning was her favorite time of day. Already dressed for their voyage, Madeleine knocked on the door of the two young lovebirds. *Arise to a most desirable morning children! Our ship awaits us!* sang the ever so lovely Madeleine De Mornais.

Having regained her health, her weight and the glow she had always exuded before her depression, Madeleine remained a picture of beauty at the age of forty two. Some did dare say she could pass for a woman in her early thirties. Lilly was proud her mother once again took pride in herself, setting an example for Lilly as well as other women.

Proudly, a generous smile sat on Valentin's face as he courteously nodded to the admirable gazes while escorting the lovely ladies to the vessel. Gentlemen scurried to relieve them of their bags, doting on them as if they were royalty. Once boarded, Madeleine became lost in yesteryear, recalling the final days she'd spent with Jon Paul on the French Riviera, overlooking the Mediterranean. Although they'd suffered, as all had during the war, they'd been spared the widespread indiscriminate massacre their poor dear child had been witness to. Nonetheless, they'd made a decision they'd thought best at the time and could do nothing to change it.

Madeleine sensed, realistically, she may be looking back at the shores of France for the very last time. As the ship pulled out of the harbor she bid her dear sweet Jon Paul a last au revoir. *Bon voyage my sweet Madeleine,* echoed in her ears as tears filled her eyes, memories of love lost, burning in her heart.

"The Serendipity" offered many comforts to those who could afford them. The enormous ocean liner was equipped with 820 tourist cabins along with those for the crew members.

Board games, cards, ladies luncheons along with entertainment in the evenings and pool tables for the gentlemen in the smoking quarters were some of the conveniences offered. It was a great opportunity to learn from those who'd been to America already. Several American soldiers were just leaving France, following their tours for the Armed Forces of the U.S. Oftentimes, a translator was willing to interpret for those in need. At least French to English translations. On rare occasions, when nobody was around, Valentin took in the salty air on deck, striking up conversations with fellow Frenchmen. Many differing opinions were shared by all.

Much time had passed since Valentin had truly allowed himself to wander back in time to his Polish roots. When living in Paris with Aunt Melanie, Valentin had privately been teaching Lilly the Polish language. Madeleine, notwithstanding her own flaws, frequently avoided joining in on conversations regarding his heritage. Knowing how very much her mother adored Valentin, she wondered why she objected so severely to his Polish heritage. Wasn't he the same wonderful man regardless of his heritage?

Lilly profoundly understood the depth of his desire to be the man he was born to be. Now, as they awaited their new conquests, he pondered his birthright quite frequently, as though it were tugging at his shirtsleeves.

Having spent quality time with Greta and Emma in Paris, a portion of his heart had been reborn. He hoped and prayed that one day they would be successful in finding Lorraine, Alina and Katya in Sweden.

One gentleman Valentin befriended onboard was a fellow Polish man. He, too, had spent time in France, although nowhere nearly as lengthy a time as Valentin. Nor had he the luxury of being taught fluent French by a lady as lovely as Lilly Mae. The two men spoke incessantly of the cruel war, their past lives in Poland, family members who'd passed on and others they'd left behind. As Valentin introduced his newfound friend, Andrew Lisowski, to his lovely wife and mother-in-law, immediately Lilly understood how Andrew had captured so much of Valentin's time throughout the voyage. How wonderful for her husband to have found a fellow countryman to share stories with.

While Lilly was sincerely pleased for him, her mother took quite a different stance on the subject. However, having been raised in the fashion she had, along with having the utmost respect for Valentin, Madeleine refrained from making any comments. They greeted Mr. Lisowski warmly, extending an invitation to join them for a special glass of vintage wine directly from their own Aunt Melanie's secret cellar. Following a glass or two of the Chardonnay they continued enjoying each other's company through dinner as well. A wonderful time was had by all until retiring to their designated cabins for the night. Tomorrow would be their last day at sea, reaching the shores of America before sundown.

With dawn on the horizon the three weary travelers awakened to spend one last day at sea. Promptly upon joining the other travelers for a buffet style breakfast, the air became electrified with the uproar of chatter among all those looking forward to their new beginnings. Time moved faster than one had expected with the excitement. Although lunch had been served the appetites of most were lacking due to jitters and high emotions. Some were expecting to join family from whom they'd been separated for several years. Others hadn't a soul to guide them in the ways of the new world.

As late afternoon approached Mr. Lisowski once again joined up with Valentin and the ladies. A discussion of the first landmark they would encounter took top rank among all. After all, it was a gift given to the United States by France so many years earlier. On October 28, 1886 President Grover Cleveland had accepted the Statue of Liberty on behalf of the U.S.A. Part of his acceptance speech read:

> We will not forget that liberty here made her home;
> Nor shall her chosen altar be neglected.

As many tried to recall the exact wording from those long ago days it somehow became irrelevant. What embraced them most was the fact their home country had given this landmark gift representing the French and their traditions, which was cause for much pride. Much to the surprise of Mrs. DeMornais and the DuBois', Andrew Lisowski offered the hospitality of his brother's welcoming hand in providing them a place to stay upon initially entering the Port of New York City.

The on slot of arrivals emigrating from Europe in previous years had proven to be a nightmare in moving their often sickly, weary bodies along, with what little belongings they owned, through the Naturalization lines. Fortunately those days were behind them. Travels were much improved over the past recent years. Still, the process was slow with hundreds of people needing to pass through the lines.

Dusk was beginning to set in as they caught sight of land ahead. Once it was confirmed to be New York City a few of the gents with violins began kicking up their heals playing jovial tunes to accompany the frolic of voices, laughter and cheers. Pulling within distance of the great Lady, The Statue of Liberty, total silence followed revered cheers for the captain of the ship.

There she stood.

<u>The land of the free and the home of the brave!!!</u>

Chapter Seven

It was advised by the captain in an announcement prior to docking that some of the guests spend the night once again on board "The Serendipity" due to the lengthy processing times. The mammoth vessels were also used to carry textile goods and other various materials to the US from Europe. These deliveries had deadlines to meet, so hired hands worked throughout the night unloading them.

Those leading the way off of the vessel initially were people with higher class cabins, having paid well for their highly convenient accommodations. Holding upper class cabins themselves, the three of them were allowed to leave that evening. However, Andrew Lisowski was not in that category. They graciously thanked him for his hospitable offer, but declined all the same.

It would feel good to stand on solid ground once again. Precautionary words of advice were shared with all, preparing them for what was referred to as *"sea legs."* Wobbly footed men, women and children made their way off the enormous ship. Some with giggles, others with a bit of fright.

Imagine entering a country where you plan to set down roots for a lifetime, not even knowing how to speak the language of the land. Much about this new adventure would prove to be challenging and intimidating.

The lights in the harbor and throughout the grand city of New York mesmerized the hundreds of emigrants and returning soldiers. Few had expected the Statue of Liberty to stand so erectly, stretching infinitely into the sky from where they docked — a promising beacon of hope and prosperity for all.

In 1948 New York City had grown into America's largest city, the nation's center of commerce and possibly, the most important cultural and political center. It was also a period of tremendous growth physically, economically and socially. Raw materials from around the globe were transformed in its manufacturing centers into products that were, in turn, shipped throughout the United States and around the world.

Its population was composed of diverse ethnic groups, some with long histories of hostilities toward one another. These groups settled in communities that attempted to keep their cultural identities ... Little Italy, Germantown, Chinatown, etcetera. Emigrants, upon their arrival, settled in these areas where their native countrymen had established themselves, reinforcing an ethnocentric atmosphere. It was very much a city composed of neighborhoods where its inhabitants seemed to prefer that insular lifestyle. Opportunity, however, was a strong elixir and when the populations of those neighborhoods grew beyond their ability to absorb their own people into the local workforce, the people were more willing to find work outside the neighborhood.

By this time the auto, truck and mass transit systems replaced the horse and carriage. Bridges, rail (both elevated and subway), and trolley services united the neighborhoods, skyscrapers among other large buildings often had subway stops within their floor plans. These modern methods of transportation allowed all of those in metropolitan areas to easily and affordably find employment throughout any area of the city.

Following the lengthy process of naturalization, several large chests and crates were loaded onto a truck to be stored until locating a new home for themselves. A taxi delivered them to the hotel where they had previously made arrangements to stay.

Soon a two bedroom apartment was leased on a limited basis, until deciding where they would set down roots. Leaving France well supplied with chests of dishware, linens, toiletries, clothing, etcetera, they needed little more than furniture for the apartment.

This task was tended to by Valentin and Lilly, while Madeleine busied herself with the removal and cleaning of all items, one by one, from the numerous chests. It was a spacious, well-lit apartment with impressive woodwork throughout. From the sizable terrace they could see for miles, providing a distant view of New York City's modern skyline. Perched on the twenty-eighth floor of a thirty story high-rise, their view, facing a southeasterly direction, they somehow felt just a few steps closer to heaven.

As Valentin set out seeking employment as a carpenter, he quickly became familiarized with the Unions that were becoming a way of life in the U.S. The unions were devised to protect blue collar workers in the skilled trades, assuring them of work whenever available and providing excellent retirement benefits, for a fee. Valentin paid his dues as he signed up for carpentry work. This gave him a great sense of fulfillment, as there was nothing more rewarding to a man of his integrity, than a good day's work.

Immediately he set out to pound nails within the city and outlying areas. Men in the skilled trades, even unskilled laborers, were in high demand throughout the entire country. The diversity of those involved in the various building projects proved to be challenging at times. Most project supervisors spoke English, however, verbal communications were not always necessary. They could easily follow along with the rest of the laborers. It wasn't long before Valentin began picking up words and phrases on the job sites, though most of his English lessons were being conducted at home by his lovely wife, Lilly.

Educated as a teacher in France, Lilly was eager to learn English so she might, once again, teach the children as she'd previously done in Europe. Every evening, following dinner, Lilly spent an hour or two instructing Madeleine and Valentin on the spoken language. No time was wasted finding a school to further her education, spending endless hours mastering the language. New York City offered endless opportunities, just as Paris had, but the hunger for a new and improved life in the U.S. was sometimes overpowering.

The assorted ethnic diversities slowly started blending together for the most part. People of all races began recognizing similar work ethics, acknowledging and respecting others' preferences and customs. This wasn't always the case, yet progress was being made over time.

Lilly made the acquaintance of a charming American woman, named Anna, who taught classes at her school. Anna would occasionally bring her mother along to join in on afternoon outings. Sharing traditions and customs was always entertaining. Madeleine especially enjoyed the company of Anna's endearing mother. It was the first time she allowed an American to befriend her and Lilly couldn't have been more pleased. *Yes, there may be hope for her here in the US yet!* she quietly mumbled through a partial chuckle.

The Americans, Anna and Louise, proved to be wonderful tour guides on many excursions. One remarkably exciting occasion was a day spent traveling to Niagara Falls. The beauty and splendor of the Falls gave way to nothing more spectacular. Numerous photos were taken, with the intention of sending them abroad to friends and family. Madeleine, it seemed, was taking an avid interest in photography. One of her photos was so visually impressive, she had it enlarged and framed as a Christmas gift to Lilly and Valentin that first year in the United States.

With Madeleine's unending assistance, or perhaps it would be more appropriately stated, with Lilly's unending assistance, they created a warm, cozy home for themselves. A stunning chandelier hung high over an exquisite cherry-wood dining table. The dimly lit glass hutch displayed delicate china that had been a part of Madeleine's family for generations.

For the first time Madeleine truly started feeling a sense of value and worth as an individual. There was no denying, life with Jon Paul had been any woman's dream. Yet she was viewed, most often, as a lovely ornament of sorts, Jon Paul's cherished prize. Now, she would started recognizing her own talents and gifts that had been so graciously bestowed upon her by her Heavenly Father.

Lilly did not know what she would have done without the steady companionship and love of her dear mother. Never was Madeleine made to feel she was not fully welcomed in their home. Quite honestly, she was in no way a guest. This was her home, the same as her daughter and son-in-law's. She contributed financially to household expenses. She would always be provided an income from her late husband's estate. This income would prove to be a great asset in times to come as well as in their current situation.

Mother and daughter spent endless hours in the kitchen experimenting with new recipes. Poor Valentin was sometimes the guinea pig used to try out new dishes on, tasty or otherwise!

Making up for lost time, they would occasionally pass an afternoon admiring the shops of New York City with all they had to offer. Madeleine had developed a fetish for hats shortly after marrying Jon Paul. Rarely did a month pass without her indulging in another colorful headpiece to place upon her head. They had great fun together, mother and daughter. Never did they forget how blessed they were to once again share in each other's lives.

Various potted flowers, bursting in brilliant colors, accompanied the lush greenery adorning their eighth floor terrace, creating a amiable garden effect in the warmer months. Windows were dressed in lush satin draperies and French lace curtains. A cozy fireplace burned red embers on many-a-frosty New York evening in the cooler seasons. Though they would likely continue recognizing their many French customs in the years to come, they commenced to becoming Americanized in a number of ways. They'd even prepared hamburgers with French fries for a meal from time to time. They questioned the name of *"French fries"* for the greasy deep-fried potatoes the French had never known. Several laughs were shared over the fries. Madeleine, accordingly, named them American fries.

Having grown accustomed to the prim and proper lifestyle he had married into, Valentin appreciated all he had. The day was approaching, however, when a family was to become a consideration. After several discussions, the couple thought it best to decide where they would set down permanent roots. Valentin most emphatically knew it wasn't in the craziness of the large metropolitan area. Occasionally, a weekend train ride would carry them through scenic mountain passes, be it a single day's tour or a full weekend, requiring an overnight stay. Those weekend tours created much curiosity regarding other areas of the vast country.

Two years had passed since their arrival in the states. Valentin's need to touch base with the openness of God's creation grew faster than the city did. He longed for the outdoors, working with the land, being one with nature as he had in his childhood. By this time all three had learned to speak English quite fluently. Particularly Lilly, with hopes of becoming employed as a teacher again. Unfortunately, she discovered women were not allowed to become employed as teachers in the U.S. if married. Only those choosing to remain single, placing their careers over marriage, could teach.

New York City's growth remained constant. Valentin became increasingly restless with the congestion of the ever-expanding city. The shoddy workmanship coming from some entering the country left little to be desired. He began disliking his work more and more. This became clearly evident to Lilly as he often returned home with a sour disposition. Lilly knew it was time to spread their wings and leave the craziness of the giant metropolis behind.

The three earnestly began their search for a permanent home. Valentin had added a sizable sum of money to their shared banking account in the past couple of years. They could now afford to expand their horizons.

The year was 1951. April offered warmer weather as they celebrated the Easter Holiday. Somehow, the past Christmas had been lacking in gaiety for them. Yet their praises and appreciation went out to the Lord for all He was providing in this new land. Everyone's health had been excellent, work was abundant, friends in the neighborhood, along with sisters/brothers in Christ, had been a welcome addition to their lives.

Nearly nine years had passed since Lilly and Valentin first set eyes on each other. Rarely did they allow themselves to slip back into those difficult years. Living underground and fighting with the Resistance Fighters seemed like a lifetime ago. Yet, they were constantly reminded of their good fortune to follow.

One of life's greatest learning lessons became apparent to all. Without experiencing the challenging times, one would never appreciate the many gifts offered to us in life.

How profoundly those words impacted each of them! They knew it was God, and only God, who forever remained a constant in their hearts, their minds and their souls. And that could never be taken away from them. When all else failed, God was still there. When life seemed lost to pain and heartache, God's promising love gave reason for continued hope once again. Even miracles seemed to come about when least expected. Some considered their good fortune luck or coincidence. But Christians do not view it that way. How wonderful it would be if all mankind recognized His endless power of love.

Many thoughts were shared about a possible a move to Quebec, Canada. There, they would have the same freedoms the United States offered. With the dominant nationality being French in Quebec, Madeleine leaned heavily in that direction. However, Lilly knew of Valentin's aching desire to return to his true self, living as Mr. and Mrs. Valentin Baranowsky. He greatly longed for his true ancestral heritage to be lived out. In explaining to Madeleine the importance of a man living his true identity, it became apparent they must do what was best in the eyes of Lilly and Valentin. After all, it was the future of their family, their children, that counted most. Madeleine would be happy wherever they settled, as long as she was near her precious Lilly.

Endless searches for Valentin's younger sisters, Lorraine, Katya and Alina, had left them with the heart wrenching, oppressive acceptance that none had survived the atrocities of the war. Throughout the many years that passed, surely some knowledge of their survival would have surfaced by now. Valentin hadn't been the only one remaining vigilant in his search for his siblings. Both Greta and Emma continued making inquisitions as well.

Lilly so enjoyed the correspondence that came from Valentin's sisters in France. A final letter had been sent to France before leaving New York. With no new home address established yet in Minnesota it was impossible to receive word from France. Lilly promised to send news of their new address immediately upon their arrival in their new home state.

Three days prior to their departure a letter was received from Emma. Lilly could not believe her eyes as she revealed the contents of the note to Madeleine.

In utter shock and astonishment, she read aloud the news of the miraculous survival of the Baranowsky sisters. How could it be they had survived throughout the past years with no record? Every effort had been made to discover their whereabouts. Reading on, Lilly learned new information had emerged in response to Emma's most recent inquiries. Letters had been sent to Poland, Germany, Denmark, Sweden, Belgium and France with each inquisition.

Likewise, Lilly and Valentin had developed a habit of sending out requests every three months to various European government agencies, seeking knowledge of his sisters' existences. But to no avail.

It appeared they'd been located after leaving the orphanage, establishing a residence of their own. Once documentation had been received by the Swedish government, along with an address on the Baranowsky girls, the exciting news had, at last, surfaced.

Proper documentation at the orphanage had not been a priority during the war. A steady flow of homeless children had entered and departed through the doors of several orphanages. Often the true names of children were never learned due to their very young ages. Prior to venturing out on their own, Lorraine saw to it all had

Swedish identifications. Seemingly, no existence of their past lives in Poland remained. Merely their own private memories, which faded further from their conscious minds as time passed.

An address in Kalmar, Sweden was provided for correspondence with the girls. Emma indicated she had just received word that very day, only minutes beforehand. After placing a phone call to Greta with the electrifying news, she had immediately written the note to Valentin and family.

* * * * *

Due to arrive home from work momentarily, Lorraine was beside herself with excitement. Madeleine listened to her adult daughter behaving just as she had as a young girl. How she relished these moments. She felt as though Jon Paul should be standing right alongside her, gently toning down the mumbling rhetoric that spilled from Lilly's mouth when overly excited. A loving laughter emerged from Madeleine.

Lilly gasped when hearing the door open, delivering Valentin safely home from another day's work. Throwing her arms around her loving husband, knowing what an enormous impact this news would have on him, on all their lives, Lilly spilled the news as fast as she could speak. This time, Valentin didn't laughingly react to his wife's girlish excitement.

The words Lilly spoke were richer than a shower of diamonds befalling him. *How can this be? How could they have been alive this entire time?* Lilly revealed the circumstances stated verbatim from Emma's letter. *I cannot believe this ... I thought all hope was lost ... Please, let me see the letter for myself.*

Lilly pointed to each word, reading aloud one more time, as her husband also read it. There was no mistaking the joyous news. At that, he grabbed Lilly, placing kisses and hugs upon her non-stop. Turning from her, he then gathered Madeleine into his arms, bestowing her with hugs galore. Laughter and tears of pure pleasure embraced them.

This calls for a celebration! exclaimed Madeleine. Leaving the enamored couple to themselves for a moment, she placed a bottle of fine wine into a bucket filled with ice.

Endless prayers had gone out to God throughout the years. The assumption the girls had most likely perished seemed almost unbearable at times. Yet, they too, had received a sense of comfort from up above, giving them much needed peace of mind. The heartbreaking pain of receiving no response, time and again, somehow allowed them to accept the obvious demise of their sisters with more ease.

But now! Now, they had every reason to rejoice in the miracle at hand. After dinner that evening, a glass or two of wine was enjoyed as they celebrated what was no less than a rebirth of these precious family members. Again, it was stated with much genuine love, God had once again given them much to rejoice about.

Chapter Eight

The decision had been made. God had spoken to each, lending His approval for a new adventure. Their chosen destination would be the beautiful state of Minnesota, land of over 10,000 lakes. Minnesota was bordered to the East by the largest fresh water lake in the world, Lake Superior. The vast, wide-open plains of Canada bordered them to the north and the flatlands and prairies of western Minnesota and the Dakotas to the west. The cornfields of Iowa was their southern neighbor. Wisconsin, to the east, also offered endless rolling hills with miles of shoreline along the Great Lakes. What would come to be known as the Midwest or the heartland of the United States spoke volumes of its diversity, with hard-working, honest, God loving people, seeking a land God had meant for them to work and enjoy.

Excitement surged as they gained further knowledge of what Minnesota had to offer. Starting from two flour mills in the 1860's, General Mills revolutionized the milling industry, producing flour with superior baking properties. Recognizing the need for a centrally located flour mill, they eventually chose the site of Minneapolis, a sprawling metropolis growing in size remarkably fast, occupied in large by Scandinavians from Europe. By the 1960's they were marketing children's products such as Play-Doh, Easy Bake Ovens, the Spirograph, Monopoly and Nerf balls, all remaining in production throughout the decades.

Another giant of industry was none other than 3M, Minnesota Mining and Manufacturing Company. Started in 1902 by five tenacious businessmen, this company flourished over the years adding newfangled products steadily.

Courage Times Three. A Novel

Still, another giant contributing to the beginnings of the industrialized revolution in America was United States Steel. Locating its eighth ore operations plant in northeastern Minnesota, it became what is recognized as the Iron Range by most today. Here iron bearing rock is mined and processed into iron ore pellets for use in steel making.

From the huge open pit mines, to agriculture, industry and logging, employment was plentiful. Brilliant displays of the four seasons, along with an abundance of wildlife and unending outdoor activities, gave Valentin every reason he could imagine to relocate to this land of abounding opportunities. And Lilly? Lilly was putty in his hands. She would follow her dear Valentin anywhere.

After carefully planning each stage of their move, something both Valentin and Lilly insisted upon, the time to depart had arrived. A large sect of land was purchased, sight unseen, by Valentin and family in northeastern Minnesota. A two hundred acre tract of forest land with rushing and trickling streams, excellent fishing and hunting, even a pond sat awaiting their arrival. They weren't intimidated by the treacherous winters that often prevailed from November through March in northern Minnesota. The rewards they would receive from living with nature more than reconciled any misgivings they might have. Valentin danced in excitement as he dreamed of their future family settling there.

It was true, Madeleine would sorely miss the hustle and bustle of the city and all it had to offer. Still, she wouldn't think twice about making the change. She had been secretly desiring to play the role of doting grandmother to a handful of beautiful babies.

Several attempted phone calls to reach the owner of the company they had hired to move them had been exhausted. In utter frustration, Madeleine set down the cumbersome black telephone, which was one of the newest modern day contraptions afforded only by those in upscale neighborhoods. Most were still using the ringer phones. One would have to ring the operator requesting her to put you through to your desired party. These telephone lines were shared by more than one customer. Often up to five individual households shared a line. Frequently they had pick up the receiver only to hear another person chattering away. This could get the hair on the nape of the neck standing upright at times. The town gossips would have to take a break from their idle chitchat. Occasionally patient users would find it necessary to cut them off on the spot. There were many operators who sat in on private conversations as well.

Invented by Alexander Graham Bell, the most commonly used name for telephone service was "Ma Bell." "Ma Nosey" was often a nickname given to operators listening in. Finally, with the widespread use of dial up phones and private lines people were rightly afforded their private conversations.

Several hours passed before Madeleine managed to reach her party. She had several questions on a list too lengthy to name. Mostly questions were in reference to the packing of precious items. Madeleine had always been a stickler when it came to organization. Every "i" must be dotted and every "T" crossed.

In three days they were set to depart the state of New York via Lake Erie. A large moving truck would carry their belongings across the state to the shores of the Great Lake, the port city of Buffalo, NY. From there they would board a large freighter carrying them and their life's treasures to their new homeland north of Duluth, Minnesota.

A sense of déjà vu overcame the threesome as they boarded the freighter. Just over two years had passed since they'd stepped foot unto American soil for the first time. New York had been all they'd anticipated and more, much more. No longer did they fear speaking their thoughts on political issues. They had complete freedom to travel from state to state, within the vast countryside, without needing permission. Food, fuel and the like were available to all without fear of rationing or hording. America was indeed a free country with liberties equally provided to all. If one worked hard, saved money, attended church and loved their neighbor they were living the American dream.

Their first mission upon reaching the Port of Duluth was to purchase an automobile. This would be the very first time Valentin would own a vehicle of his own. It was the first time he owned any piece of property in his lifetime as well. He truthfully could not conceive of the fact that he was able to purchase 200 acres.

Daydreams darted through his mind as he imagined just what he could do with that much land. Sometimes he needed to pinch himself in order to realize this wasn't a dream, but reality. With Lilly at his side, life had done nothing but improve. How he cherished her each and every day. Lilly reciprocated those feelings as well. Without him, her dream of coming to America may have never come to fruition.

How strangely life moved in the fashion it did, she thought. Surely the events in her lifetime that had caused major upheavals, then ended on a positive note, were not simple coincidences. Only God could move mountains the way He had, allowing one's life to change on such a grand scale. There was something, somebody out there with a power beyond anything we, as mere humans, could ever fathom. Wasn't the Bible written proof of a superhuman creator?

After spending a couple years in New York with freedom of religion available to all, Lilly began to wonder about her upbringing as a Catholic. Surely there was something to be said for the beliefs of the Jews, Evangelicals, Muslims and all other religions.

Given the opportunity to attend their church of choice, Lilly, Valentin and Madeleine often found themselves at the doorstep of various churches and synagogues, briefly witnessing the beliefs of others, studying God's Word from various perspectives.

Lilly often marveled at how people could live so peaceably within the confines of a small town, while differing on their religious beliefs so enormously. On occasion she would approach this subject with Madeleine or Valentin but never the both of them together in the same room, at the same time. This was too complex a subject for group discussion until she had formed a more unwavering objective about it all herself.

She prayed fervently for God's wisdom. The word she received in response remained the same. John 14:6 Jesus said to him,

"I am the way and the truth and the life. No one comes to the Father except through Me."

No, she didn't hear his voice speaking to her from out of the skies. It was far more subtle than that. It was that still small voice recurrently returning to her mind. Perhaps it was her subconscious mind. She knew this subject would be a source of much interest throughout her lifetime. What most pleased her, however, was the freedom of choice to honor God in whatever fashion she chose. Surely this matter would be wide open for family discussions with their children in the future.

Spring had arrived in the northern tier states. As the ship carried them from port to port, loading and unloading people and cargo, they relished the warmth returning the land back to life. Never did they perceive the northern hemisphere negatively when the cold weather set in for a long winter's nap. It was always more of a necessary sleep, providing rest to many of God's living creatures and plant life.

As sometimes said of those living in northern climates, the long cold winters could be emotionally draining for some. Others frolicked in the pleasurable activities offered by snowy weather. Each season presented its own varied outdoor activities for all. Consequently, the DuBois' favorite time to travel outside of New York City was autumn, when Mother Nature featured a spectacular showing of her best works. Nothing could surpass the beauty and splendor of the gold, peach, coral, crimson, orange and red colors provided for all to enjoy. It was truly a sight to behold!

Word had it colors of Minnesota's autumn season were comparable to that of Upper State New York. In only a matter of months they would judge for themselves. For now they waited in anticipation for all Spring and Summer would provide.

Seeing the last of Lake Michigan the megaton ship on to Lake Superior, of Duluth, MN and Superior, WS. Spring provided generally milder weather with lesser chances of turbulent storms while navigating this ocean-like body of water. Lake Superior was well known for swallowing more than one great freighter within the cold depths of her soul over the years. She bore the brunt of early winter's nasty demeanor, when the gales of November could turn on its predators or friends in a moment's notice. Only the fool-hearted would venture out onto those November waves, even the most masterful of captains.

The Indian name for the *"little pond"*, aka Lake Superior, another endearing term given the lake by those who most loved her, was *"Lake Gitchi Gummi."* Indian folklore had many a story to share with those visiting the shores of this magnificent lake. One would simply have to sit quietly with nature to hear her whisper tales of old. On the northern banks, several small waterfront communities dotted the shoreline. Marinas offered sailboats, fishing boats and the like for tourists to take advantage of. Southern shorelines boasted of the many miles provided those locally as well as tourists from throughout the world with powdery sand dunes to squish the toes and fingers into or provide dune buggy escapades throughout spring, summer and fall.

Endless hours could be spent scaling rock ledges on the craggy shorelines exploring coves, hiking trails, rock climbing and simply connecting with nature, looking into the face of God. Truth be told, those who shared a commonness with the great outdoors, stood on heaven's doorway when enveloped by all of God's creation. The serenity, tranquility, beauty and spiritual connection occurring between man and nature cannot be denied. It is there, where man can bare his soul, tantalizing and embracing every inch of his flesh and bones.

Sometimes women find it difficult to understand why men enjoy getting into the deep woods hunting, fishing, portaging, etc. Perhaps this is why ... Females, at times, have the blessed ability to find peace within more easily than men by bonding with other women, cuddling their newborn babies, nurturing their children or sharing testimonials with each other. Whereas, the male species often finds his peace in nature. Men may brag about the great kill when going out to hunt, yet, it's not that alone ... This is where many men have their own private opportunity to touch base with God reaching deeper inside, fully acknowledging His presence within their souls. Man was taught from early on to be the bread winner and major decision maker; to be strong, withholding his emotions; yet he must treat a lady gently, allowing her to tenderly ease him back into timidity over the years. God knew what He wanted from us before He formed us into humans, His many children. All this we are witness to, with reverence and awe, as time molds and shapes us, thus better understanding Valentin's desire to raise his family within the beauty and splendor of nature.

As the vessel dragged its creaky bones into the bay, ending another arduous journey, Lilly, Valentin and Madeleine smiled, holding hands as they reached their final docking. Oh what adventures lie ahead of them.

Duluth, sitting on the edge of a rocky hillside, displayed her beauty with pride. With trees, shrubs and bushes joyously coming to life in May, all of nature had taken on the bright green shades of Spring. What a delight to see, to feel life returning after a good winter's rest. The lungs of this western-most port of all the Great Lakes, expanded its walls, inhaling new life once again.

Minnesota is recognized for its fast moving thunderheads rolling in and out throughout the days of Spring and Summer. Low pressure systems dipping out of Canada could sit in place for several weeks. While remaining motionless, high pressure systems would climb up from the south colliding with the stationary front. This would provide beautiful sunny mornings followed by fast moving afternoon storm cells, rolling in and out within minutes.

This day, however, gave way to nothing but clear blue skies, void of a single cloud, temperatures in the mid seventies and a light breeze flowing off the lake. Before leaving the grand vessel, they paused to give thanks to their Heavenly Father for guiding the boat and crew safely to their destination.

Having spent so much time traveling on water caused all three of them to develop sea legs. As the women initially de-boarded the vessel, just ahead of Valentin, hearty laughter spilled out in a roar from within as he watched the women get their legs back, wobbling about, hanging on to anything stable to prevent them from toppling over. Lilly gave Valentin a growling frown quite unlike anything he had witnessed before, causing him even further laughter. She simply did not see the humor in it. Once they had regained their land legs however, it did, in fact, place more than a grin on her face. Abruptly all burst into vigorous laughter, escalating to the point of tears. What a magnificent way to begin the final trek to their new home site.

Valentin promptly instructed the men from the moving service to deliver their belongings to a storage unit fifty five miles north of Duluth. Handing them a well drawn map, the movers shouldn't have any problems locating the units. Next they hailed a taxi, directing the driver to the nearest car sales lot. After purchasing a shiny new 1951 Ford Custom Deluxe Country Squire, including white walled tires and a body dressed in wood striping, their personal belongings were loaded into the rear of the vehicle.

It was a proud moment for Valentin as he slid behind that steering wheel. Proud indeed! He had purchased his very first automobile. As always, Valentin had planned ahead. He'd had the foresight to obtain driving lessons from a fellow church member prior to leaving New York City, enabling him to acquire a license just prior to their departure. Sitting behind the wheel of that shiny new Ford Squire, Valentin shared a most satisfied look with his dear Lilly. Thus far the trip had gone precisely as planned.

Courage Times Three. A Novel

    Steadily ascending the steep hills of Duluth Lilly wondered if they might just reach the clouds. Duluth reminded the threesome of photos they had seen of a city in the state of California named San Francisco. Ultimately reaching the top of the hill Valentin followed directions straight through Duluth unto Highway 53, proudly maneuvering his brand spanking new automobile north to a crossroad just south of the town of Eveleth. According to directions, they would proceed exactly fifty five miles north until reaching Highway 37, which turned in a westerly direction only. At the three mile marker they would be sitting on the very property they had purchased, sight unseen.

    Whatever would they do if the land turned out to be skunk land? Nothing but swamp and mosquitoes? The party he had dealt with was a reputable company, as Valentin most definitely had investigated. He had learned of a man who had purchased property in the same area. Word was, he was an upstanding citizen who would not steer a man wrong. More than pleased with his purchase through the land realtor, Valentin was strongly advised to take his chances in purchasing the property. Either he was about to become deliriously ecstatic, or nauseatingly crushed. Faith that God had steered him in the right direction held strong though.

Chapter Nine

Northeastern Minnesota was not only the land of over 10,000 lakes but a land filled with forests as far as the eye could see. With as much underbrush as trees, Lilly and Madeleine became quite curious as to what kinds of wild animals could be lurking in those forests. It was very unfamiliar territory for the ladies but they kept an upbeat attitude.

Along the roadway wildflowers galore grew in shades of yellow, lavender, blue and orange. June offered wild strawberries and chokecherries while late July and early August offered bushes full of blueberries and raspberries, not to mention countless other berries and herbs. Minnesota's lakes and streams flourished with fish which could be caught at any time of year.

Once the ice on the lakes thickened to the point of safety, where it held a good amount of weight, a frequent sight would be ice fishing houses scattered about. These fish houses were pulled out to the middle of the lake with trucks. Those living in warmer climates could not imagine driving on ice out to the middle of a lake. It was commonplace for these hearty Northlanders however. Not only was this a means of providing families with their main course for dinner, it also served as a great sport year round. Holes were drilled through layers of ice with augers right in the middle of the fish house where hours could be spent pulling them in while awaiting the *"big one."*

Another frequent sight would be the *"grand prize"* caught by the man of the house, stuffed and mounted on the wall in the front room. Many a fishing tale were told over a brewskie or two.

The overall livelihood for most families residing in this area of Minnesota was the iron ore mining. An approximate one hundred mile stretch of iron ore lay beneath the ground waiting to be excavated over years to come. Most towns had their humble beginnings in the various locations where a new mine was started. The economy was robust with new homes, businesses and schools being steadily erected.

The beauty of the lakes, scattered frequently on each side of the highway, were a breathtaking sight. Valentin already felt a sense of home there. It was often referred to by many as God's country.

Following directions they soon approached the exit to Highway 37. Just three miles to go! Valentin tried his best to breath, hoping the over sized lump in his throat would shrink back to normal. Reaching out for Lilly's hand, he came upon the mile marker which told him they had arrived at last. How far he had come. From Poland to France to New York to Minnesota. Valentin reached out for Lilly's hand, a moment of joy overtaking him, as they pulled alongside the road to their property.

Their first up-close look at a doe and her fawn greeted them immediately. Forests, fields, a stream running right in front of their eyes, flowed out of a body of water appearing to be substantially larger than a pond.

Approaching the water by foot they soon came to realize it was not a small pond, but a lake. Unrolling the paperwork he had grabbed from the trunk of the car, Valentin double checked to be sure he wasn't mistaken about the location. As far as he could tell all appeared to be correct. Had they actually purchased land including several feet of lake frontage? Having a lake at their doorstep meant he could farm if his carpentry skills did not find him work otherwise. Valentin could not be more pleased with his purchase, sight unseen. Tomorrow morning he would confirm his investment. They would also come to learn the name of the lake as Long Lake, aptly describing the length of this body of water.

Pushing their way through the dense woodsy thick, Lilly, accompanied by Madeleine, made her way back to the new automobile to rest for a short time. It had been a long day. All were ready for a warm shower, a tasty meal and a good night's sleep.

As the ladies awaited Valentin's return, Lilly began realizing the tremendous task that lay before them. Many months of labor would be required by all to turn this raw land into a home for themselves. Questioning Valentin, upon his return, Lilly seemed distraught and overwhelmed by it all. Inquiring about their accommodations until their home was built and habitable, Lilly's precious husband assured his wife she need not worry her pretty head about such matters. As they drove into the first town of Eveleth they found a cozy motel for showering and refreshing themselves from the long journey.

Following a few phone calls, Valentin drove the ladies to a local restaurant where they dined on fresh walleye for dinner. Then it was back to the motel for a good night's sleep. Much lay ahead of them tomorrow and in the days to follow.

Early the following morning Valentin was off on business to the City Hall in Eveleth with his land description in hand, seeing to it the layout of the land was properly drawn up and registered. After just a few minor corrections his next stop was the Carpenters Union Hall to confirm his request for laborers and machinery. No time would be wasted as the crew was to begin immediately, clearing and excavating his land. Making plans in advance from New York City, Valentin was a step ahead of himself, as he preferred whenever possible.

His next stop would be back at City Hall, where he would make inquiries about a name change. Having discussed the matter at length with Lilly, Valentin felt strongly about taking back his true name of Valentin Augustus Baranowsky, his given Polish name. Although the process would be timely, needing verification from records in Poland as to his true identification, he was more than happy to wait. After all, he had lived with the surname of DuBois for several years. A few months wouldn't change anything. Yet, he and Lilly did introduce themselves as Valentin and Lilly Baranowsky to their new acquaintances. Madeleine had no qualms about the name change. She only wanted what was best for her family. Nothing more.

Meanwhile, Lilly and Madeleine slept in until finally feeling a bit of life enter back into their bodies. Still, Lilly was pale, lacking the enthusiasm she'd expected to have. Apparently more rest was needed to boost her energy and enthusiasm.

Conveniently located very near a grocery store, Madeleine walked the short distance purchasing a few items of food for a light continental breakfast. Pulling Lilly out of bed, Madeleine instructed her daughter to freshen herself before joining her for breakfast. Lilly did as instructed, but when it came time to eat she had no appetite. She was never much of a breakfast eater anyway so a small glass of orange juice sufficed just fine.

Courage Times Three. A Novel

Stepping outside the motel room at 10am, the ladies walked to the downtown area, window shopping as they had in New York City. Not long into their browsing the mother/daughter duo became inevitably aware of the major changes in the lifestyle they were about to embark upon.

Left far behind were the cozy coffee houses, cobblestone streets lined with numerous storefronts displaying the latest fashions, ice cream parlors, flower shops, but most importantly, no hat shops ... not a single one ... Madeleine was heartbroken without having her choice of a new hat each month. Little did she know there would rarely be use for such items in their new way of life. Perhaps Sunday church would be her only weekly opportunity.

As the days passed, mother and daughter would accompany Valentin to the property occasionally, anxiously watching the progression of the property shaping into what would be their yard. With a full crew at their disposal, the land was cleared, developing a winding roadway to the location where the home was to be built, just fifty feet from the shoreline. The home front would face east on the west end of the bay overlooking the water. Mornings would welcome the brilliant sunlight into their living room and kitchen daily.

Madeleine and Lilly eagerly sought out information as to what types of plant life were best suited to the climate, while also learning which flowerbeds would grow best in the sun or shade including perennials. Rich fertile soil would provide hearty growth for most any flowers, vegetables or herbs that could sustain the climate's cool nights. Disappointed it would likely be another year before they could plant the flowerbeds, they found other methods to provide robust color in lovely decorated flowerpots placed accordingly upon the sizable deck. Madeleine kept busy photographing the progress of the home building for the many scrapbooks, full of memories, she would one day present to her grandbabies.

Valentin was sent out to earn a living through the Carpenters Union Hall, which kept him busy 5 - 6 days out of the week. The ladies located the Resurrection Catholic Church in town for Sunday services, followed by pot luck luncheons. This was their opportunity to become acquainted with fellow townspeople, many of whom had emigrated to that location from Europe. From the Nordics to the Slovenians', Slovakians, Italians, Germans and French to the

Catholics, Protestants, Jewish and agnostics, people gathered together in harmony, cherishing their many freedoms in America.

Two weeks of hotel accommodations began to wear on them, as the quarters were tight and they had been living like sardines on the ship that brought them and their furnishings across the country to Minnesota. Only a small apartment was required for the short period of time until the new home was livable. Immediately a small, lower level two bedroom duplex apartment in the town of Eveleth was leased. Removing only a small portion of furnishings from storage for the apartment, the majority of their belongings remained untouched, waiting to be unpacked for use in their new home.

Immediately upon receiving the address of their rental apartment, telephone service was requested to be installed. An uncomfortable anxiety had rutted itself in the middle of Valentin's stomach. The timing could not have been worse. His desire to receive any written word from his long lost sisters was, at times, overwhelming. His joy in learning of their survival was often recklessly preceded by the angst he suffered. He must make a long distance telephone call to Emma. It was of much urgency he confirm the survival of his younger sisters in Sweden. He couldn't bear to wait any longer.

Lilly and Madeleine were fully aware of Valentin's anxiety. He always seemed pre-occupied. Understanding there was much to be dealt with regarding their future home was one thing. But the added pressure of not knowing if Lorraine, Katya and Alina were indeed alive was tearing him up.

The day the telephone service was installed Madeleine urged Valentin to make whatever calls he deemed necessary to gain further news. She assured him she could cover whatever costs were incurred from the overseas calls. So, without further thought he placed the long distance call to Paris through the operator.

Only two rings brought Emma's much desired voice to his ear. Valentin delighted in hearing her voice once again. He felt as though she was standing right next to him, carrying out a normal everyday conversation. This call held, however, a great deal more importance than everyday chitchat.

Once the overseas operator allowed the connection to go through, Valentin asked the ever so important question ... *Have you received any affirmative response to the correspondence sent to our sisters Emma?* Emma wanted nothing more than to give him a positive response. But she knew that was impossible. She had not received any reply as of yet. Heartbroken, but certainly not defeated, a plan was devised to expedite the process of confirmation.

Lorraine obviously had gainful employment providing a means of support. Even Katya and Alina would now be old enough to have jobs. A few telephone calls might just provide a work sight for one of them if they still used the same surname as given at birth. First things first, however, locating a home telephone number was where they would begin their search, given they had not married, no longer using their maiden names. Many did not yet have the means to afford a home telephone. Only scant information had been gained, giving the basic information of an address used by a Lorraine Baranowsky in Kalmar, Sweden.

Keeping expenses at a minimum, Valentin said his goodbye to Emma, promising to notify her immediately upon gaining further knowledge.

Earth to Valentin! ... earth to Valentin! ... please come in Valentin! As if snapped out of a trance, Valentin lovingly approached the mother of his child, placing his head upon her womb. Lilly's response, filled with warm affection, stroked his hair gently. So very much to digest in one single day. Tears of joy filled his eyes, a strong sense of gratefulness overtaking him at that moment in time. A prayer of much appreciation went out to their Lord and Savior. Lilly, herself, was still dumbstruck at the thought of having a child growing within. Numerous precautions had been taken in avoiding pregnancy throughout the years, but at times they had wondered if God had other plans for them. It just seemed as though their far-from-foolproof method of birth control had been compromised more than a few times. Lilly warned Valentin not to get his hopes up too high before confirming it with the doctor. Still, he now had two possible dreams coming to fruition at once. If the news they were awaiting from Europe and from the doctor both came to be, he would be the most blessed man on earth. Mother Madeleine's hopes, too, hung on firmly, as the dream of a precious grandchild played repeatedly, over and over in her mind.

No telephone call was received before the three found themselves yawning at the end of a highly emotional day. Nothing could deny the presence of loving smiles in each of them as warm embraces replaced their anxiety, bidding a goodnight to one another.

Hope for word of Valentin's sisters within the next twenty-four hours, avoiding the lengthy time it would have taken via postal service before the telephone came into existence, was much appreciated. A peaceful night's sleep for all was just what the doctor ordered. Tomorrow would bring another day filled with excitement and anticipation. Special prayers of thanks were sent to their awesome Father above for the many gifts he bestowed upon them. Valentin held Lilly close to his heart, warmly wrapping her in his arms until their dreams carried them away.

Heavy sleep caused an abrupt awakening. With vague awareness of what was ringing in her ears, Lilly shook her husband to answer the ringing telephone. Valentin frantically searched the base of the bed for his bathrobe. Swiftly tying the belt around his waist, no time was wasted as he charged into the kitchen where the ringing box was located. As expected, the overseas operator from France was on the other end of the line.

Both Lilly and Madeleine followed Valentin into the kitchen. A look of anxiety beheld curiosity while silently listening. *Please Lord, let it be good news,* whispered Lilly.

Blinking his eyes repeatedly, Valentin appeared to be hearing more clearly, as though his eyes struggled to clear cobwebs, better enabling him to absorb the words he was hearing. A faint voice could be heard in the background as Emma asked the operator to inquire if he would accept reversed charges for the call. Valentin refused the charges and the line was disconnected, just as they had planned to do. A five minute delay in response prompted his direct return call back to Emma in Paris.

Madeleine filled the coffee pot with water and coffee grounds, setting it on the stove to percolate while Lilly read off the telephone numbers to Valentin while he repeated them to the operator. Two rings again brought Emma's voice to his ear.

Without hesitation Emma chattered on rapidly, filled with vigorous enthusiasm. Yes, yes! We have located Lorraine's place of employment along with a telephone number. Valentin shared each word, verbatim, with Lilly and Madeleine. Could they truly be hearing the voices of his beautiful baby sisters momentarily? Absent from his life for so many years, the reality of the moment was difficult to wrap his head around.

Another promise was made to Emma before disconnecting the call. He would notify her as soon as he had made contact. Tantamount to everything else was the knowledge of their truly being alive.

This is all too good to be true Lilly! He couldn't believe he was so close to hearing his sister Lorraine's voice for the first time in over a decade.

Yes operator, I would like to place an overseas call please. Lilly hustled to bring the number to Valentin at the kitchen table. Madeleine poured a steaming hot cup of fully-leaded coffee for Valentin and herself. Lilly thought it best to avoid any caffeine at that hour of the night. Valentin listened as the Swedish/American speaking operator asked to be connected with Frau Lorraine Baranowsky. It was 9 o'clock AM in Sweden. Lorraine would surely be at work by this time. Hopeful glances tossed from one face to another spoke of the angst within the four walls.

Valentin waited for what seemed to be an eternity. Then, suddenly hearing her voice, words could not describe the overwhelming relief, the joy, the intense shock waves, that vibrated through him like a zap of electrical current. His loving eyes, instantly misting over with tears, was nearly too much to bear. Finding his voice on demand seemed a task too terrific to achieve. He opened his mouth to speak yet no sound came forth. A second but not altogether futile attempt, after clearing his throat, finally produced a strained and broken uttering. On the other end of his line, a crackly connection, somewhat diminishing the voice in clarity, produced a Swedish speaking woman.

Hello? Lorraine? Speaking in Polish, he stated, *this is your brother Valentin!* A clunking of the phone and a loud thud was all Valentin heard. Soon, voices echoed throughout the room. Someone picked up the telephone speaking in Swedish. All Valentin could do was repeat Lorraine's name. *I, brudder to Lorraine. I, big brudder to Lorraine.* It was apparent Lorraine had lost consciousness upon hearing his spoken words. Was it possible this could be the voice of a brother she had long since given up for dead after all of these years? The shock of hearing him alive on the other end of the telephone was altogether too shocking for her.

Just as suddenly as she had dropped the telephone, Lorraine quickly recovered from her fainting spell, respectfully requesting the telephone receiver to be returned to her, thanking those now surrounding her for their care and concern.

Valentin! Is it truly you my brother? Years of prayer and hope had, at last, been answered. He could hear the many questions coming from those nearby. He pleasured in listening to her courteously sharing the good news with them. An applause broke out as heaving sobs overtook her. Valentin took a quick moment to tell Lilly and Madeleine it was indeed his Lorraine. Tears of joy were shared by all.

In their native Polish tongue, the two exchanged personal information of their whereabouts. Valentin praised God Almighty when hearing Katya and Alina were alive and well. Lorraine was stunned to learn of his move to the USA. She sobbed even further when he shared the wonderful news of their sisters, Greta and Emma.

Understandingly, the tragic news of their parents and brother, Hugo, was upsetting to Lorraine. Exchanging addresses and telephone numbers, as well as their sisters' personal contact information both cherished each moment with their newly rekindled siblings, their words and voices never leaving their thoughts for long. Saying goodbye proved to be more difficult than either had anticipated. A promise of continued correspondence was undeniably guaranteed by both.

Before placing his last call to Emma once again, Valentin, Madeleine and Lilly held hands in prayer of appreciation for the enlightening truth that had, at last, been revealed. Following a cup of coffee, the quick and final call was made to Emma, sharing the marvelous news of their dearest siblings survival. A request was made for Emma to call Aunt Melanie, thanking her, not only for her heart-warming assistance, but in sharing the almost inconceivable success in finding their sisters.

* * * * *

Madeleine worked anxiously, cleaning the apartment with great vigor while awaiting the return of her beautiful daughter and son-in-law. Today was Lilly's first visit with the obstetrician. While nobody had to prove to Madeleine the validity of her daughter's state of health, still, a definite confirmation would be the frosting on the cake, so to speak.

Moments later, walking in the door of the apartment, hand in hand, smiles strewn across their faces, they delivered the joyous news of their first child's arrival. At ten weeks pregnancy she should deliver in late March of the following year, 1952. With a delivery date in late March, Lilly had likely conceived on their journey through the Great Lakes while in transit to their new home.

Madeleine was overjoyed with the ecstatic news. At last she would become a grandmother. The three stood together, beaming proudly, as Valentin expressed his deepest gratitude to their Heavenly Father for the greatest gift of all, life!!!

Standing in the narrow hallway of the small apartment, with little space and fewer amenities than they had been accustomed to, their hearts could not be any more full knowing of God's greatest treasure right there within them. Something money could never buy. The true meaning of love and joy ... an infant child! And no less miraculous, the renewed life of his precious sisters.

Only a few weeks remained until the house was ready for habitation. Back when the blueprints were drawn up for their home, the Baranowsky's undoubtedly planned, not only for their own bedroom, but for Madeleine's room and two additional bedrooms for future family needs.

How delighted the women were to begin decorating the baby's room. They spoke incessantly of the necessary furnishings required to complete the nursery. Everything from clothing needs, blankets, bonnets and playpens were included in the planning. Choosing room colors, curtains and carpet were also such exciting elements mother and daughter discussed for days. Having the new Sears and Roebuck catalog along with J.C. Penney's, provided shopping right at home, even in their nightwear if so desired. How they reveled at the wonder of God's greatest gift every night as they would solemnly lie down for another night's sleep.

This was one of the happiest times Lilly would recall in her elderly years. Time spent bonding with her own mother while becoming a mother herself. Not until having children of her own would Lilly ever encompass the full extent of her mother's love. Still, they considered themselves ultimately blessed to be sharing their many achievements with each other now, leaning on one another for love and support. Madeleine and Valentin were becoming much more than in-laws. The mother/son relationship could not be stronger. How the Lord had blessed them all.

*****

At last, Lilly's morning sickness began to subside. She was thankful to be moving into the new lake home without being plagued by nausea.

Autumn was most definitely in the air. Their anticipation of the awesome colors Minnesota's Fall season had to offer had now fully arrived. True to its word, it certainly did reach their expectations with a vast array of maple, poplar, oak and birch leaves, among others, highlighting the decorative forest and lakeside in varying shades of auburn red, burgundy, coral, peach and gold. The three anxiously anticipated their near move into the home while Mother Nature displayed her finest workmanship.

Lilly dreamed of one day buying riding horses, similar to what she had ridden as a child in France. Land was no deterrent as 250 acres provided enough space for several grazing horses and a full sized barn, filled with stalls. She, too, would teach her children to ride just as Madeleine and Jon Paul had taught her, not so many years earlier.

Chapter Ten

    The time had arrived for the Baranowsky's to empty the storage unit, filling their newly built home with their many treasured belongings. The unpacking got underway and before long mother and daughter seized moments, here and there, to venture into yesteryear. Endless chatter ensued while unveiling trinkets, knickknacks and various cherished mementos from crates and boxes.
    Cautiously removing a small jewelry box, Lilly knew well of its exact contents, one of her nearest and dearest possessions. The treasured locket she had received from her parents before entering the underground so many years ago. Always making sure the locket remained in place around her neck during her lengthy time underground, it had acted as a constant reminder of her parting moments with her parents early in the second world war. Only after seeing her mother once again in Paris did she remove the locket, placing it in safe keeping for a lifetime. She was sure to always check the content of the box as she moved from Paris to New York to Minnesota. A timeless reminder of extreme pain and loss, Lilly used that memory to strengthen her from time to time, rather than allowing the memories to bring her down. Somehow, it served as a source of hope, forever encouraging her trust in her true Father. It would always remind her of the time and place she first met her loving husband. Lilly knew if she could survive those years of misery, she could withstand any challenges in her lifetime.
    Frequent thoughts of her father carried her to another place and time, especially now that she carried his first grandchild. Madeleine often assured Lilly of her father's likely approval regarding her choice of a husband. There wasn't a man alive who loved her more, who cared about her every need, or who wanted to please her more

than Valentin. So much had happened in those past ten years since first meeting her husband.

It is utterly intriguing how God brings love to those who least expect it in the most peculiar of ways. Never would Lilly have dreamed she would meet her knight in shining armor while barely surviving her very own life underground during an inconceivable war.

Additional memories would creep into their minds here and there, only to be forcefully pushed out, sometimes wishing they could permanently be extracted as they continued unpacking belongings. Before long they had set up shop to the extent they could until further work on the interior was completed. Window trim and baseboards needed to be stained and varnished before Valentin could complete those interior jobs. Lilly could not be exposed to the potent fumes of those products while carrying their child within her womb, otherwise she and Madeleine would have jumped into the project full force.

Once completed, however, the women would carry out their duties, dressing the windows in elegant coverings. The lavish satin draperies they had purchased for their New York apartment had been carefully packed away for future use in the home. This was taken into consideration when sizing the windows for the house as the value of the satin ran into several hundreds of dollars. Such an expense could never be squandered.

Larger pieces of furniture, such as the grandfather clock and piano, were now being carried into the home by dear friends from the church. The heavy items took more than two men to maneuver through the doorways. A layout of the room with its furnishings had been created prior to even the initial building of the home, avoiding any errors that would cause additional work for the movers. Valentin rarely left any stone unturned, one of his admirable qualities greatly appreciated by both daughter and mother.

The ladies applauded with cheers as the last piece of furniture was placed into the living room. In payment for their hard work a huge batch of spaghetti, with the necessary fixings accompanying it, was served to the hard working, famished men. They certainly had worked up a voracious appetite. Father Perk had even lent his muscles on that beautiful Sunday afternoon. Before delving into their heaped piles of spaghetti, he led a prayer blessing the young couple's new home.

What endearing friends they had acquired in such a short period of time in Minnesota. Their reception in New York City didn't hold a candle to the generosity and kindness shown by the small town people they had come to love and respect.

Autumn ended all too quickly as they busied themselves daily, placing the finishing touches on their home. Gone were the cool brisk days of Fall. Winter had ushered itself in by mid November with its first snow of the season.

Thanksgiving day seemed to appear in a flash. Lilly's abdomen further revealed her pregnancy as their first child blossomed within her womb. Occasional flutters of butterflies created a warm, affectionate sense of motherhood early on. How earnestly they looked forward to the joy of a little one in the house.

Late afternoon brought Valentin home once again in his fancy Ford Squire. The ladies of the house were nearly finished preparing dinner as he walked in the door. Removing only his work boots in the entry porch, he scurried into the kitchen with a single yellow rose for the beautiful mother of his child-to-be. Lilly had always been attracted to yellow roses as her husband well knew. Those little things were what Lilly treasured so much about her dear husband.

Finishing the last of their scrumptious dessert, New York style cheesecake with strawberry sauce, Valentin thanked the ladies for another delicious meal. Looking out the window at the gray, ice-covered lake, Madeleine caught sight of the season's first snowflakes, falling ever so softly to the ground. Not a single sign of wind was present as each flake grew to the size of dimes, gently floating feather-like through the air. An awe-inspiring sight, no doubt.

Snow accumulated steadily as daylight gave way to the western skies, the solemn darkness inviting itself in. A soft glow upon the snow, highlighted by outdoor lanterns, provided an amazing display of sparkling diamonds; each flake gently resting, one upon the other. How dynamic was the Lord as He blanketed the earth in magnificent white, each flake unique in itself, invoking breathtaking awes from the three of them. One could gaze for hours, mesmerized by the glimmering beauty.

That night, as the grateful couple entered their bedroom for the night, both knelt on bended knee at their bedside, praising Him so wholeheartedly for their many blessings.

Thanksgiving came and went leaving newfound memories for all to cherish. Additional new coming emigrants, attendees of the Resurrection Catholic Church, were cordially invited to the home of the Baranowsky's for a delightful meal of turkey with all the dressings.

In all, ten guests joined in the festivities for their first Minnesota celebration in the year of 1952. Each couple had prepared a favorite dish or dessert which complimented the plump, mouth-watering turkey. Following grace, plates were filled with various ethnic specialties completing a hearty, ten-course meal. pumpkin pie was the hit of the desserts topped with light fluffy whipped cream.

As the couples departed the home of the Baranowsky's that evening, they spoke of the upcoming holiday, Christmas Day, in which all desired to once again join together in celebration.

*****

Madeleine had taken to spending much time outdoors photographing the beauty of the winter wonderland. As promised to their families abroad, frequent photos were generously included with all other correspondence going to France and Sweden, keeping them abreast of their lives in the USA.

Lorraine, Valentin's only single sister in Sweden, had made it her solitary, individual pursuit to improve the lives of children less fortunate in life than many. Her quest to improve their lives molded her own character into something reminiscent of a saint. She matured in spiritual growth immensely, as a Lutheran, in the capital city of Stockholm.

The port city of Kalmar, sitting just south of Stockholm on the shores of the Baltic, was where Valentin and Lorraine's younger sisters had settled. Alina and Katya had both married, residing with their respective Swedish husbands and children. Photographs and letters provided this family, so brutally torn apart by the monstrous war, a method of re-connecting. With little cognizance of understanding the ramifications those tragic years had on them, how it had shaped them into people they likely would not have become under other circumstances, they vowed to keep constant communications with one another. Hopes of one day embracing their siblings in person, dreams of sharing their new lives and families together, were often at the forefront of their thoughts. Be it God's will, perhaps time would allow the luxury of those embraces.

Sisters Greta and Emma remained living in Paris, affectionately keeping in close contact via the postal service with their beloved brother in the United States and sisters in Sweden. Lilly and Valentin, too, hoped to one day return to Europe, reacquainting themselves with their dearly beloved siblings. However, that day was in the far distance, with a new family in America just being established. Thus, life would move forward, as it always had.

Greatly appreciative of Madeleine's photographic abilities, Lilly and Valentin steadily encouraged her to continue pursuing her hobby with vigor. What a treasure it would be having so many visual memories to revisit while later passing them along to future generations of Baranowsky's. Surprisingly, both mother and daughter had adjusted to this major change in lifestyle incredibly well. When one has endured extreme hardships, the ability to pick oneself up increases tenfold. These courageous Europeans had indeed endured the worst of times. Rather than allowing it to destroy them each made their own conscious choices, using it to boost their stamina, driving them to succeed in whatever goals they would set for themselves. Never did they fear life's challenges. Unending love, along with the promise of hope and faith, ultimately kept them afloat.

Chapter Eleven

The Holy Day of Christ's birth was near. A lovely Norway pine stood centered in front of the large living room window, waiting to be decorated. One day for thawing before dressing it in its finest attire was the plan. Valentin cautiously began the process of intertwining the colorful lights through branches, while the women proceeded to adorn its bows with ornaments, candy canes and garland.

Night fell upon them, enveloping the dimly lit magical aura of the tree. Smiles and hugs provided additional warmth to the already soft ambiance. A subdued moment of golden silence rested upon them.

Turning to sneak a candy cane from one of the bows, Lilly suddenly gasped with delight, placing her husband's hand on her abdomen to feel the infant moving within. All agreed this child could sense the joy residing within Lilly. At this same time next year they would be holding a precious baby child in front of the glittering tree.

* * * * *

Snow, with bitter cold temps and ferocious northerly winds blew down from Canada. Valentin bundled himself in winter garments made of wool, heading outdoors to move the automobile beneath a tree with long extended branches, shielding it, somewhat, from the weather.

One of the great conveniences of living in snow country was having a garage for housing the family automobile. With having invested in two major purchases, an automobile and a newly built home, within the past six months, a garage would have to wait for some time to come.

Tucking the Ford Squire beneath the tree, Valentin then proceeded to laboriously heave shovels full of snow up against the base of their home. This acted as an insulator against the icy north winds that had already given them a heavy dose of arctic blasts. With temps dipping to -18 degrees Fahrenheit, accompanied by gusting winds, the wind chill factor would reach a dangerously low (*feels like*) temp of -42 degrees.

How does one survive those kinds of frigid temps? Turn up the heat, dress accordingly, close down the schools and even some of the businesses. Those unfortunate souls unable to stay indoors were always advised to wear layers of clothing, protecting the body from head to toe.

Emergency cold weather kits were advised for all to keep in their cars. Those kits, meant to be kept in the car, not the trunk, included a blanket, flashlight, matches, a few snacks and water, to name a few. A bright red piece of material, used to tie on the top of the antenna, was always wise to keep on board, a means of notifying passers-by of their situation. In blizzard conditions, snow could blow high enough to cover the entire car. The odds of surviving life-threatening cold temperatures increased ten-fold.

It takes hardy people to live through the cold Minnesota blizzards. Fortunately, old man winter would only toss out the ravaging storms a few times each winter, generally quite short lived. Oftentimes, people rejoiced with the Spring thaw, greatly appreciating the warmer seasons each year.

Completing his shoveling chores, Valentin headed for the lean-to, a sloped roof added to the side of the house for cover. After placing the shovel in its designated spot, he turned toward the house, ready to call it a night. But he stopped in his tracks when he saw headlights approaching down his driveway.

Wondering who would be paying a visit at 8pm on this freezing, blustery night, he waited to greet the visitor. It was, undoubtedly, a woman, as she struggled to maneuver her way through the snow. Even as she grew nearer he struggled to identify her inside the bundles of clothing.

In broken English, the approaching woman if he was Valentin Baranowsky. Neither had the ability to identify the other as they were both bundled beyond recognition. Courteously he replied, with some trepidation, he was, in fact, Valentin Augustus Baranowsky. Upon hearing those words, the woman collapsed to her knees.

The hair on the nape of his neck stood at heightened shock as his very instincts told him who this might possibly be. Quickly raising her to a stand, seeking out the others eyes, both confirmed the answer they desired. *My dear, could it truly be??? Are you my sister Lorraine?* he nervously inquired. *Yes, yes ... it is me ... Lorraine!* she cried.

How many years had it been? He had not seen her since she was twelve years of age. When he left Poland for France he was merely sixteen years old. Just a boy. Today he was a man of twenty-eight. Which would make Lorraine twenty-four. Twelve long years had passed between them, without a hug. Without a single smile. With no physical contact whatsoever.

The bitter cold was immediately forgotten as they stood frozen in time, embracing one another continually. Gently releasing her from his embrace, Valentin sent Lorraine into the entryway while he removed her luggage from the car. Per her instructions, he graciously thanked the driver for delivering his dear sister to him on that frigidly cold December night, sending him back onto the ice covered roads. She explained her intentions to brief him on her traveling partner once they got indoors, allowing her driver to complete his journey to his destination that bitter cold winter night.

Stomping their feet, freeing them of excess snow, they stepped through the doorway into Valentin's warm, inviting home. Immediately Lilly scurried into the room at the sound of stomping feet. Who on earth had come in with Valentin?

Expecting, perhaps, to see a neighbor in need, Lilly was about to speak when Valentin gently hushed her with a gesture to his lips, requesting her silence for just a moment. Removing their head wear, vaguely familiar faces revealed themselves. The tears, no longer capable of being withheld, streamed down bewildered faces. *This, Lilly, is my dear sweet sister, Lorraine, all the way from Sweden.*

Valentin gazed upon his sister intently, envisioning her as the twelve year old girl he'd left behind all those years ago.

Madeleine, hearing the commotion from her bedroom, entered the room just as Lilly leaned into Lorraine, embracing her as though she were her own sister. She, too, shed tears for the joyous moment upon them.

Standing just behind Lilly, dressed in her evening wear and looking every bit as beautiful as ever, Madeleine soon realized who this tall, attractive woman was. Indeed, it could be none other than a Baranowsky, likely one of Valentin's siblings. The striking resemblance between brother and sister was apparent. High cheekbones, similar shaped emerald green eyes accented by deep chocolate-brown hair spoke volumes of their shared Polish heritage. Even their smiles matched one another's.

Madeleine offered an enormous hug to Lorraine before instructing her to free herself of her heavy outdoor clothing. Following suit, Valentin refused to turn his sites away from his most welcomed visitor as he removed his own outdoor wear.

He could not believe his good fortune. Lorraine had given him the best Christmas gift one could ever receive, the gift of her presence. Madeleine set the teapot on the stove to heat before slicing several pieces of zucchini and pumpkin breads, freshly baked just that afternoon. Not sure if they would be burning the midnight candle, getting acquainted and reacquainted, Madeleine set out a few blends of tea. Chamomile for rest or lemon zest for energy, along with a favorite blend of coffee.

Lorraine instantly felt a relieved sense of comfort with the unfamiliar faces. After freshening herself in the bathroom she was shown to the guest bedroom, allowing her time to unpack a few necessary toiletries and such. Soon, the four of them locked into conversation taking them to Europe and back, time and again, throughout the next few hours.

Lorraine explained her good fortune in meeting an American professor in Sweden who was studying animal life in the Nordic countries. It ironically happened to be that his family lived only 100 miles north of the Baranowsky residence in International Falls, Minnesota. Informing her of his plans to return to his home for the holidays, it occurred to Lorraine she quite possibly could make a surprise trip, herself, to finally see her long lost brother and family. She certainly could afford the trip and was in good hands with Professor Thuringer assisting her along the way. She had been given a two week paid vacation along with a Christmas bonus for her years of devotion to the endless needs of homeless children.

The threesome were assured of meeting Professor Thuringer when he came through to pick her up for their return trip to Sweden. As midnight struck its melancholy chimes, a yawning Lorraine found it necessary to excuse herself for a much needed night's sleep. Amid good night hugs and kisses, Valentin once again expressed his deepest pleasure to Lorraine for the most wonderful gift she had brought him.

Regardless of late night conversations all were quick to rise the following morning. Lorraine was fully familiar with cold winters as a resident in one of the Scandinavian countries. She had well maintained the wherewithal to tolerate bitter cold temperatures unlike her fragile French counterparts, Lilly and Madeleine.

Following a most stimulating conversation over breakfast and coffee, Valentin and Lorraine excused themselves from the company of the ladies to step outdoors for a bit of private time together. While the temperature still hovered below zero, the north winds had substantially lifted providing a brisk but invigorating walk as they explored the beauty of the property. Each felt much pride in the other as they lightly spoke of life at this time in their lives. There would be plenty of time to cover past losses. For now, Lorraine hoped to hear more about Valentin's plans for his future with Lilly and her mother.

Keeping well informed through letters, Lorraine had been fully briefed on her new niece or nephew due to arrive in late March. Her heart longed to be near her brother's family now that she had found him again. Having sisters in Sweden, Lorraine had, most definitely, found time to spend with their families. However, there was so much she had missed out on in Valentin's life. A strong sense of profound guilt seemed to surround her now, lingering ominously, like a cloud she couldn't quite find her way out of, regarding the atrocious deaths of their baby brother, Hugo, and their precious parents. Shame would manifest itself within her very soul it seemed, charging her with accusations of neglect, even abuse, for not finding some way to prevent their deaths. Satan had a way of celebrating his many achievements, like inflicting self-loathing within on numerous lonely souls in a time of war, when hatred seemed to run rampant amongst many. She would manage to alter those thoughts, however, by handing them over to the Lord, time and again. As written in scripture, His yoke is light, He is not burdened by it.

She was sure she could sense her brother's curiosity as to why she had never settled down to raise a family as her other siblings had done. In the early 1950's it was uncommon not to marry and begin a family by the age of twenty. Many women were not yet accepted in colleges or they pursued what was expected of them, playing the role of homemaker and mother while the men went out to earn a living for the family. Wishing to avoid being questioned on this matter, Lorraine quickly changed the subject. Valentin sensed her avoidance, leaving it for another time to be addressed.

Standing still for several moments, admiring the beauty of the white splendor, listening to melodic chirping coming from the barren tree tops, the two siblings reached for each other's hand, cherishing the moment. Just a few feet in front of them two squirrels scurried across the snow, from one tree to another, chattering away about last night's wintry storm.

As both siblings opened their mouths to speak, a nervous laughter prevented them from going on. There they stood, after so many years, somewhat unable to make general conversation with each other. So much had happened! There were just too many crowding thoughts invading their minds, making it difficult to find a place to begin sharing their personal lives.

Valentin eased the moment with a tender word of understanding. Cuddling together, embracing his sister's shoulder, the two stood silently, pondering their younger years together as family and their separate lives following the start of WWII.

Two black hawks flew high above, screeching as they searched for food below. The sky remained a steely gray, threatening additional snow at any moment. The forecast called for a high temperature of merely -2 degrees Fahrenheit for the day. Only the very hearty would spend much time outdoors today. Soon the temps would rise to 20 - 30 degrees above zero, making outdoor fun enjoyable once again.

Before trudging their way through the snow, back to the house, Lorraine asked Valentin if she could pray with him. He was so pleased of her close relationship with the Lord.

Upon his smile and nod of approval, they lifted their heads to the open skies in prayer. As she finished, such a strong sense of love surrounded them, they could never deny the presence of His Holy Spirit! Their Heavenly Father would give them the strength needed to bear their souls to one another when the time was right.

* * * * *

Christmas Eve had arrived for many throughout the world. Having spent Thanksgiving with church family from the Resurrection Catholic church in their own home, warm thoughts of that pleasant day still remained fresh in their minds. Carrying on with tradition the foursome attended Christmas Eve mass.

The weather was in agreement with all, providing safe, mid- winter travel. A few minutes were spent after mass introducing Lorraine, with great pleasure, to their dear new friends, afterward returning to the blissful solitude of the Baranowsky household.

A quiet exchange of personal gifts between this immensely grateful family followed a late night dinner. Materialistic gifts were of minimal value on that particular Christmas Eve as all appreciated the divine presence of Spirit and family.

Christmas Day in December of 1952 would hold a lifetime of cherished memories for this family. Valentin excused himself from the ladies stating he had a quick errand to run that morning. Soon he returned carrying a delicately carved wooden cradle.

Lilly's husband glowed with pride as he presented the cradle to his wife. Precious countless hours had been spent making the swinging cradle for their firstborn child. That gift would provide unending hours of quiet solitude rocking their newborn to sleep. It would be placed alongside the sofa, in the infant's earlier months, providing peace of mind with the child within sight at most times.

Lorraine gifted the threesome with edible specialties from the land of Sweden, having withstood their days of travel well.

Madeleine, having discovered yet another gifted skill from God, retrieved a painting from beneath her bed, presenting her daughter and son-in-law with a future glimpse of their completed home, nestled alongside the blue waters of Long Lake, surrounded by the vibrant colors of autumn. Although Lilly knew her mother had been up to something while spending numerous hours in her bedroom, she had no idea of the extent of her gifted artistic abilities. The painting would be proudly displayed on the living room wall, providing an autumn background, year round, behind their comfy crimson-colored sofa.

Lilly wasn't without gifts of her own to share with her family. For her mother, she and Valentin had tucked away nickels and dimes to purchase three exquisite hats directly from Paris. Madeleine had refused to hide away her beloved hat collection, instead choosing to wear a different one each Sunday to church or on the rare occasions spent dining out. Her genuine giggles of excitement warmly pleased Lilly.

Lorraine's surprise visit allowed little time for a personal gift to be made for her. All was not lost to the constraints of time however. With Madeleine's photographic talents she and Lilly purchased a lovely locket similar to the one given to Lilly by her parents. One side of the locket held a smiling and happy couple with Lilly in her fifth month of pregnancy. The other side presented a lovely outdoor shot of Madeleine that Lilly had managed to snap on the deck one autumn day. This gift could be worn by Lorraine any time she needed them near to her heart.

Valentin, too, had found the time to whittle a miniature squirrel holding a nut to its mouth as they had witnessed outdoors, that first day following his sister's surprise arrival. It would remain, forever, a heart-warming holiday for all.

Lorraine, being the organized woman she was, kept a list of the old fashioned customs at Christmas which flourished for years in the countryside of Poland. On Christmas Eve there were a lot of fortunes told and customs performed for the following year. Most were related to weather, health and matrimonial status, observed to ensure a plentiful year. She was sure the French women would find the customs entertaining, to say the least.

On the quiet, peaceful evening of December 26 the foursome basked in the warmth and comfort enveloping them within the soft ambiance of the room. Stories were shared of Polish and French Christmas traditions alike. Lorraine was first to share a few customs related to health at the Old Polish Christmas season.

First, upon awakening, you'd better not go back to bed - this would certainly bring illness. Next, a crust of bread and a coin placed in a basin with cold water ensured plenty of food and physical strength for the following year. Also, the first person entering the house on Christmas morning should be a man, to guarantee health for the whole household; a woman entering would mean sickness.

Hearty laughter erupted as she continued to read from her list of traditions. She continued on.

Christmas tree decorations used were apples, which brought beauty and health. Ornaments made out of straw brought wealth.

Weather, wealth and marriage were very important in the lives of the whole villages, so some customs were strictly observed. A sunny Christmas Eve day guaranteed lots of eggs as well as a marriage for the young and poor.

Every dish had to be tasted; if not, it brought bad harvest to a certain product. Going to visit a neighbor and trying to steal a small item would ensure wealth. You had to return the item on St. Stephen's Day. After a mass on St. Stephen's day (12/26), people threw wheat or rice at each other to bring good harvest and wealth in the coming year.

There was a belief that on Christmas Eve water in a well turned into wine. At midnight, animals spoke in human voices, but it was bad luck to overhear. Winning at card games that day brought happiness for the whole year. In a region threatened by wolves, leftovers from Christmas Eve supper were placed outside the gate to invite the wolves, which when treated well, would not harm the host.

Hysterical laughter abounded as Lorraine read aloud another seemingly ridiculous old custom. Brother and sister would recall one or two customs their own parents had managed to hang on to during their childhoods.

Next came the stories of French customs and traditions from mother and daughter. Before moving on, cups were filled with hot eggnog and rum for sipping. Then, all ears widely opened as Madeleine spoke of her own memories.

Christmas in France had many unique holiday customs, such as Pere Noel and the Christmas Crèche instead of a Christmas tree.

In France, Christmas goes by the name of *Noël*. This stems from the French phrase *les bonnes nouvelles*, which means *"the good news."* This is in reference to the gospel and spreading the word of Jesus Christ's birth. Santa Claus is called Père Noël, meaning *"Father Christmas."* He dresses in old fashioned robes trimmed with fur, and carries a sack of gifts.

Like many countries in Western Europe, the Christmas season in France begins with Saint Nicholas' Day, December 6th. In eastern areas of France, particularly Alsace-Lorraine, parents give children their Christmas gifts on Saint Nicholas' Day, as opposed to Christmas Day, which is reserved for religious services and a family dinner.

In other parts of France, Père Noël comes bearing gifts on Christmas Eve for the good children. He places small treats and toys in the children's shoes, which they leave by the fireplace. Adults often wait until New Years Day to exchange gifts with one another.

Christmas trees can be found in France, though they are not as popular as they are in Germany, Great Britain and the United States. By far the most popular Christmas symbol in France is the nativity scene, or Christmas Crèche. Introduced by Saint Francis of Assisi in 1224, the Christmas Crèche did not really catch on in popularity until the time of the Renaissance of the 16th Century.

Many regions of France also use *Santons* in their Christmas decorations. Translated, *santons* mean *little saints*. The small village of Aubagne, in the Provencal region of France, is considered the world capital of santons.

The traditional French Christmas dinner usually takes place after the midnight mass on Christmas Eve. Called *Le Reveillon*, the main dishes of this holiday dinner vary from region to region.

In Alsace, goose is served as the main dish, while in Brittany buckwheat pancakes with sour cream are a featured dish.

Turkey and chestnuts are popular in Burgundy, while in Paris and the Il-de-France region oysters are served. Of course, no French Christmas dinner would be complete without the traditional log shaped cake, Buche de Noel.

In Provencal, children skate outside during Twelfth Night (*the day before the Epiphany*) to meet with the three kings who were on their way to give the Baby Jesus his gifts. The children would give the three kings food for them and their pages. In return, the kings would give the children gifts.

In honor of this occasion, another popular Christmas dessert, known as the Cake of The King, was served. Decorated with designs of stars, crown, dragons and flowers, a special bean or trinket was baked inside. Whoever got the piece with the bean was "*king*" for the following year.

Popular up until the 19th Century, the Cake of the King still graces the holiday tables in French-speaking Quebec, where old world customs are still practiced. A similar cake, simply called Kings Cake, is served in Louisiana, to mark the start of the Mardi Gras season.

* * * * *

Lorraine's version of rural Polish customs extended back many a year, customs no longer practiced in the 1950's of course.

Madeleine spoke of traditions old and new alike. A delightfully entertaining evening was spent learning of each other's traditions and customs.

Poland had been one of the European countries severely lacking in the finer things of life. The country lived under poorer conditions than the majority of Europeans did throughout the years, continuing to do so to this day. The comparisons in lifestyles was so vastly differing it was difficult to fathom.

Madeleine had not forgotten her younger years when raised in Germany, which had been her birthplace. Those memories were best left behind. Unheard, unspoken pain, tucked away into a locked closet, never to be re-opened. Revealing those painfully cruel memories of mere survival, of extreme poverty, then ending with the untimely deaths of both parents, warranted no mention to anyone for any reason. Life for Madeleine in early childhood had no place in her world of today. She chose to remember the comfortable manner in which she had been so privileged to receive once beginning life over again under her Aunt's roof in France.

Lorraine had also learned a few Swedish traditions over the recent years as well, mostly from Katya and Alina's families as they had adapted themselves to through their husband's traditional Swedish ways. She did share a few simple traditions she had found enlightening. All in all, the time they had shared at Christmas bonded these intriguing souls forever.

Chapter Twelve

The New Year of 1953 offered unlimited opportunities in the United States. The day presented reasonable temperatures with lightly scattered snow.

Valentin quickly responded to the knock at their door. On the other side stood a handsome young professor by the name of Famous Thuringer. Taking his coat, scarf and gloves, Valentin cordially invited Professor Thuringer to join them for a tasty New Year's luncheon prepared by the women. Lilly immediately made the introductions as each seated themselves at the kitchen table.

Light chatter ensued as all avoided the inevitable moment at hand, Lorraine's departure back to her very distant home across the miles. Valentin abhorred thinking about not seeing Lorraine, likely for many years to come. Sharing life under the same roof for ten days, Lorraine found it extremely difficult saying good bye to her hospitable, newfound family as well. The offer was extended, more than once, for Lorraine to consider moving to the U.S. permanently, even living with their family for awhile if necessary.

Valentin had never learned of her reasons for delaying marriage, respecting her privacy as she had so chosen to do. It was somewhat apparent, however, that Professor Thuringer and Lorraine shared slightly more than a simple platonic relationship. This spiked the interest of not only the women, but Valentin as well.

Finishing their luncheon, the gentlemen moved into the living room allowing the women to quickly tend to the cleaning of the dishes. Having their privacy for merely precious few moments, Lilly and Madeleine instantly pumped poor Lorraine of any possible interest in this fine, educated young man from Minnesota.

Throughout giggles and laughter these mature, adult women were seemingly behaving like teenagers. They battered her endlessly with question after question. At last, Lorraine admitted she just might be somewhat interested. Twice Lilly peaked around the corner of the kitchen doorway sneaking in another glance of the professor.

This most certainly heightened their desire for Lorraine to, perhaps, one day marry this most eligible handsome man, returning to Minnesota with him upon completion of his studies abroad. Giddily, Lorraine waved them off as being entirely silly. However, mother and daughter could see beyond her front, try as she may to hide the truth.

In a round-about way Madeleine cleverly found a few private moments with Professor Thuringer before their departure. A quick inquiry as to whether or not he and Lorraine had frequented many eating establishments there in the capital city of Stockholm was one approach. Smiling from his response, he confirmed her suspicion of some kind of dating history, something Lorraine had been too shy to share quite yet.

Ah yes, Madeleine and Lilly may just have to play cupid from this point forward if they were to hasten Lorraine's marriage plans, moving her closer to her newfound family. Not a moment was wasted dropping a few subtle hints in the Professor's lap regarding their utmost desire to have dear Lorraine living close at hand. Famous remained somber in his demeanor never giving way to his intentions. Still, the women had their instincts which often bore much truth.

A solemn departure accompanied by tears of sadness overtook smiles as they waved goodbye until fully out of sight. So precious were the days they had spent together. The three made it well understood Professor Famous (most often referenced as "*Fame*") Thuringer would always be a welcomed guest in their home.

Fame came from a strong Lutheran family of Swede and German ancestral backgrounds. Attending a Lutheran church while in Sweden he had made the pleasurable acquaintance of Miss Lorraine Baranowsky. Through her association with the professor she had furthered her English speaking abilities on the rare evenings she was free of work commitments. She had vowed, to herself and the professor, to lighten her workload following the overseas vacation to the U.S.

Commencing their drive on an ideal traveling day, brisk but with a sky full of sunshine, the first several miles of thoughtful silence appeased both following the tearful departure. Once settled in for the two hundred mile drive ahead they began sharing their own individual stories of time spent with beloved family members.

How rewarding it was for both to connect with loved ones from childhood. Vastly opposing circumstances and upbringings profoundly impacted the character and personality each had developed throughout their individual lives.

Fame had rather recently celebrated his 26th birthday just two months prior to his Minnesota visit. Having lived through a few struggles of his own, Famous shared how he had lost his mother to pneumonia at eleven years of age. His father, disinterested in marrying again, remained a single parent throughout Fame's teenage years. He had often hungered for her warm voice and the comforting touch his father could not quite replace.

A good father, nonetheless, he remained vigilant in raising his son to be a good Christian man, all the while driving him to succeed in his quest for a higher education. Having graduated from the University of Minnesota in Minneapolis, Fame was the first in the Thuringer family to receive a college degree, offering endless opportunities for stable, secure white-collar employment anywhere in the U.S.

His father, Harold, had worked numerous hours of overtime in the lumber mill to cover his son's educational costs. Fame would always be indebted to his dad for all he had provided both himself and younger brother James. Never had he or James caused their dad any grief or pain following the untimely demise of their mother. They well understood the heartfelt loss of his wife was just as difficult as their own loss of their beloved mother. They did manage to navigate their way through the years bonding together as a three-man unit until the boys could comfortably provide for themselves.

Fame often sensed the restraints Lorraine obviously bore, keeping a safe distance, barring her ability to show even the slightest affection toward him. Wondering what had caused her profound mistrust in men he guessed it had likely occurred during her time living as an orphan in her younger years on the eastern shores of Sweden.

The three youngest Baranowsky sisters had survived the brutality of a merciless war, but at what price? Against the odds at hand, any assurance of her opening up seemed slim, but Fame knew there was a loving, affectionate woman within, struggling to escape her past. He would continue all efforts to win her full love and trust.

Following a restless night's sleep, Lorraine asked Fame if he objected to her taking a quick nap on the five hour drive to Minneapolis which would then place them on an eastbound train. With a smile, he lazily gave her the okay to do so. Before lying her head upon the window Lorraine placed a sweater against it for added comfort. Closing her eyes she lightly drifted off for a much needed rest.

There was nothing new about Lorraine's frequent nightmares. Relieved to be haunted with fewer now, than in past years, she considered the possibility of it happening here in the presence of the kindly professor. Shrugging it off she decided to take her chances. However, beyond her ability to control her dreams, she did exactly as she had feared.

Awakened by her own life-curdling scream Lorraine shook herself out of the nightmare. Reacting with instant fear, Fame hit the brakes bringing the car to an immediate halt alongside the highway. Without giving Lorraine an opportunity to turn away he embraced her as best he could, given the tight quarters they were in. With uncontrollable sobs Lorraine covered her mouth with the handkerchief Fame had offered, pressing her face against his shoulder until at last maintaining her composure.

Explaining it was a ridiculous nightmare Lorraine made every attempt to shrug it off while feeling extreme embarrassment in front of Famous. The professor refused to drive another mile until she agreed to share the frightening dream with him. Explaining why the in-depth story was too lengthy to discuss right then and there he agreed to drive until reaching the next town. She knew the time had arrived to share her horror with this very caring man. She had, at last, reached a point of trust with him, enabling the necessary strength to finally reveal her ugly, shameful secret.

Upon reaching the next town, Fame followed through with his plan to stop in a safe place, allowing Lorraine to unload the burdensome weight of twelve oppressive years, still remaining deep within for much too long.

Courage Times Three. A Novel

As the eldest of the younger Baranowsky sisters, Lorraine, barely thirteen years of age, was forced to grow up overnight. Immediately following the death of their parents by the German Gestapo in Krakow, a nearby neighbor tossed the girls into a filthy railway car filled with sheep being transferred to the north coast of the Baltic Sea. The kindly neighbor did the only thing he could think of, possibly saving them from torture or likely death. Had they remained in Poland, they surely would have been raped and beaten by the cold-blooded Nazi soldiers. Unknowingly, he took a chance in sending them away on the first train passing through Krakow.

The three frightened, nearly hysterical, young girls cuddled together in a dark corner covering themselves in straw. A few crumbs of bread and cheese were all that had been spared them. Fearing even more intense hunger down the line, they postponed eating what little they had for hours, taking merely a single bite of their meager rations until Katya, the nine year old, began crying relentlessly from the fear and hunger that plagued her. After deciding to eat only half of the food, they eventually fell asleep upon each other's shoulders. The late night hours allowed them a much needed escape from the dreaded, never-ending fear that had overtaken them.

* * * * *

Lorraine hastily awakened to the sound of men's voices nearby. Lifting her head just slightly, she flinched as three men swiftly jumped into the same car as the girls. Speaking a language unknown to her, she had no awareness of what they were saying.

Shaking violently, she remained hidden beneath the straw, protected, as well, by the vulgar smelling sheep between them. She never thought she would become thankful for the presence of those sheep. All she could do at that point was pray! Pray, as she had never prayed before in her life, that the men would not suspect their presence in the darkened corner of the rail car.

Generously allowing the younger girls their much needed sleep, she also bought them time before finding it necessary to finish off the last of their morsels. Lorraine became lost as to what their next move would be. She had no idea if they were still in Poland but she doubted it by the unfamiliar speech of the undesired riders.

Abruptly awakening from a nightmare, Alina jumped up letting out a curdling scream. Most likely the severely broken child was reliving the past couple days of her life. Startled from hearing Alina's scream, the three mangy, haggard looking men discovered the three desolate children stashed beneath the straw. Lorraine prayed, with every ounce of her being, for these unsavory characters to treat them with kindness and respect.

Sobbing began to overtake Lorraine as she reached far into the depths of her mind to reveal the remainder of the story to the professor. Famous was sure he knew the very direction she was headed, but thought it necessary for her to speak the words out loud of that horrifyingly crippling event. After a brief reprieve Lorraine continued on.

At once, the callous behavior of the men threatened any remaining sense of hope for the young, innocent girls. One of the men, however, responded emphatically to the horrendous behavior of the others, shouting for them to cease their unspeakable conduct in the name of God.

Chaos ensued for what seemed to be an eternity. Amidst the shrill cries of the girls, the bellowing sheep and the grunts of the struggling men fighting, Lorraine covered her baby sisters, trying to protect them from what she feared may possibly take place.

The kind man was losing the battle with two against him. Recognizing his defeat, while fearing all three of the girls would be irreparably damaged for life, he bartered with the other men. In exchange for the younger girls' safety he offered the oldest of the girls, Lorraine, to the men for their disgusting desires.

Tears filled his eyes as he uttered those words, continually pleading for God's forgiveness. Repudiating their actions repeatedly, they could only cry as the innocent thirteen year old was pulled to the other side of the railcar. The kind man gently took the younger girls into his protective arms, doing his best to prevent them from hearing the horrendous cries of their older sister. The sadistic madness of those next few hours would silently haunt them forever.

Lorraine knew his curiosity would have to be pacified one day regarding the next several years of their teen-aged lives, being parentless and alone. That conversation would have to take place on a future date as the emotional upheaval of the moment had already left her well spent.

Fame apologized to Lorraine for prompting her to speak of the tragic occurrence. He continued to hold her close as her sobbing slowly subsided. He assured her that releasing the pent up agony of her secret to someone else would likely help lift the weight of carrying it alone.

Reaching the end of the vulgar truth, Lorraine hung her head in shame, stating her full understanding that no man would ever want such used goods. Famous realized the full extent of the broken woman's torture. He equally understood her reasons for caring so profoundly about those children suffering from the lack of loving and caring parents.

Gently easing her away from his shoulder, he spoke authoritatively, instructing her to look into his eyes. Hesitantly, in shame, she did as he demanded.

The pain he saw in those beautiful emerald eyes brought him to tears. He would never be fully able to understand the depth of her pain. But as he spoke, the words that stumbled from his mouth no longer held an authoritative tone. They were the most tenderly spoken words Lorraine had ever heard.

Never ever consider yourself spoiled goods, softly whispering his love for his beautiful Lorraine into her ear. Tears continued to escape their eyes as Famous gently leaned into Lorraine placing a warm and promising kiss upon her lips, an indication of his true-spoken words. It was a time to begin healing from those menacing and cruel memories for good, gaining defeat together with the encouragement and trust of this understanding and loving man and God's assistance.

Chapter Thirteen

The two had driven as far as Minneapolis, Minnesota where they promptly caught the passenger train carrying them to the East coast. In the early 1950's a respectable single woman would never entertain the thought of traveling together with a man, posing as a couple. She would be scorned ruthlessly for her behavior. Despite having separate compartments they still enjoyed dinner with one another nightly before retiring. No disrespectful behavior played into their socializing during their travels.

Immediately upon arrival in New York City they proceeded directly to customs. All checked out for the two travelers as they boarded their final means of transportation, braving their way across the mighty North Atlantic through iceberg laden oceanic waters. January was the coldest time of year to be traveling the particular route they were on. Once reaching the westernmost ports of northern Europe a short trip into the Baltic Sea would carry them to the Scandinavian country of Sweden.

Assisting Lorraine in locating her cabin first, Fame then proceeded to his own cabin, but not before making plans to meet for dinner in the formal dining room at precisely 6 o'clock pm. No signs of affection were shared between the two for fear of idle gossip. Complete respect and proper behavior was undeniably expected between an unmarried man and woman at all times.

Entering his own cabin, Professor Thuringer found his quarters small but sufficient. Instantly freeing himself from the confines of a suit jacket, the discomfort of a tie and a stiffly starched dress shirt, Fame felt like he could breathe freely once again. The liberating of his neck spoke volumes as he dropped lifelessly to the firm cot which served as a mattress in most cabins. He unquestionably could use a couple hours of sleep, that he was sure of. Yet his mind slid instantly back to the earlier conversation he'd had with Lorraine. Exposing the burdensome truth of her past took a great deal of willpower on her part. He could not, however, cast off her words, her unwarranted look of embarrassment, her thoughts of somehow being unworthy of any man's love and respect because she had been so violently violated. How could she believe she, herself, was somehow responsible for the inconceivable behavior of those miserable men of Satan? Precious Lorraine. Will she ever be able to trust another man to love her for all the right reasons? He hoped, over time, he would be able to convince her she was entirely a victim. She was, in no way, spoiled goods.

* * * * *

Lorraine had always worn her hair drawn back, wrapped into a neat, orderly bun at the nape of her neck. Fame envisioned her now, her deep chocolate hair loosely undone. He could envision himself gently caressing her shoulders. A man of good height himself, he enjoyed admiring her long lean legs covered in nylon hosiery. More pleasurable thoughts of this dear woman filled Fame's mind as he lie upon his cabin cot. They weren't erotic thoughts, simply warm and affectionate ones.

Packed in with other items of clothing was a floor length evening gown she'd had hanging in her closet for a few years. Worn only once, she had hoped for an opportunity to wear it during her stay with her brother's family. Never having that opportunity, she decided the time had arrived for her to present herself in a more feminine fashion to Professor Thuringer. As always required, formal dining included formal attire.

Unlike the fashion sense of the late 1900's Lorraine decided to wear her hair down with her enticing floor length gown, giving way to a much softer womanly presence. Her heart seemed to skip a beat, here and there, as she envisioned Fame's response upon first seeing this revised version of herself. After brushing her hair 100 times, shaping and painting fingernails and applying a light amount of make-up, Lorraine proceeded across the room to her baggage. Removing a new set of nylons, just moments later she had attached each to the garter belt worn to hold them up. A final check, and recheck assured her of the satisfaction she demanded. Although her dress would fully cover her legs, it was imperative each back seam run straight up the back of the leg. At times Lorraine would chastise herself for being so overly particular in everything she did. She knew psychologists had a name for this seemingly harmless issue. It was referenced as OCD, or obsessive compulsive disorder. Tossing that thought to the wind, it was now time to finish dressing, not concerning herself with such trivialities.

Seating herself on the edge of the cot, Lorraine guardedly slipped into the bold wine-colored, sequin-studded dress. The gown, boasting of silk and taffeta both, hugged her body accordingly, revealing only a mere glimpse of cleavage.

Completing her spectacular evening attire, simple, yet elegant jewelry adorned her neck and ears. A light spray of expensive French perfume, a parting gift from Lilly and Madeleine, was applied before stepping into her low heeled footwear.

Checking the time, Lorraine had only a few minutes to spare before meeting Fame in the dining room. Taking one last look at herself in the mirror, then a second and a third look, one would barely recognize this remake of a feminine woman looking back upon her. For the first time, Lorraine was understanding the confidence that accompanied a highly feminine woman. Plainly written, even in the words of the Bible, God speaks of woman's empowering abilities to entice and allure the strongest of men. Not that these were Lorraine's intentions for Professor Thuringer. Simply pleasing him with her beauty and femininity was all she hoped for. She wanted to make him feel like she was the only woman in the room. Her desire to impress was only meant for this one very special man.

Upon reaching the doorway of the dining room Lorraine thought her heart would jump clear out of her chest, leaping directly overboard. With perspiring palms, she entered the softly lit room. Never in her life did she recall feeling so entirely overwhelmed in this way. A few moments earlier she had stood in front of the mirror with total confidence, pleased and proud of who looked back. Suddenly, she felt the urge to turn around and run as fast as her legs could carry her, back to the security of her room. Alas, it was too late. Their eyes locked at precisely the same moment.

Behaving like a love-struck boy, Fame approached the vision of loveliness, bowing slightly toward her. Reaching out to take her hand, he raised it to his lips, kissing it gently, allowing himself a few extra seconds to catch his breath. Her womanly scent and staggering beauty triggered sensations in him unlike anything he had ever experienced.

Both of their hands trembled upon the tender touch. Aptly choosing not to embarrass her by over flattering her womanly appearance, Fame used extreme caution.

Miss Lorraine Baranowsky? I have never been witness to a more breathtaking sight in my life!

A pleasing smile extended across Lorraine's face as she accepted his compliment. Interestingly, she recognized the return of confidence that had momentarily escaped her. Rather than being full of herself Lorraine shyly inquired, *Do you really like it?*

Her innocence and honesty were absolutely refreshing. Having met a few beautiful women in his years, all had exuded most annoying mannerisms, a cause for him to keep his distance from them. In Lorraine's case, not an ounce of arrogance presided within this diamond in the rough, pleasing him immensely.

Lacking somewhat in the dancing department due to her simple lifestyle, Lilly's frequent smiles spoke softly of her appreciation in his ability to graciously coincide with any misstep on her part. Other couples gazed admiringly at the obvious young love swaying to and fro on the dance floor.

A highly pleasurable evening of dinner and dancing filled them both with a sense of magical sentience. Never had Fame expected Lorraine to present herself so femininely that evening. She truly was most beguiling in his eyes.

At evening's end, he respectfully returned her to her cabin quarters with another light kiss to her hand. It was, indeed, a memorable evening for both.

Chapter Fourteen

Spending her first full winter in Minnesota gave Lilly a hardy taste of what to expect each year. Mother nature had tossed in numerous snow days as well as her share of sub-zero temps with gusty north winds. The Baranowky's, along with Mrs. DeMornais, managed to fill their days with endless projects throughout the snowy season.

Mid March was soon upon them leaving a mere two weeks before reaching the delivery date of the baby. Madeleine, alone, had knit three blankets for the infant in colors of blue, yellow and green. Without knowing the sex of the child they would be safe with those colors regardless of gender.

In long past years pink was actually worn on infant boys as they wore clothing in red, that faded quickly, leaving them pink. That had changed somewhere along the lines of infant fashion. No longer were boys ever allowed to wear pink. Pink was for girls only! Not only had Madeleine made three blankets, she had also managed to whip out six pair of booties in varying colors.

Cloth diapers, baby pins and rubber pants were purchased in bulk. Breast nursing was Lorraine's choice of feeding versus formula. A crib, along with rocking chair and changing table filled the room, while families of stuffed animals established residency throughout as well.

The excited couple were about to be proud parents after nearly eleven years together. Soon their good night's sleep would be invaded by hunger cries and wet diapers. Lilly would become accustomed to keeping a dry clean cloth perched on her burping shoulder to avoid clothing changes for herself throughout each day. The wringer washing machine would be kept humming at a steady pace with diapers and baby clothes. Washed garments would be hung on the outside clothesline in the warmer months and in the basement on lines during the winter. All clothing required ironing, some sprayed with starch to firm them up. Most often clothing was pressed while still damp to remove wrinkles easier. If fully dried they were sprinkled with water then rolled up until being ironed shortly afterward, making laundry duties laborious and time consuming.

In mid afternoon, on March 14th, Lilly surprised everybody by going into labor early. A nervous called was placed to Valentin's boss requesting her husband be sent home immediately. The time had indeed arrived to drive her into the city of Virginia for the new infant's entrance into the world.

Following twenty-two hours of labor Lilly gave birth to a beautiful baby girl who they named Tia Lee Baranowsky. Weighing in at six pounds even, their newborn baby girl stretched a normal length of 19 inches. Lilly had endured a lengthy labor, but once their little angel started making her way into the world it was swift and efficient work on Lilly's part.

Following a three day hospital stay the loving family drove their first baby girl to her new home, where she would live throughout her childhood and teenaged years.

Life on the lake that summer proved to be a productive, yet fun, season. Valentin took on the burdensome task of turning the soil in a nearby field to plant their garden. Potatoes, tomatoes, lettuce and cucumbers {for pickling and fresh salads} were planted, along with several rows of corn, beans, peas, beets, onions and pumpkins, not to forget the potatoes.

A few apple trees were planted along with rows of tame raspberries. Nature provided as many wild berries as they could pick on their vast two hundred acre spread. Flower beds galore were planted with perennials as well as annuals.

Madeleine embarked on the task of dressing the deck in pots of geraniums, gladiolas, petunias and pansies.

Fiscally equipped with only enough money to build a garage or purchase a boat, the former took precedence, as it should have. It would undoubtedly serve them well, housing their auto with protection from the long Minnesota winters.

A dock was put into the water along with a raft assembled of 2x4 lengths of wood atop empty 50 gallon barrels to keep it afloat.

In their free time occasional picnics would highlight the weekend, entertaining other young couples, some with children and some without. Barbequed burgers and hot dogs, beans, watermelon and chocolate cake with ice cream usually topped the menu list. Once the apples and berries came of season, decadent pies baked with love accompanied each meal.

The economy continued to soar throughout the United States. Newfangled electrical gadgets were entering the market daily. The mid to late 1950's offered much growth and progress in transportation, communications, industry and manufacturing.

Their young baby girl, Tia Lee, forever proved to be a daily blessing. Having a slight bit of colic in her primary months, she later adjusted well.

Madeleine became obsessed with photographing baby Tia. Valentin set up a darkroom in the basement strictly for Madeleine's photo processing. Families abroad felt as if they were watching her grow right alongside them. Standing and hanging 8"x10" frames held numerous photos of their first born. Madeleine was the most excited when Tia's first tooth pushed through at only 4 months of age. She was loved dearly.

* * * * *

Having attended services at various churches or synagogues in New York City, they again made their decision to do the same in Minnesota. On Lorraine's second Sunday with them, over the holidays, they attended Christ Lutheran Church for her benefit as she was a practicing Lutheran. Thoroughly enjoying that service, they continued attending for several weeks until one day opting to make it their home church.

They meant to offend nobody in their choice of religious beliefs, yet there were those who adamantly refused to understand their reasons for turning away from Catholicism. There is some truth to the fact that although some Christians tend to believe they are not prejudiced when it comes to practicing God's word, sometimes true colors are revealed.

The Baranowsky's continued to treat those past friends with kindness and respect revealing the genuine love of God within. Wanting to believe we are not prejudiced when it comes to religion, race or ethnic background, there sometimes lurks, in the depth of our souls, a lack of genuine discernment.

August started winding down with early signs of autumn in the air. Cooler nights took the place of summer's warmer evenings. The sight of golden leaves, dotting northern Minnesota's lush green forests, were the first to begin the yearly autumn ritual of shedding themselves following a summer's worth of greenery. The families of poplar and birch trees were the first to produce and first to lose their foliage each year. Madeleine and Lilly learned the process of canning fruits and vegetables for storage in their cool dark basement for winter's use. These previously refined women had certainly transformed from high society city women into genuinely simple country pioneers.

Brenda Brown Elliott

Chapter Fifteen

Bath time for Tia was most often enjoyable. This day, however, she was a bit cranky with two additional teeth pushing their way through her sensitive tiny gums. Running a low grade fever didn't give Lilly reason for alarm as it had been typically normal with her teething.

Forever thankful to have Madeleine's help around the house, Lilly called for her mama to answer the ringing telephone while she continued bathing with soapy hands. Hastily, Madeleine ran into the living room answering on the fourth ring. *I have a long distance call for Mrs. Jon Paul DeMornais. Is this the party they wish to reach?* With a quick response Madeleine answered that she, in fact, was Madeleine DeMornais.

A slightly familiar voice greeted Madeleine in French. The connection was poor, creating difficulty in understanding the caller. Immediately Greta, Valentin's sister, identified herself. Somewhat stupefied, Madeleine covered the phone's mouthpiece, calling for Lilly to come quickly.

Bundling baby Tia in a heavy towel, Lilly hurried to see what the problem was? She instantly asked if it was regarding Valentin ... *is he hurt? Is it Valentin?* Shaking her head she hushed Lilly momentarily. Solemnly she listened as Greta informed her of the grave illness that had befallen Aunt Melanie. Apparently she'd waited too long before seeing a doctor for what she had assumed to be a nasty cold. Upon examination, she was admitted into the hospital with severely infected lungs. Little hope remained for Melanie's survival of the fatal illness. Requesting the telephone number of St. Germaine Hospital, Madeleine quickly jotted it down. Madeleine sincerely thanked Greta for her kindness in her swift notification. Sending love with God's blessings, they hung up the phone, disconnecting the disturbing call.

Fretfully informing Lilly of the disheartening news, Madeleine impatiently dialed the endless long distance numbers. In such a frustrated frame of mind she repeatedly misdialed, forcing herself to begin again and again. Finally, on her fourth attempt, she reached her party explaining the situation at hand, requesting information of Aunt Melanie's current status.

After a momentary lapse a Dr. Anton Revelle began speaking into the telephone. As in previous long-distance conversation, the crackling connection made it difficult to hear. Covering her left ear with her hand she spoke clearly and loudly into the mouthpiece. *I see. Yes ... Are you sure? Absolutely positive? Oh dear ... Yes, I understand doctor! Thank you for your time.*

Slowly placing the telephone back unto its receiver, Madeleine began to cry. Lilly wrapped her free arm around her mother's shoulder. It was apparent the news was not good. Lilly began to tear up as Madeleine explained Aunt Melanie's likely demise within the next few days.

How their hearts broke over the sad news of their dearly beloved Aunt Melanie. As Lilly proceeded to diaper and dress baby Tia, she realized, with Melanie's passing, she would never have the opportunity to have her Aunt spoil and love her beautiful daughter.

Aunt Melanie always had a soft spot for children throughout her lifetime. Robbed of the pleasure of giving birth herself, she had missed out on the joys of rearing her own babies, thus taking to spoiling her nieces and nephews, and later her great-nieces and nephews. Lilly knew, when she left France, she would forever miss her Aunt's tender loving care she so cherished. Now she must be satisfied with the many blessed memories that would forever remain in her heart and mind.

Three days passed before receiving word from the hospital that Melanie had departed the life of the flesh and entered into her eternal resting place with God. Madeleine knew the estate and vineyards would be left to her as this had been Melanie's wish. She would likely find it necessary to deal with legalities involving the property. Melanie had informed her years earlier, however, that all paperwork was prepared in the event of her death. After discussing matters thoroughly with Valentin and Lilly the decision was made that Madeleine travel to France, taking care of the business at hand.

It was mid September when Valentin, Lilly and Baby Tia delivered Madeleine to the Minneapolis/St. Paul International Airport. Since the end of WWII a huge leap in international aviation occurred over a ten-year period. By 1952 it was becoming the preferred method of overseas travel, cutting traveling time from five days by sea to one half day by air.

The ladies stared in amazement at the size of the jumbo jet that would carry Madeleine to France. **Air France** was boldly written across the silver body of the big bird. This would be Madeleine's first time to fly. Valentin and Lilly seemed to be more tense and jittery over the flight than Madeleine herself.

Having been a very free soul throughout her lifetime, Madeleine believed God's timing controlled everyone's life. She believed He had our lives drawn out for us before ever bringing us to life on Earth. Thus, in her eyes, if her life were to end while flying the blue skies, let it be God's will.

What a delightful way to view life, or perhaps better stated, to view death. To honor the Lord by doing our best each and every day; to bestow kindnesses unto others; to live each day for Him, as Jesus directed us to do numerous times throughout the Bible; to never fear death, knowing it will lead to an awesome eternal life, full of His glory and free of the pain endured in the physical realm; having complete faith in our Lord while here on Earth.

Tears escaped the eyes of mother and daughter as they separated for the very first time since their re-union in Paris several years earlier. Madeleine assured her daughter all would be well, confirming her strongest belief they would see each other once again in the near future. She would be sure to call Lilly and Valentin within a few days.

Butterflies galore fluttered through her tummy as the enormous jetliner, filled with over one hundred travelers, ascended higher and higher into the skies. Madeleine was utterly amazed at the sight of the earth below as they climbed continually upward into the heavens. Soon she found herself in the midst of thick fog, later realizing they had just flown through the cloud cover.

Amazing! Astonishing! Madeleine continually repeated the words to the nervous looking woman seated beside her, whose eyes remained closed for some time. Never had she dreamed she'd ever be flying across the mighty Atlantic. She wondered what other impossible dreams would one day come to life in her years on earth. Pausing momentarily, she spoke to her late husband, Jon Paul, about this amazing flight. A sense of closeness with Jon Paul embraced her as they soared high above the earth in all its glory.

Following a smooth landing in Paris, Madeleine was greeted by Jon Paul's sister, Chantelle, at the airport. Having spent many years living across the roadway from one another, these two women shared numerous memories together. Good, and sometimes not so good, as it was for all living in the physical realm.

With warm smiles they clutched one another closely, placing a kiss on each cheek, as was, and still remains, a French custom. Chatter ensued as Madeleine vividly described her flight. It was simply amazing that just earlier that morning she had been standing on American soil, only to find herself back on French soil merely hours later.

It wasn't long before she learned of the mental and physical fatigue following a lengthy flight. At first, she believed she may be getting ill. Within a couple of days, however, all was back to normal.

Anxious to see Valentin's dear sisters, Greta, Emma and families, she placed a call inviting them to join her for dinner at Melanie's home the following evening. For the girls, as well as Madeleine, bittersweet memories pulled at their heartstrings. So dear, Melanie had been to all she had loved. She would surely be missed.

Chantelle was quick to point out to Madeleine the importance of keeping the vineyards in the family. Having brought her own vineyards back to life once again, as Melanie had, they'd gained a further sense of pride, as all vineyards had not been restored to their previous productivity following the second war.

Consequently, further discussions with Melanie's attorney, Valentin, Lilly and Chantelle proved to cause even more confusion for Madeleine.

Wholeheartedly believing she would likely never return to her homeland, Madeleine had resorted to the fact her remaining life would be spent in the United States. Once she had returned to France, however, a long-denied aching for her homeland overtook her. Of her own accord, she decided to return to the French Riviera, where she and Jon Paul had spent their last days together. Once arriving in Marseilles, Madeleine spent a week on the beautiful shores of the Mediterranean, perusing her choices of what to do with her newly inherited vineyards and estate.

By weeks' end she came to her final, unwavering decision. The vineyards would be sold along with the estate. Proceeds from the sale would provide many opportunities in life. The first being the purchase of property on the French Riviera. Enough time had lapsed since her husband's death, allowing her to fully enjoy all the Riviera had to offer. She would find a large enough villa to house her daughter's family, forever providing them the luxury of a French vacation any time they'd so choose. It would also enable her grandchildren to remain familiarized with their French heritage. Yes, she knew with every ounce of her being, this was the wisest choice.

Secondly, she would discuss the possibility of having a lovely summer cottage built on Valentin and Lilly's property, right alongside Long Lake. This would provide the young couple their privacy in raising their children without having a meddling mother or mother-in-law within the confines of their own home. Madeleine had to admit, she wouldn't mind having her own private quarters once again. She realized she had never lived in a home of her own. It was time to spread her wings, if only a few hundred yards from her daughter.

Thirdly, she would place a sizable amount of Francs into savings bonds, yielding substantial interest throughout the years and providing a college education for each of her grandchildren.

Pleased with her decisions, she felt the very spirit of Jon Paul prompting her to make the right moves. France, with all her immense beauty, including structurally magnificent historical buildings and aesthetically pleasing terrain, would offer the opportunity to advance in her oil painting and photography skills. It would ignite her desire to move forward, continuing her own personal quest to utilize her recently recognized, God-given gifts. Madeleine was just learning how to be strong, independent and successful.

How exciting was this? Truly coming into herself at middle age? Discovering her feel for the arts, venturing out on her own, making major life-changing decisions that would influence the future of not only herself but numerous others? All this spoke volumes of her newfound courage.

Madeleine De Mornais now knew exactly who was in charge of her life, only second to her Heavenly Father. She'd sometimes been aware of God serving her, but she'd rarely given Him the credit in her younger years. If anything, she'd blamed Him at times for taking her precious Jon Paul away from her after too short a marriage.

With the passing of time, Madeleine eventually eased away from those negative feelings, discovering there was no rest for the weary who single-handedly excluded the Lord from their everyday lives. She was living proof the load doesn't lighten until finally handing it over to Him, announcing with great pleasure, that she could no longer carry it by herself alone. Letting go and letting God! He wanted her to lean on Him always, so she would never walk alone in life again. This would be Madeleine DeMornais' greatest of life's lessons!

Some of these realities hit Madeleine like a torpedo during her stay in Marseilles. It was time for her to return to Paris, place the property on the market for sale, and call Lilly with the exciting news.

First instincts were to share the news of the sale of the property in Paris with Lilly via telephone. On second thought, it was probably best to relate the news through a letter. Sensing Lilly might possibly question her abrupt decisions, Madeleine expressed her deepest, most sincere thoughts and wishes in a five page letter.

Upon receiving the letter, Lilly was quite surprised by the uncommonly independent choices her mother was making. Yet, it was her mother's life alone and she respected her wishes. In all honesty, it was most exciting to be handed an opportunity, as such, to vacation in the south of France at any time. She also believed it would be beneficial for her mother to have her own private quarters if she so desired.

How proud she was of her mama, taking life by the horns and running with it now. Taking time that very afternoon to write a letter in response, with her utmost approval, became a priority.

Chapter Sixteen

Sweden was enjoying a pleasant entrance into the month of October. Lorraine and Professor Thuringer were most definitely addressing each other on a first name basis. In fact, they were well beyond that stage of the dating game. They had become engaged in the last week of September. The joyous couple had posed, with loving smiles on their faces, for an engagement photo that would be available for their viewing in a few days.

A wedding date of December 20th would accompany the engagement announcements. Notes of their plans to wed would be sent to family and friends in Sweden, France and the United States.

How Lorraine looked forward to being the wife of an accomplished, devoted professor of higher education. Having received only a minimal education herself, Lorraine had managed to work her way up in the field of social services in Sweden for the needy children. Though finding her work pleasing at most times, she knew she had the ability to excel in higher education with the encouragement and support of her fiancé.

Fame's Nordic animal studies were due to wrap up in late October. With her family scattered throughout Europe and the U.S. they chose to have a small, private wedding requiring a minimal amount of money. They preferred to put that money to better use, traveling for a short time visiting her sisters in Sweden and Paris, France. Following her familial visits they planned to permanently make their home in Minnesota.

* * * * *

Walking to the end of her winding driveway in October, Lilly looked forward to the one week in northern Minnesota that would provide nearly summer-like temperatures, a time known as Indian Summer. Already chilly mornings and nights had replaced the warmer ones. Summer seemed to fly by in the blink of an eye.

Opening the mailbox at the main road, Lilly placed the return note for Madeleine into the mailbox for the postal carrier to take. Opening the box, Lilly saw he had already been there that day. Still, she set the little red flag upright, notifying him to take her outgoing mail the following day.

Baby Tia slept soundly in her crib while Lilly made her brisk jaunt to the mailbox. Entering the house she rubbed her barren arms to warm them from the chilled air.

Sitting down at the kitchen table, she scanned their day's mail. Finding a letter from Lorraine, she cautiously opened it, knowing it contained more than simply a letter due to its extra weight.

Seeing the endearing photo of Famous and Lorraine pleased Lilly greatly. She did not, however, expect to find an engagement announcement along with it. Jumping in delight she released little yelps so as not to disturb Tia's nap. Not only was Lorraine getting married but she and Fame would be making their permanent residence in Minnesota.

* * * * *

Valentin walked in the door of the house at precisely 4:50 pm every day. Lilly allowed him the time to quickly shower prior to setting dinner on the table as she did every workday. Afterward, feeling refreshed, Valentin lightly kissed her forehead as he turned to seat himself at the table. Slowly pulling something from her apron pocket, Lilly teasingly handed her husband the envelope. Wearing a smug smile, he knew she had something up her sleeve.

What's this all about? he smugly inquired. Barely able to maintain her silence, he waited for her to burst. *Lilly, Lilly Lilly! Come, come now, let it all out!*

Unable to hold her tongue another second, she blurted out the words so rapidly he couldn't understand a single thing she said. Roaring! Valentin was absolutely roaring with laughter as he pulled out the photo and engagement announcement, reading the message of Lorraine and Fame's upcoming wedding plans.

What astounding news he proclaimed, with a broad smile across his face. Nothing could have pleased Valentin more on this fine day. The following evening he had just learned of Madeleine's future endeavors. Now, just one day later, more exciting news. So much to absorb within merely two days' time. The world certainly had a way of changing overnight and they knew it very well from firsthand experience.

October nights frequently left frost on rooftops, yards and car windows. Even the pumpkin patch would be painted in white. Valentin was thankful to have his auto housed in the new two-stall garage this winter. Erecting the building was a quick project with many good friends pitching in to assist.

It never failed to astonish Lilly when so many folks generously gave of their free time. Of course, they both offered their services when others were in need as well. But those in the small town and rural communities, in that particular region of northeastern Minnesota, seemed to take great pride in generously sharing and graciously giving.

Raised in a household of some privilege, Lilly was always taught to be courteous and friendly toward others, but there had been a lack of genuine giving from neighborhood friends and acquaintances. The same held true in her Aunt Melanie's neighborhood in Paris. An air of stuffiness or arrogance was often exuded by most.

Regardless of her upbringing, however, Lilly's entire being had been changed by the war, as was the case with many.

Genuine acts of giving had affected her most. Appreciating the kindnesses of others sat at the top of her list of do-goods.

Bundling baby Tia in layers of blankets Lilly set out for the pumpkin patch pulling Tia in a large red wagon from behind. The time had arrived to pick out a couple of unshapely pumpkins, used to prepare a few delectable pumpkin pies. The best shaped ones would be left to carve faces into for the festive Halloween celebrations. This was not a tradition celebrated in France but Lilly thought it to be great fun, having learned about it just the year before.

Finding themselves back in the warmth of the house, Lilly removed the seeds from within the gooey flesh of the pumpkin after carving a hole in the top. Setting Tia down on her favorite blanket on the living room carpet, surrounded by a few of her toys and stuffed animals, Lilly busied herself with the kitchen duties. Peeking in on her frequently, she would smile, appreciating her infant's superb behavior. Lilly certainly was fortunate to have such a well behaved baby the first time around.

Allowing more time to lapse than she'd realized, Lilly shuffled her feet, in her loosely fitted slippers, into the living room, only to find no baby. Instant panic set in! *Tia ... Tia ...* Lilly called frantically!! She began running in circles about the house, in and out of every room, looking behind the sofa, under the coffee table, even in the closet, which had tightly closed doors. Tia had never even crawled as of yet. Where could she possibly have gone?

Just as Lilly prepared to place an emergency call, she heard Tia's soft little voice coming from somewhere. But where? Where was she? Quietly she listened to hear her voice again. A minute, maybe two, had passed, but to Lilly it seemed like an hour.

Searching again, this time more thoroughly, Lilly's heart skipped a beat as she lowered herself to the floor in the baby's bedroom, finding Tia playing with a soft, fuzzy green turtle, named Elmer, beneath her crib. What relief! Lilly lay on the floor, inhaling deeply and grinning at her little angel. Reaching out for her, she gave baby Tia a stern lecture about running away from mommy.

Scratching her head, wondering how she'd managed to get into her bedroom, Lilly set her down on her blanket once again. No sooner had she done it when Tia propped herself up on all four, scooting herself along like nobody's business. Laughing and clapping her hands, while praising Tia for her newfound accomplishment, Lilly astonishingly watched as she crawled along. An occasional *"oops"* would happen, leaving Tia on her nose, but she was a tough one. She would get back up on all four hitting the unbeaten path once again.

Lilly was so excited to share the news with Tia's daddy. This milestone would have to be recorded in her Baby Book. It also meant Lilly would now have to begin sternly teaching her child not to touch certain items, especially the few plants that were within her reach. This is when parenting truly becomes a full-time assignment. Mommy and daddy would never want to see their precious little one take a tumble down the stairs or fall into the bathroom toilet.

Brenda Brown Elliott

* * * * *

A week had passed since Tia began venturing through the house of her own accord. What freedom that newfound accomplishment had afforded her.

At Halloween the Baranowsky's attended a small gathering of friends bobbing for apples, playing games and eating caramel apples while drinking fresh apple cider. All were dressed in silly or scary costumes hiding their true identities. Lilly found the celebration as much fun as the Independence Day celebration on the Fourth of July.

The day after Halloween the Baranowsky's drove to the Minneapolis/St. Paul airport to pick up the returning Madeleine from her lengthy travels. Immediately returning to the Iron Range on the same day created a long day for all. Still, Madeleine spoke incessantly of her many adventures and accomplishments while in France.

Delighted with Tia's advancements, namely crawling, grandmamma spent endless hours with her precious grandchild. It was good to have her mother back home with them, Lilly thought. They had truly missed her daily presence in their lives.

Madeleine had returned with a few fashionable and trendy Parisian articles of clothing for the family. Lilly felt so blessed for all she had in life. Her mother never failed to think about Lilly and her family.

* * * * *

The 1950's were witness to great advancements in the United States. People were encouraged to conform. Religion became more important. In 1954 "*Under God*" was added to the US Pledge of Allegiance. In 1955 "*In God We Trust*" was printed on all money. Music was making history as never before. Some top stars of Rock n' Roll were Elvis Presley, Connie Francis, Chuck Berry, Jerry Lee Lewis and Buddy Holly.

Lilly and Valentine purchased their very first hi-fi stereo bringing clear sounding music directly into their home. Valentin would often swing Lilly about, stocking footed, on the tiled flooring when a lively tune entertained them. The music provided many hours of enjoyment along with daily news events of the nation, even the world.

Also, before the end of the decade they purchased their first black and white television set. Placing rabbit ears on top of the TV set would provide a clearer picture, but oftentimes the screen would remain quite snowy. It enabled TV viewers to pick up three television stations, ABC, NBC and CBS. A few nightly news anchormen spent years broadcasting to American citizens. Names like Douglas Edwards, Chet Huntley and David Brinkley highlighted the screens throughout the 50's. Walter Cronkite later replaced Douglas Edwards in the early 60's.

McDonalds was franchised in the 50's. In 1954 penicillin and the polio vaccine were developed. These were huge advancements medically speaking, saving countless lives from sure death related to infections or paralysis from polio.

Chrysler, Ford and GM were the top three auto makers, producing eight million new cars per year. In order to accommodate travelers needs, the Interstate System was built in 1956 connecting north to south and east to west. In 1957 the first nuclear plant was built.

The Mickey Mouse Club, I Love Lucy, American Bandstand and Ozzie and Harriet were the top rated television shows, while James Dean and Marlon Brando topped the list of actors highlighting the movie screen.

Dwight D. Eisenhower was elected President of the United States that November of 52 with Richard M. Nixon presiding over the Vice-Presidential position.

Lilly's favorite new fashion wear was pedal pushers, which were a leap forward for women, not only showing their barren legs from the knees down, but allowing them more comfort from the stifling hot summer days. Patent leather shoes were replacing Buster Brown saddle shoes while polyester became the fabric of choice. Men began sporting woolen plaid work shirts in the northern tier states along with Rayon pullover casual wear.

Hoola hoops, hop scotch and Simon Says were favorite pastimes for children, even teenagers. Civil rights movements became the topic of conversation at many dinner tables daily. Motown got its establishment in the mid 1950's as well.

The Olympics were held in Helsinki, Finland in the year 1952. The Russians decided to enter her athletes after having withdrawn from the competitions in 1912. The athletes were not allowed to have any communications whatsoever with Westerners, going to the extent of setting up their own training facilities in order to avoid risking communications with the West. The competition of East vs. West dominated the games. It was said there were many more pressures on US athletes because of the Russians. The feeling was strong that the Americans just had to ... absolutely must ... beat them. Approximately 5,000 athletes participated, representing 69 countries.

* * * * *

Winter had ushered itself into Minnesota once again. The Christmas of '52 would provide an entirely different atmosphere than the previous Christmas. However, before reaching Christmas they first would celebrate Thanksgiving in late November with the company of Mr. and Mrs. Famous Thuringer.

Lorraine and husband had greatly enjoyed their visits with her family members. In Sweden, Katya had married Nicholas Osterholm. Without delay three healthy vibrant boys were born into their family by the names of Bjorn, Christian and Hans. At the ages of four, three and one, Katya had her hands full twenty-four seven. With her husband, Nicholas, being a fisherman on the Baltic Sea, parenting alone could become stressful at times. However, Alina's husband, Axel Johannson, worked arm in arm with Nicholas out on the sea. Axel and Alina bore two beautiful baby girls by the names of Katarina and Asa, ages two and three at the time of the Thuringer's visit. The two sisters were always available to each other in times of need. For this they were extremely thankful.

Lorraine spent endless hours cuddling and caressing her playful, endearing nieces and nephews. Time seemed to fly as the sisters shared their lives with one another. Even Nicholas and Axel set aside free time to spend with their sister-in-law and husband. Sweden had also suffered throughout the war with limitations on food, supplies, and communications. Fortunate to have been spared any bombing raids, however, they'd managed to keep their historic buildings and monuments intact as a legacy to their Scandinavian heritage. Living so near the island of Bornholm had had its disadvantages however.

The Nazi's held tight control over the Baltic waters. The fishermen found it necessary to redirect their fishing boats into open waters further north of the island, causing them to be away from home even longer during wartime, say nothing of the fear they lived with daily of being bombed by the Germans.

By 1952 much of Sweden had returned to her previous lifestyle. From Swedish shores, the Thuringers crossed the Baltic to the northern shores of Germany where they caught a passenger train taking them through the German cities of Hamburg and Essen. From there they continued onward through a corner of Belgium until reaching France, depositing them directly into the hands of Lorraine's sisters in Paris.

It had been 13 years since the five sisters had been alienated from one another. Although Greta and Emma would not have an opportunity, as of yet, to personally bond with sisters Alina and Katya, Lorraine would, at least, be able to share stories of the time she'd spent in Sweden with them.

As the train pulled into Paris, Famous thought he may have to sit on his precious wife, Lorraine, to keep her from jumping off too early in her excitement. Lorraine's eyes searched desperately, trying to recognize those ever-so-dear faces in the gathering crowd. Too many faces, just too many faces, she said again and again. Soon one face looked the same as the next. She was getting lightheaded and couldn't breathe well. She must maintain some control of her emotions. Pausing for a few moments allowed Lorraine to maintain control once again.

Having shared occasional photographs with one another through the mail, all three sisters had some idea of the others' appearances. Photographs don't always portray one's looks accurately, but when Lorraine and the Professor stepped foot from the train, squeals could be heard for blocks around. Instant recognition danced within their eyes. They would have known each other regardless of any recent photos. Warm, passionate hugs spoke volumes of their strong familial bonds, in a fashion only understood by true sisters. Love shared between them started at birth and extended throughout lifetimes.

Although brothers can truly bond in a masculine fashion, sisters seem to have that emotional glue the good Lord bestowed upon them at birth. A natural sense of nurturing, providing the gentle fixes of life's aches and pains through touching, cuddling, and hugging. Lorraine promptly introduced her new American husband, Professor Fame Thuringer, to her sisters. Heartfelt Warm embraces were shared among all.

Retrieving their baggage from the train, Greta and Emma guided the couple to the bus stop, transporting all to Emma's villa. There, the husbands and children of these long lost sisters, awaited the arrival of long-denied family members.

Paris presented no sunny skies on this Saturday in November. Vacations to this European destination were not the norm at this time of year, avoiding inclement weather. Numbing cold rain and chills, with low temperatures approaching freezing were not pleasurable weather conditions conducive for outdoor frolicking. Factor in wind chill and fewer daylight hours, a trip to the Mediterranean provided much more enjoyment.

But this wasn't a vacation of sorts. The weather could have been a staggering fifty degrees below zero as far as Lorraine was concerned. Besides, she'd lived in an even colder climate herself in Sweden for many years. Suffice it to say, Fame's upbringing in the northernmost area of Minnesota, sitting right on the Canadian border, had thickened his skin just the same, enabling both the ability to withstand the cool damp weather of Paris in November.

In 1947 Greta had married a French gentleman by the name of Gerard Moreau from whom she bore two sons, Rene and Andre, ages four and five.

Emma, it seemed, had caught the fancy of a Masseur Anton Bonnet, also marrying the same year. Shortly thereafter they welcomed a strapping baby boy into the world named Dominique, now age four and a precious baby girl named Anastasie, age three.

As Emma removed her coat a bump of a tummy revealed evidence of her third child due in another five months, an expectant due date in early April. Lorraine smiled with pleasure reminding her sisters of Valentin's baby Tia's birth date in late March. This one-time separated family was beginning to come together once again. The perils of war had stripped them of the years they would have spent together. Still, their bonds would overcome any negative circumstances threatening their shared love, uniting the once poor, uneducated siblings forever. Time and the miles between them would only prove to unite them even further.

Following the typical non-stop chatter that would ensue within any family getting re-acquainted all shared a satisfying blessing, thanking the dear Lord for reuniting them. Now it was Greta's turn to share even more exciting news with Lorraine and Fame.

With events occurring in a rather brief period of time, Lorraine hadn't had an opportunity to learn of Madeleine's sale of the vineyards and estate following Aunt Melanie's death. Greta anxiously shared the wonderful news that Madeleine had purchased a sizable Mediterranean villa for the Baranowsky family to use at their own discretion.

You mean they can fly over to vacation in the south of France at any time? asked Lorraine. What thrilling news this was for the family. Perhaps they would all have the opportunity to engage in an entire family gathering within a few years.

As a French wine vendor, Emma's husband, Anton, traveled frequently throughout the Western European countries, distributing fine French wines throughout. Numerous business trips to the Mediterranean familiarized him with the weather, thus suggesting June or September as the preferred months of vacationing. Of course, July and August supplied tourists with ample sunshine and warmth. The Wine harvests, called vendanges, were held in mid-September. Winters held less appeal for visitors with the mistral, a biting, moaning wind rumored to drive people insane, or at least off the beaches. Springtime was said to be pleasant, but only offered temps up into the mid 50's. How intriguing it was for these family members, who had spent years apart, to come together in their adult lives, with new spouses and children from all parts of the world. Certainly God had His hand in all of this.

Chapter Seventeen

Lorraine could not believe where the time had gone during their stay in Paris. Having fallen in love with the city of fashion and prestige, she insisted Fame promise to return them once again to the grand city. Viewing the Eiffel tower, along with the many other spectacular sights in the Spring, while all was in bloom, was something to greatly look forward to.

Although she admired the beauty of the city, Lorraine secretly preferred the quaintness and solitude of the small town or rural setting, such as that which Valentin and Lilly had acquired.

What little Lorraine had for furnishings in her tiny Swedish apartment were sold off at auction prior to their departure from Stockholm. She did pack her personal belongings in a few large crates, shipping them to the Baranowsky residence in Minnesota for safe keeping until their arrival.

With overseas flights available to all interested travelers in 1952, Fame and Lorraine boarded a Pan Am jetliner in Paris destined for New York City. From there they would immediately catch a connecting flight to Minneapolis/St. Paul, bringing them within two hundred miles of their final destination, Eveleth, Minnesota.

Valentin, Lilly and Madeleine remained busy, as ever, raising Baby Tia and preparing for the long winter season ahead while keeping involved with numerous church activities.

Valentin could not have chosen a better area of the country for hunting and fishing than northern Minnesota. Deer, moose, duck and grouse were vastly abundant. Every and any kind of fishing was available and plentiful.

Early November marked the beginning of deer hunting season. Valentin looked forward to his days in the brisk northern woods, awaiting the time for that perfect shot. Building a deer stand in the trees before the season opened enabled him to head out early each morning, situating himself comfortably, preparing to take out the first big buck.

Minnesota's deer population in the northern half of the state often resorted to eating the birch off trees in the cold winters, leaving their meat with a wilder taste than those in central and southern Minnesota. There, corn fields were abundant, providing them feed for several months out of the year. Still, a freezer full of venison, throughout the entire winter, took top priority when it came to feeding a family. Often, the toughest parts of the meat would be ground up with pork and spices, making it into venison sausage. Having a basement cellar to keep the numerous jars of home grown and canned vegetables and fruits, along with a freezer filled with venison, the Baranowksy's would be well prepared with food throughout the winter and spring seasons.

Trans World Airlines landed in Minneapolis/St. Paul International in snowy conditions, causing some intense discomfort in the Thuringers for just a moment. Fame unexpectedly let out a yelp as Lorraine firmly squeezed his hand, causing slight pain. She then followed up with a prayer, thanking the Lord for seeing them through the flight coming to a final stop Lorraine silently thanked the man upstairs for seeing them through the entire flight from France to Minnesota. This first flight ever for Lorraine had caused trembling from time to time while flying at such high speed so very close to heaven. Fame had flown once before, however, that didn't prevent him from dealing with shaky nerves as well. Each released a deep breath of relief, pleased to be back on solid ground.

Reaching the baggage claim area they identified their own baggage, snatched it up from the rotating carousel and stepped outdoors into the snow and cold winds. Raised collars, hats, scarves, gloves and buttoned up winter coats were in place, preparing both for the arctic blast.

Standing at the curb of the street, Fame hailed a taxi to drive them to the car rental agency. In little time they were on the road heading north to the Baranowsky's for a short visit before Thanksgiving Day. Plans were to spend a few days with Lorraine's family before continuing onward to International Falls, Fame's hometown, joining his father and brother for a Thanksgiving dinner.

The Thuringers were joyously greeted upon arrival at Long Lake. Following hugs and congratulations on their wedding, the newlywed couple blushed as Lilly handed them a few packages to open, compliments of the Baranowsky's and Madeleine on their blessed marriage.

Lorraine politely excused herself before opening the gifts, finding her way into the guest bedroom to quickly change into something more comfortable than her traveling suit. Opening her largest suitcase she immediately discovered it was the wrong case. Looking at the others sitting on the bedroom floor, she was sure she'd simply grabbed Fame's bag. Frustration began setting in as she opened all three additional bags, realizing she'd somehow ended up with another traveler's bag. The wrong bag held women's clothing, but much smaller in size than Lorraine's long- stretched body. Rejoining the others she explained the obvious error in confusing her bag with another's.

Having sent crates carrying her personal belongings in advance to her brother's home, Lorraine knew she wouldn't be without any clothing completely. Still, it was a large bag containing many of her favorite articles of clothing, and a monetary loss as well. The other bag was hers, for sure, yet held mostly sleepwear, undergarments and toiletries.

Lilly and Madeleine were both smaller framed than Lorraine, making it impossible to offer their own items of clothing for temporary use. It was rare to see women in full length pants in 1952. Most commonly worn garments were dresses or skirts with a blouse. For the time being, she would have to settle for wearing a pair of Fame's trousers along with a sweater of his. A belt, wrapping itself nearly twice around her tiny waist, held up the trousers, but remained hidden by the long draping sweater. Fame smiled as he rolled up her sleeves. Feeling even more humiliated and detecting a smug look on his face she instantly popped out her bottom lip in a pout while stomping her foot on the floor. *You are laughing at me!* Removing the smirk, he appeared to be quite contrite in his apology, all the while remaining somber in assuring her of his genuineness. However, upon turning away he burst into laughter while making his way back into the living room.

Following closely behind Fame into the living room, Valentin half expected his sister to smack her husband one good. After all, that was how she'd reacted to him back in their younger years, when he had teased her about the boys.

At first, thinking she had matured substantially, Valentin let the thought slip away. That is, until she snidely vowed to get even with her dearest husband sometime soon. Laughter burst throughout the room, as Lorraine found a place on the floor with Baby Tia.

The unwrapping of wedding gifts took place on the floor allowing Baby Tia to amuse herself with torn paper, ribbons and bows. The warm air within the comfortable confines of the home, gave a sense of fulfillment to all. Accepting the lovely gifts which would serve them well in their new home gave Lorraine a sense of belonging she had never known. Thanking them graciously, Fame started filling them in on their future plans.

Becoming part of the University of Minnesota in 1947, the U of M Duluth branch had apparently requested Professor Famous Thuringer to join their staff. Recognizing the opportunity to expand his animal studies in the northern climates of the U.S., along with earning a comfortable income, Fame informed the family of his decision to accept the position.

What pleasing words to Valentin's ears. With an enormous sense of gratitude, he wrapped his arms around both Lorraine and Fame. It would be grand with Lorraine living so near his family, sharing in the holidays as well as occasional weekend visits. Duluth was a nice sized city with much growth opportunity. Lorraine may not have exactly what she'd planned, living in a rural setting as her brother did, but she had other plans for herself as well.

Numerous conversations with Fame regarding higher education prompted a sense of confidence in Lorraine that she, too, could succeed in furthering her goals. Lorraine became greatly enthusiastic about checking into classes offered at the Univ. of Minn. Duluth. ever in life had she imagined attending a University. Fame recognized her capabilities, encouraging her, as his own father had encouraged him. Confident in his ability to cover the additional educational costs, he proudly extended full support in her quest to learn, to better improve herself.

While enjoying a lengthy dinner, Madeleine and Lilly convinced the young couple to invite Fame's father and brother for Thanksgiving dinner in late November. What a pleasure it would be to become acquainted with the professor's family. After all, they were extended family now. A quick phone call that evening ensured their desire to join in on the family festivities. This year would prove to be quite different from the prior year. At that time, the Baranowksy's never imagined what joy lay ahead with a beautiful baby daughter, Lilly's joy having her fully recuperated mother with them, a rekindled relationship with three of Valentin's sisters, the gift of Lorraine's new marriage to a fellow Minnesotan, establishing residency so near their own home. Soon, those strong family ties would envelope several additional people into the womb of their hearts and homes. How very blessed they were.

The following morning the men ventured outdoors and into the garage hunting for the crates that transported Lorraine's clothing from Sweden. Not far beyond the garage was their own small landfill where garbage and trash were discarded. This was commonplace for rural residents in 1952, as no type of garbage pickup was provided at that time. They would burn the piles occasionally, being their only means of elimination.

Tightly closing the door of the garage behind them, the gentleman turned toward the house with arms full. Before realizing it, a large black bear stood up in defiance of their presence. Reaching a good eight feet in height as he stood on his back legs, the wild animal sounded equally ferocious. Both men were mostly hidden behind the large crates they carried. Stopping instantly in place, they decided their best move would be to slowly turn around and return to the garage. In doing so, the broad furry creature let out a growl that would have awakened the dead.

Slowly, the two re-entered the garage through the man door. Having studied bears in Minnesota and Sweden, Fame knew they were likely in no danger, as the black bear was known to be quite timid, usually leaving mankind to himself, unless searching for food. It had been a dry summer, leaving little for the animals of the forests to feed on, so the bear was likely hungry.

Deciding to wait it out in the garage, the two brothers-in-law started up a conversation regarding Fame's studies of animals. Soon, however, they heard Lorraine's voice yelling at the bear. Familiar with the bear's timid nature, Fame couldn't help but laugh once again as his wife made an effort to scare it off. However, the ladies had no idea where the men might be.

Stepping just partially outside the porch door, Lorraine tossed a large venison roast toward the bear in the hope of satisfying him. Lilly held Tia firmly as she and Madeleine watched the crisis unfolding outside the kitchen window. Never would they have had the courage Lorraine was displaying. The men, all the while hearing what was taking place outdoors, opened the door just enough to get a peek at the bear's present location. Still too close for comfort, they remained in the garage until the coast was clear.

At last the bear meandered along toward the landfill after finishing the tasty venison. Valentin and Fame resumed their previous endeavor to carry in the crates of clothing, again tightly closing the door behind them.

A sigh of relief emerged from the women, while Lorraine was bestowed the great honor of saving the men from what could have been a very ugly scene.

Teasingly, Lorraine boasted she'd considered letting the bear have its way with Fame after his mocking behavior the previous night. However, considering Valentin's well being at the same time, Fame received Lorraine's generous sympathy, sparing her poor husband from certain fatality. Hearty laughter filled the home for several minutes along with Fame's deepest appreciation of his wife's gracious mercy. Valentin and Fame simply didn't have the heart to inform the women of the unnecessary waste of venison, as the bear likely would have shied away from the men anyway. How could they deny Lorraine her due glory at that moment? Smiling appreciatively, both men greatly thanked their sister and wife for her courageous behavior.

Another large venison roast was removed from the freezer that morning, allowing it time to thaw before placing it into the oven to bake for their evening meal. A favorite method of cooking the roast would be to pile it high with onions and seasonings, later adding fresh potatoes from the garden and canned carrots from the cellar. There wasn't much that pleased a hungry man more than a good hot dinner baking in the oven, especially after working hard outdoors.

That day, Lorraine whipped together homemade cornmeal biscuits to accompany the main course. Madeleine removed a container of frozen blueberries for a delectable mouth-watering blueberry pie, the likes of which no other could hold a candle to. That same afternoon the women busied themselves with baking apple, pumpkin and mincemeat pies for tomorrow's Thanksgiving menu. Homemade vanilla ice cream, prepared by Lilly, would complement the delicious warm pies, every bite being savored by each individual until not another crumb was left to be seen on their plate.

Lorraine rejoiced when learning of her clothing being located. A phone call was placed to the international airport in Minneapolis regarding the suitcase. Reaching the lost and found department, Fame learned the party with Lorraine's baggage lived in Grand Rapids, MN. Thankfully that was only an hour west of Eveleth, making the transfer of bags easier than they'd thought. Actually, they believed they would likely never see the right bag again.

Exhausted from their lengthy trip, Lorraine agreed to wait until the day after Thanksgiving to meet and exchange the baggage. However, the other party agreed to drive the distance to Eveleth immediately after speaking on the phone with one another. Both parties were pleased to have their own proper garments back. They would be sure to check more cautiously the next time they traveled.

The women knew tomorrow would be an early day as the 24 lb. turkey needed to be stuffed and slid into the oven by sun up. Television would afford the men the luxury of watching professional football throughout the afternoon while the women would join together in chatter while cleaning the kitchen.

Receiving a few inches of snow the previous night, Fame took it upon himself to shovel the walkways, as well as banking the snow against the base of the house. Shortly afterward he greeted Harold and James when they arrived. Everyone was introduced before partaking in a glass of wine prior to their feast.

A pleasant day was had by all, particularly for Madeleine and Harold. It seemed the two had especially enjoyed each other's company that afternoon. Lilly's eyes didn't miss a moment of Madeleine's flirtatious behavior. She'd whisper a comment or two into Valentin's ear, trying her best to remain inconspicuous. Fame, too, noticed his dad's somewhat flirtatious responses to Madeleine.

Harold had taken a special liking to Baby Tia. There was no shortage of arms in the house, carrying her around to her heart's content. Nor was she denied itty bitty samples of the delicious turkey dinner. Madeleine, always the photographer, was sure to snap plenty of photos during the festivities, especially those of Tia and Harold together.

At day's end, Harold and James Thuringer headed north with full tummies and pleasant thoughts of that most blessed day. *Madeleine is a really nice lady, huh dad?* James inquired of his father. *Yes, yes indeed she is ...* was his one and only response. James left the subject of Madeleine DeMornais at that.

Following his personal introduction to the Dean of students at UMD, Fame was then introduced to various staff members. Professor Thuringer felt a great sense of belonging as he toured the campus, meeting additional staff members. He felt equally comfortable knowing his new bride would flourish nicely there. It was of great satisfaction to him that Lorraine would be only moments away if any problems arose.

As anticipated, the excitement of finding a home in Duluth was all they had expected. Having spent a sizable amount of money traveling in Europe after their wedding, the couple considered it wise to purchase second hand furniture, still in excellent shape looking nearly brand new, for their first home.

The decision to rent for the time being, until they were sure of Fame's security at UMD, outranked their desire to purchase a home just then. Besides, it would take time to build a nest egg for a down payment on a home. Money would also be needed to cover Lilly's education.

Each weekday morning the couple would leave home together, headed for the University. He, as a professor and she, as a student. Lorraine did, at times, sense some discomfort when questioned by younger students about her educational aspirations at her age. Professor Thuringer instructed her to simply use her foreign upbringing as a reason for her late start as a U.S. college student. With the exception of very few, the majority of women Lorraine's age, in their mid twenties, were well on their way to having their third or fourth child. Large families were the accepted norm then. Birth control for women had not yet been introduced. The only way to prevent pregnancy was by abstaining or using condoms, which was fully the responsibility of the male.

The newlyweds were fully settled in before Christmas arrived. Lorraine created simple decorations for the holiday season. The weekend prior to Christmas was spent entertaining the

Baranowsky's, Madeleine and Harold Thuringer. James was spending time courting a girl of his own interests in International Falls, where he was employed as the business manager of a flourishing hardware store.

It had become obvious to all that Madeleine and Hal were indeed enjoying one another's company. Apparently the two had exchanged a few letters between themselves. Madeleine took great pride in the fact she'd very skillfully learned to write in English. French was still spoken between mother and daughter occasionally. The women also planned to teach Tia how to speak fluent French as well as English.

The girls spent a full day shopping for Christmas gifts in Duluth where a greater variety of items were sold, being a larger city than Eveleth or the small neighboring towns. Meanwhile, the men went in search of a Christmas tree after completing a game of Chess that Saturday morning. Later in the afternoon all participated in the decorating of the tree. Sunday morning the three couples, along with Baby Tia, attended services at the Hillside Lutheran Church. Hal, (Harold's nickname) had been a Protestant all his life. Yet, he felt the message was the same, regardless of specific religion and Madeleine admired that quality in him.

Christmas season was Lilly's very favorite time of year. The world seemed so much at peace when recognizing and celebrating the birth of dear Baby Jesus. One of Madeleine's most precious keepsakes was the Nativity Scene, or as described in French, the Christmas Crèche, that was handed down to her from Aunt Melanie when she married Jon Paul. Halfway into the month of December she removed them from safekeeping, beautifully displaying each piece beneath the handmade animal shelter for the Nativity Scene. Valentin took great pride in preparing a manger within, using dried brown grass pulled from the ground prior to the first snowfall of the year. This served in place of the hay as described in the Bible of Jesus' birth.

Christmas Eve, once again, was spent in the home of the Baranowsky's. That evening, however, was a bit noisier than the previous year, with Baby Tia tearing open packages for others. Everyone appreciated the gifts exchanged between themselves. That Christmas Eve ended early as all laid down for a long winter's nap, preparing them for a busy Christmas Day filled with festivities.

The pleasant aroma of a large juicy ham wafted throughout the house that day, giving cause to growling stomachs. Most avoided eating anything else until the 10 course meal was served, at precisely 3 o'clock PM.

When saying *"MOST"* that is exactly correct. Somebody sneaky, by the name of Valentin, frequently found his way into the kitchen, acting as though he were innocently chatting, until his fingers would snap up a cookie, or a bar, or anything looking tasty at the time. More than once, Lilly would give a playful tap to his fingers with her wooden spoon, teasing him that no food would be left for their guests. Blending in with the aroma of various dishes cooking, the scent of pine from the Christmas tree lingered lazily throughout the home.

Joining in on that Christmas Day of 1952 were Harold, James and his girlfriend, Nicole, Lorraine and Fame. With eight adults and one baby girl the home was filled with chatter, laughter, blessings and hope. Hope, for another bountiful year filled with God's love, everlasting peace and heartfelt joy.

Christmas cards were exchanged by all, including those from overseas families unable to share together in the festivities. Valentin and Lorraine were overwhelmed with excitement when hearing Alina and Katya's families had traveled to Paris, for the first time, spending Christmas together, getting re-acquainted once again. God had certainly blessed each and every one of them this joyous Christmas season!

Lorraine did have reason for concern regarding Alina however. It became apparent while visiting with her sisters, just a couple of months earlier, that Alina had lost all faith in God. She still held bitterness and anger over the break-up of her family, the death of her parents, and the ugliness, the emptiness, she'd felt throughout the difficult years of the war.

With her own life taking such enormous leaps within the past few months, Lorraine had managed to put her concerns for Alina in the back of her mind. Now, however, with life settling down somewhat, thoughts of her baby sister crept into her mind more often. There was no time better than the present to share a family prayer for Alina. Lorraine asked for everyone's attention as she expressed her concerns.

Responding with heartfelt concern, Valentin immediately formed a circle with his family, asking God to seek her out, as He had done with each of them. Continuing around the circle, each family member addressed the Lord, requesting He touch the heart of dear Alina. Fully aware she must be open to Him as well, they prayed for His all-knowing wisdom to enlighten her, guiding her back into His loving arms. This was their utmost important prayer request in this ending year of 1952.

Courage Times Three. A Novel

Chapter Eighteen

The winter of 52 - 53 was already coming to an end. Where had the time gone in that past year? With eight teeth in her mouth Tia was eating many grown-up foods. She had already started walking at eleven months of age. Lilly had taken to shutting all of the bedroom doors as well as the bathroom. Electrical sockets were covered with tape and the trash was kept beneath the kitchen sink. LOL! Preparedness! Prevention! All in the Baranowksy household were faring well.

Lorraine and Fame were taking in all the activities at the University campus. Spring break at the college was just beginning, giving the Thuringers a chance to relax for a short time. The demands of being a professor at a college didn't end when Fame left the school at the end of his teaching day. The Thuringers had taken an avid interest in the UMD Bulldogs hockey team that winter. They looked forward to late summer when football season would kick into gear as well. Lorraine was doing extremely well in her classes, her husband so very proud of her achievements. She had taken a special interest in working on the school newsletter, which led her into the field of journalism.

Madeleine continued seeing Hal Thuringer from time to time. Both were learning fun and interesting facts about the French and the Scandinavians from each other, even how to prepare chocolate soufflé or lefsa.

As per earlier discussions in that Fall of 1952, Madeleine's wish to have a cozy cottage built on the lake near Valentin and Lilly became more than a wish, it had taken on a life of its own.

Melting snow, warm days with dripping rooftops, slush and mud from the thawing ground marked another end to a long winter.

Ground breaking for Madeleine's year round cottage had begun. Hal was a few years older than Madeleine, therefore an *"Over The Hill"* 50th birthday celebration took place in May. Valentin bestowed Hal with the nickname of *"Old Coot"*, as they *"roasted"* his life throughout his 50 years.

Lilly and Valentin found this an opportune time to share their fun news with the family. Lilly was with child once again, expecting on December 20th. Hugs and kisses were shared by all as they toasted the happy couple. While secretly hoping for a son the second time around, Valentin kept those wishes to himself. After all, Lilly had no control over the sex of the infant growing within her. He would feel blessed with any gender as long as it was healthy and strong.

The building of Madeleine's cottage was only one of the projects proposed for construction late this Spring. When, at first, the proposal to pay for the barn and horses was suggested by Madeleine, Valentin felt somewhat uncomfortable accepting such a large gift. Once explained that her own desire to ride also played a factor in making such a generous offer, she convinced Valentin to accept. Mother and daughter exuberantly looked forward to riding together once again as they had in years past. A vast spread of open field sat just to the west of the home, a perfect layout for the two new mares. Endless hours would be spent grooming and riding. Lilly and Madeleine both looked forward to teaching Tia and the upcoming new bundle of joy to ride one day.

As the construction of Madeleine's cottage neared completion, Madeleine wondered if anything permanent would become of her relationship with Hal. Having tossed feelings, she wasn't sure if she wanted to take on the task of learning how to live with another man's habits and lifestyle. Yet, it would be very nice to have the love and devotion of a man throughout her elderly years. Much time had passed since Jon Paul's death. Rather than being left alone and lonely, she had been blessed with the love and kindness of her daughter and family. What more could any mother ever want from her child? Truth be told, Lilly and Valentin felt exactly the same way about Madeleine. What more could any child want from a parent?

Madeleine had been an outstanding mother, mother-in-law and grandmother to their Baby Tia. Never had she pushed her weight, correcting them in their choices of nurturing and disciplining Tia, asking for anything beyond the norm, only sharing the good times along with the bad, always taking life in stride. They'd all grown together in their Christian lives, learned much about the true meaning of life and adjusted well to life in the United States, both in New York City and northern Minnesota. Yet, so much life lay ahead.

One very lovely Spring evening, Madeleine and Lilly sat upon the swing made for two after putting Tia down for the night. Valentin was out in the field plowing the garden for the summer crops that would soon be planted. Gazing out upon the lake, mother and daughter became mesmerized as the soft breezes caused tiny ripples upon the blue waters, leaving the impression of diamonds dancing on it.

Turning their heads to the sound of an approaching automobile, Madeleine smiled when she recognized the unexpected guest. Greeting Hal rather quickly, then excusing herself, Lilly left the two to themselves on the deck. Hal apologized for dropping in unexpectedly then had a seat next to the lovely Madeleine.

No time was wasted before getting down on his knee, looking Madeleine in the eyes with a look of love and nervous excitement. *My dearest Madeleine, would you do me the honor of becoming my wife?* As he spoke those words, Hal pulled a velvet box from the pocket of his trousers, opening it to display the breath-taking diamond ring.

Realizing exactly what he was up to the second he bent down on his knee, Madeleine didn't know if she dared breathe. There was no way on earth she had expected this proposal. Sitting quite numbed, with her mouth gaping open, she suddenly burst into laughter. *Are you serious?* The words barely squeaked out of her. Not sure just how to respond to her abrupt bout of laughter, he assured Madeleine he was, indeed, serious.

Madeleine, I never even considered dating a woman since my late wife's death. From the first day we met, I was taken by your beauty and kindness. You've given me a reason to smile when I awaken each morning. You fulfill an emptiness I never expected to be filled again. I love you and will continue to love and cherish you forever, if you will accept my proposal of marriage.

Madeleine could see the genuine love and admiration Hal had for her. She knew she was beginning to grow in confidence more now than at any other time in her life. Something told her Hal was ready for changes in his life at this time as well. And she had to admit she found him very easy to communicate with.

Her first words to Hal in reaction to his proposal were kind and warm. Taking him gently by the hand, Madeleine exposed a big smile as she eased him back up unto the swing to sit beside her. *You are the only man who has even remotely sparked an interest in me. I believe it is quite possible for us to, perhaps, fall deeply in love one day. On that note, I must tell you I would like to continue seeing one another. I have no interest in dating another man, but I cannot, in all honesty, state I am already in love with you. I pray you will understand this dear Hal.*

Feeling slightly let down by her refusal to accept his marriage proposal, Hal gently replaced the blue velvet box into the pocket of his trousers. He still remained optimistic however. She had not accepted his proposal but she also had not outright refused the possibility of it ever occurring either.

Hal was certain, over time, he could romance the lovely Madeleine, enticing her into reciprocating his love equally. At her suggestion the two began walking along the lakeside, hand in hand, visually absorbing the glassy waters while catching the sunset in the western skies, displaying an array of colors behind them. Madeleine wanted to learn more about this only man who had given her reason to consider love once again in her life.

* * * * *

Another busy summer came and went. Madeleine and Hal, along with Valentin, Lilly and Tia had spent a weekend shopping in Duluth for new items to furnish Madeleine's quaint new cottage alongside the lake. A beautiful sunshiny day blessed their July 4th celebration on the lake that year with everyone taking turns trying their luck on water ski's behind the new speed boat that had been purchased.

Children from the summer Bible Camps invaded the lakes in late July, pulling Lilly away from home to teach classes to the fifth and sixth graders. Madeleine was more than happy to appease Lilly when it came to caring for Baby Tia in her absence.

Summer turned into autumn with winter landing right on its heels. Fame and Lorraine had become very actively involved in both football and hockey activities at UMD. Lorraine continued her interests in journalism while working on the school newsletter. Those interests greatly intrigued Lilly. After all, she had learned much about the production and printing of newspapers in her underground life. Lorraine had no knowledge of that, as those difficult times were left mostly unspoken. So she was quite astonished when Lilly chose to share tidbits of those times with her.

Lorraine hadn't shared her difficulties as a younger woman with anyone other than her husband, but she sensed that one day she might be able to share that pain with Lilly. Oftentimes, when we learn of others' misfortunes in life, it somehow enables us to stand stronger in ourselves.

The fragility of our human mind and soul is forever tempted by the Evil One. How odd it all is, to learn life's greatest lessons through the most heart-wrenching tragedies in our lives. Tragedies can make us strong or make us weak. We are the only ones who have complete control over our own minds. Many allow others to do it, but in essence, we are the sole controllers. No matter how often someone may tell you are weak, that you are worthless or you cannot do something, they are striving diligently to control your mind. Only you can stand up to that, only you can walk tall in your shoes, a lesson worth always remembering in life. Most importantly, however, letting God walk with us at all times, is worth more than all the gold on Earth.

Something both Lilly and Lorraine had learned to do for themselves, was to spend time reading God's Word from the Bible. The longest chapter in the Bible is Psalms. Psalms and Proverbs are continuous words of wisdom for us to use in our everyday lives. Whenever the horrors of their past began to sneak into the forefront of their minds, spending time with God, simply by reading His Word, was so consoling they knew they could never survive in this cruel world without Him. For this, they would feel forever blessed.

Madeleine absolutely loved the warmth and coziness of her own private cottage. She immediately began to invite guests from the church as well as her special guest, Hal Thuringer, into her home for entertaining luncheons and dinners. Being very financially comfortable, from the inheritance of Melanie's vineyards and estate, Madeleine began making plans for her first vacation to the south of France. She felt it best to make the trip alone this first time. Her feelings for Hal had grown immensely, even to the point of possibly accepting his marriage proposal. However, she felt she owed it to herself to test the waters, so to speak, as a single woman, while vacationing on the Mediterranean.

Her departure would not take place until after the Christmas season. With Lilly due to deliver their second child on December 20th Madeleine felt the necessity to remain in Minnesota to care for Tia throughout Lilly's hospital stay. Her plan was to remain in France for a full month. That would allow her time to come to a definite decision regarding a future with Hal. It wasn't at all as it had been the first time around for her in love. So young and beautiful; so fragile and naïve, Madeleine's romance with Jon Paul swept her off her feet from the day she'd met him. Understanding that love can change immensely in the way it is given and received as we grow older, accounted for the slight loss of giddiness and skipping heartbeats that accompanied her first love. So, she had to be entirely sure that what love she did feel for Hal would be enough to sustain a marriage for the remainder of their lives.

Lilly was very proud of how Madeleine was dealing with the relationship. In years past her mother might have jumped at the opportunity to have another man care for her every need. Doing a double check of her feelings before taking that gigantic leap assured Lilly of her mother's undoubtedly strong security and stability in herself. Valentin was in full agreement with the women. He had come to love and respect Madeleine in much the same way he would have loved his own mother, had she survived the war.

In the late hours of December 19th Lilly went into full labor. With her water breaking and contractions coming every seven minutes that night, there was no time to waste in getting her to the Virginia hospital. At 6:18 a.m. on the morning of December 20th the exact delivery date estimated by her doctor and herself, Lilly gave birth to another bouncing baby girl. But it didn't stop there. Following the first, came a second. Another baby girl. Lo and behold, the Baranowsky's were blessed with identical twin daughters.

Lilly often thought she must be carrying a boy within her as she continued to expand in leaps and bounds through the last two months of her pregnancy. Two more daughters. Valentin's excitement over having twins so overtook him, he never thought twice about that son he had been wishing to receive.

Courage Times Three. A Novel

The happy couple had already picked out the name of Robin Loreen for a girl. Now they must think of another girl's name. One that had frequently entered Lilly's mind was Rhonda Lou. With Valentin in full agreement to name her Rhonda, the blessed couple snuggled closely, each holding one of their precious newborn twins, Robin Loreen and Rhonda Lou. Both infants were perfectly healthy, with strong lungs and enough weight to be sent home right along with their mother after a five day hospital stay.

It became absolutely necessary for Madeleine to postpone her French vacation to a somewhat later date. Lilly would need her help twice as much now.

Never had they imagined the chaos that would ensue in caring for identical twins. Not only did they need double of everything, they also found it necessary to give each a color of their own, enabling parents and grandmamma a means of identifying just who was who. Lorraine and Fame wasted no time in driving the sixty mile distance to see their precious new angels. Harold, as well, found his way through the one hundred mile stretch to shower the happy couple with gifts for their second and third bundles of joy.

Somehow, this magnificent miracle of twin births convinced Madeleine her feelings for Hal were most genuine. Genuine enough in fact, to warrant a wedding in the near future. Hal couldn't have been happier when she shared the magnificent news with him.

Swinging his feather-light wife-to-be into the air, six month's worth of holding his breath, praying diligently for his Maddy's long awaited acceptance of his marriage proposal, allowed a huge release of tension he had not even been fully aware of.

At their advanced ages both agreed a very small, private wedding was appropriate. Rather than purchasing a new outfit for the occasion, Madeleine made no fuss over trivial garments for a private ceremony. Nor did time allow for it, as endless hours were required in caring for the twins while Lilly got back on her feet. Even then, with Tia still under the age of three years, both women worked steadily throughout each day tending to three children.

Madeleine DeMornais joyously became the loving wife of Harold Thuringer in February. Harold, of both German and Scandinavian heritage, carried the proud name of his paternal grandfather, who was almost entirely German. Just a hint of Austrian accompanied his heritage. Madeleine had been mostly raised in

France following her parents' deaths, but her younger roots came Germany, as a Jewish citizen. Once Hal had learned this bit of information, he urged Madeleine to touch base with her very humble beginnings.

She shared what knowledge she did have of her young childhood days. Recalling she and a younger brother had occupied a small apartment under the loving care of poor but kind parents, Madeleine rarely allowed those memories to surface. She did recall living very near a large river and freezing in the cold winter months with little to no heat to keep them warm.

While in France following the death of Aunt Melanie, Madeleine ran across a large book filled with photographs and letters. Aunt Melanie had always become quite fidgety and nervous when Madeleine approached her with inquiries of her past history in Germany. *Oh dear, I just haven't time to venture into all of that nonsense right now!,* would generally be her Aunt's response to her inquisitions of earlier childhood with her biological parents. Obviously happy with the privileged lifestyle she lived, Madeleine easily let the matter slide. Upon finding the book full of memories from her past, she'd simply tucked it aside until packing it in with other belongings being sent to her Minnesota residence.

She'd considered leafing through the remnants of her past when she moved her personal belongings into her new lake cottage. Now, with Hal's urging, she would finally delve into her long-past life in search of her true identity. Somehow, with him at her side, her fears seem to have subsided for the first time in her life. She'd enjoyed being a French woman. The upstanding citizens of France were refined ... and debonair, exuding a sense of elegance and sophistication. She'd always taken pride in being part of higher class society as a French woman.

Now, life had changed in so very many ways. No longer did she smart of arrogant sophistication. Madeleine had learned how to be very down-to-earth in her demeanor. The petite 5'3", 110 pound woman would likely always portray a bit of feminine sophistication. And, of this, she was quite proud. One need not lose their sense of pride and dignity, even after learning how to humble themselves in life. She also knew Harold likely would not have fallen in love with the woman she had once been. Realizing it possibly may have been her very own arrogance that had often sent men in another direction, she grimaced at the somewhat humiliating feeling of embarrassment it caused her now.

How very much she was enjoying the discovery of her newfound self. Throughout this time of immense growth in Madeleine's life, she also developed a much closer relationship with God. A relationship she had no idea even existed here on earth, as many don't throughout their entire lifetimes.

As these middle-aged lovebirds prepared to live out their future years with one another, Hal moved some of his personal belongings into the lake cottage. While taking care of business regarding the sale of his long time home in International Falls, Hal's youngest son, James, expressed an interest in purchasing the home for himself and possible future wife, Nicole, as it held many loving memories of his childhood with his mother and father both. Hal and Fame could not have been more pleased with the outcome of the home's future. For years to come it would continue housing the strong bloodline of their dear family.

Chapter Nineteen

Comfortably seating themselves in front of a cozy burning fire in the living room, Madeleine and Hal began sorting through the memorabilia dear Aunt Melanie had so painfully preserved for her daughter's future knowledge. Like the hands on a clock rolling backward rapidly in time, Mrs. Madeleine Thuringer allowed herself to return, for the first time in numerous years, to her young childhood years.

The city of Cologne, Germany sat on the banks of the Rhine River. The sister-cities of Cologne/Bonn suffered substantial damage as much of Germany did throughout WWI. Although France and Belgium had sustained more material damage to their territory, Germany received longer lasting economic damage from which it could not recover for several years. This had such an impact on the livelihood of so many German citizens, it left little hope for many regarding their futures.

This was the reality of Madeleine's existence in the first eight years of her life. So dirt poor, they'd barely been able to stay alive, let alone sustain good or even fair health.

Madeleine was the oldest of two children born to Freidrich and Germaine Dietrich early in the first decade of the 1900's. With one brother, Gustav, 4 years her younger, Madeleine often spent her days caring for his needs. The small barren quarters they'd merely existed in, did little to nothing in providing them warmth throughout the never-ending months of icy cold temperatures. Madeleine slightly recalled snuggling together with her brother as they fed off of each other's body heat on many nights. With the warmer weather of summer, sharing a home with a barrage of insects was commonplace for this family. Madeleine's mother would comment occasionally about the bugs being in the wrong place if they, too, were in search of a few measly crumbs.

Struggling merely to keep the family alive, Germaine Dietrich would venture out daily in search of work, any kind of work she could find for that particular day. When nothing could be found, begging for eggs or potatoes wasn't beneath her in the daily ritual of walking the streets of Cologne and Bonn. Her husband, Freidrich, would occasionally find employment in the agricultural areas just outside of the city. There were also times when he would spend the day fishing on the Rhine in the hopes of catching just one good sized fish to ease the hunger of his family that day. So very many hungry vagrants lined the shores of the river in hopes of feeding themselves as well.

The reasons were many as to why Madeleine never wanted to return to those blatantly excruciating times. So blessed to have been taken in and raised by her Aunt Melanie and Uncle Marco in France, she always thought it best to never look back.

Life had humbled her now causing her to reach back to those native roots once again. The fact her younger brother, Gustav, may still be out there in the world, was weighing heavily on her mind.

In the 1890's, eastern European citizens experienced widespread death from cholera, famine and influenza. It was influenza on top of famine that took the lives of both Madeleine's parents. A paternal uncle took the children into his own home for approximately six months following their parents' deaths. In 1914 WWI overtook them so fiercely it was all he could do in feeding his own family, let alone two additional mouths in Gustav and Madeleine.

Tears were shed by her saddened uncle's heartache as his task to send away his brother's children, in separate directions, never knowing if they would once again meet up in life, played like an old movie in Maddy's mind. She knew he had no choice, yet the pain of losing her brother, as well as her parents, overtook her for quite some time. She still did not understand why life must be so challenging, so very painful.

Madeleine was the first to be sent away at the age of 10. Feeling lost and lonely in a world completely unknown to her, she retreated into seclusion during the first few months of her life in France. Aunt Melanie's steady and loving encouragement slowly enabled her to break down the barriers that stood between herself and her dearest young niece. Melanie oftentimes felt the Lord had blessed her with the very needy, broken child. Her own inability to bear children cast a heavy weight upon her shoulders. At that time in history, a man could divorce a woman who was unable to bear his children. Knowing this, Melanie strived endlessly to appease her husband in every manner possible, to keep his faithful love from fading.

Fortunately, she'd been blessed with a sizable dowry, so to speak, serving as financial security for herself and her husband. An astute businessman, Franco made wise choices, mostly in Swiss investments, providing them additional income over and above the vineyard's hefty profits. Later in life, when WWII wreaked havoc on most northern vineyards in the early 1940's, those investments proved to be a huge asset, providing Melanie and Madeleine the ability to stay afloat financially. Later it would provide them the necessary funds to reinvest into the vineyards following the second world war.

Once Madeleine began letting down her guard with Aunt Melanie, she eventually grasped the opportunities available to her, learning the French language and customs. Located in a very prestigious neighborhood, on the northeastern edge of Paris, the home afforded her privileges unlike anything she had ever imagined.

However, Franco was consistently demanding when it came to her adapting to the highly expectant role required of any child of theirs. Had it not been for the warm and nurturing affection of Aunt Melanie, she wasn't sure she could have withstood his stern demeanor.

* * * * *

The first letter Madeleine and Hal came across was addressed:

"For Madeleine's eyes Only"

My Dearest Madeleine,

It is with deepest regret you have found this note prior to my sharing this information personally. If, indeed, you are reading it, one can safely assume I have passed on from this Earth. Yet, I must confess the guilt and shame I carry with me daily, in hiding your one and only brother's existence from you.

You may or may not recall having a brother, by the name of Gustav, who is four years your younger. All the while, knowing I was wrong in keeping this from you, I remained true to my promise to Uncle Franco that I never reveal the letters of correspondence to you that continually arrived over the years.

I live with only one single consolation, and that is the fact that instead of my destroying the letters, I hid them away until the day arrived for them to reveal themselves to you.

Fully aware of my selfishness in wanting you to need only me, I denied you your God given right to share in your only brother's life. I pray, with nothing but genuine sincerity, that one day you'll find it in your heart to forgive a selfish and cruel old woman.

Enclosed within the pages of this book are all of his letters to you my dear. You have been, and always will be, the light of my life, dearest Madeleine. Please know Uncle Franco loved you with as much intensity as I, myself, have. We always wanted what was best for you.

May God guide you in your search for Gustav.

Your Loving Aunt,
Melanie

Madeleine could not refrain from shedding many broken tears as she considered how her life would have been so very different, had she been given the opportunity to share in his life. Knowing Aunt Melanie's love for her was, without a doubt, genuine, she still did not understand her Aunt's reasons for keeping her from her beloved brother.

Written in very broken French, Gustav stated he wished to begin corresponding with her. The letter stated nothing of his current living conditions, yet it was common knowledge that many hard feelings had developed between the Germans and the French following WWI.

Franco and Melanie had harmoniously strived to mold their lovely Madeleine into a respectable lady, a refined woman of grace and high moral principles. Franco was not about to take a chance in returning unnecessary discord to her renewed lifestyle. She had lived long enough without him in her life. He could only bring embarrassment and shame to the family name.

Jon Paul and Madeleine had been bestowed a sizable spread of land, covered with rich, fruit bearing vineyards for their wedding gift. Settling along the edges of Reims, France, they remained within close proximity of her Aunt Melanie's very sizable estate. No time was wasted in beginning their family. In 1923 Lilly was born into the life of privilege, providing her all of life's materialistic conveniences along with much love.

Sadly, however, the very small framed Madeleine ran into difficulties when delivering her first child, nearly losing her own life. For Jon Paul, the very real and frightening possibility of nearly losing his precious wife in childbirth, gave him great cause to do all he could in preventing another occurrence of that nature. Madeleine had also been instructed by the midwife to take great strides in preventing another life threatening pregnancy.

In the year 1930, some years after marrying Jon Paul DeMornais, Madeleine's Uncle Franco was killed in an untimely accident. Thrown from his horse, while traveling at a high speed, he fell to his instant death.

After sharing this incredible story with Hal, the two sat, motionless, considering their good fortune, having found one another at this time in their lives.

Hal was beginning to absorb the many hidden treasures lying within this woman of great courage. Born and raised in the U.S., he had served his country proudly in WWI. In fact, he offered just a slight peek into his own past when familiarizing her with his brush with the Germans. He had been stationed onboard the USS Battleship Division 9, serving with the British Grand Fleet against the German High Seas Fleet. He had also been present at the surrender of the German High Fleet in 1917 - 1918.

Madeleine and Hal sat somewhat bewildered as they considered the vast differences in their histories. Five years had passed after her departure from Germany to France to live with Aunt Melanie by the year 1917. They'd wondered if their paths had crossed way back then, would they know each other today? If someone had told her, back in those younger years, that she would fall in love with and marry a man in the USA, she would have enjoyed a great laugh. That kind of silly talk would have been absolutely preposterous.

Then again, had he been told that one day he'd meet and marry a beautiful mature French woman, he'd likely feel the same exact way about such gibberish.

That is what is so outstanding about this small world. Have you ever been hundreds or even thousands of miles away from your roots, only to run into a familiar face from your younger years? And you try to determine exactly what the odds are of running across that particular person so very far away from the home you had both once known?

God always has his reasons for intentionally causing certain people to cross each others' paths in life. Are there lessons to be learned in many more instances of our lives that we actually never even grasp unto? Likely so, I would imagine.

It's hard to believe Lorraine and Fame simply happened to meet one another while he was in Sweden. What were the odds that he would live a short 100 miles distance from her only brother in the USA? What were the odds that Lilly would meet the love of her life while living underground during the war? What were the odds Lilly and Valentin would move to northeastern Minnesota, out of all the areas in the vast United States, only to end up just 100 miles from their future brother-in-law and future husband to Madeleine?

The complexities of life truly are too vast to comprehend much of the time. For those who have no concept of having the power of the Lord working for them in their human lives, much loss is suffered. There is nothing more spectacular than the miraculous occurrences that take place every day in a Christian's life. Because a Christian is more likely to recognize that power from a higher source versus the non-believer.

Following the review of numerous letters to Madeleine from her dear brother, Gustav, the couple intended to look into his whereabouts in the very near future.

One letter, in fact, mentioned an ancestral tie to a Swedish grandfather. This certainly raised the eyebrow of both Madeleine and

Hal. *Perhaps you've got some of this good Swedish blood in you too!* commented Hal.

Life was full of surprises, and as time drifted onward for the lovely Madeleine DeMornais Thuringer, she realized the likelihood of many more surprises to be encountered down the line.

The following day Madeleine was anxious to share her new discoveries with Lilly and family. Late March was providing a touch of Spring in the air. The warmth of the late winter sun reminded Hal of the upcoming days to come, spending time outdoors developing a beautiful rose garden as he'd had in his previous yard near the Canadian border.

Hal had always been good with his hands. He enjoyed building fun birdhouses, picnic tables and other useful objects from wood. Plans to erect a large enough garage to house his automobile, as well as provide him the space for a workshop, rummaged through his mind. He spent endless hours outdoors estimating the size and design of his garage, bird watching, or shoveling snow. He looked forward to the change in seasons, allowing him to use his varied creative gifts in other areas that could only be carried out in the warmer months in Minnesota. He often remarked, *Idle hands create idle minds!!* Having spent over 25 years working for the lumber company up North allowed Hal to retire early with a full pension. Still, he felt way too young to lazily whistle his life away in a rocking chair.

Madeleine's photography had fallen to the sidelines for the past few months as she adjusted to her new husband and new home. Learning of her brother's desire to contact her for all those years, sent her mind racing in all directions. Lilly was amazed to hear the news of her maternal uncle. Trying to keep her ears and eyes wide open to all the activities and demands of three children often required three heads, each providing her two sets of ears and eyes for each individual child. Of course, when mother entered the house, the load would lighten immensely, as she always provided Lilly with much assistance. Hal, too, would make his way over to the Baranowsky's frequently, offering to take one of the kids off her hands for an hour or two.

With the twins, Rhonda and Robin, being only three months old, Hal usually bypassed the responsibilities of feeding and changing the infants, instead opting to take Tia outside for a ride on the sled, or to make snow angels or a snowman. Always engaging in such adult conversations, Tia would astonish the adults time and again with her intelligence. One wondered how a three year old could be so observant at times. Occasionally, Tia had heard her grandma complain of the bird poop that would end up on the car, absent mindedly giving Madeleine cause to use an inappropriate word or two in the company of a young one's ears.

As Hal and Tia approached the car sitting in the driveway of the cottage, she looked at Grandpa Hal with a questioning frown? *Grandpa? Are those damn birds at it again?* Before Hal had a chance to think, he burst into laughter hearing the innocently spoken words roll so easily off the tongue of their precious little one.

Yes, yes indeed Tia, it appears those birds have been up to no good again.

Still chuckling as he entered the house, Tia shared a warm smile with her grandpa, *That's funny ha grandpa?*

With another good chuckle, Grandpa took Tia's hand, assisting his little angel through the heavy door of the cottage. Equipped with snow pants, boots, jacket, hat and mitts, Hal helped the ever so grown-up Tia free herself of the many garments. Static electricity shocked them both time and again. Little Tia's hair looked like she'd just poked a finger into the electrical socket. Grandpa Hal lifted her up to the mirror in the bathroom to see her silly hair, causing bunches of giggles.

From there they made their way to the cookie jar for a few of the delicious chocolate chip cookies Grandma had baked just the day before. A fine tea party was enjoyed by both until Grandma walked in with explicit instructions from Lilly to return her lost daughter for her afternoon nap. After all, when her daddy got home from work, they would all enjoy cake and ice cream after Tia blew out the candles on her birthday cake. But the best was saved for last, when the wrapping on the gifts were torn to tidbits, revealing her fun new toys on her third birth

Chapter Twenty

Lorraine removed the day's mail from the mailbox sitting alongside the front entrance doorway. Quickly shutting the door to prevent the cold wind from slicing through her barren skin, she noticed a letter from her sister Katya in Sweden.

Always excited to hear news or receive photos of the family, she immediately tore open the envelope. No photos accompanied the letter from Katya this time but that was okay. She still enjoyed hearing from her. Except this news wasn't what Lorraine had hoped to read.

It appeared that Alina, in her desperate search for peace of mind, had turned to alcohol as a crutch. Katya explained she'd been aware of Alina's light drinking from time to time, but never felt it was an issue until now.

It had become profoundly apparent when Katya stopped by to see her sister one day unexpectedly. It was two o'clock pm. Her two young nieces, Asa and Katarina, napped solemnly on the sofa. What Katya found when entering the house was shocking. The home was in total chaos. Dirty dishes, with food stuck to them for what looked like days, were strewn about the house along with clothing, books, toys and ashtrays full of cigarette butts. Two empty bottles of vodka sat on the metal kitchen table, covered with so much litter, one could not even find a spot to set down a plate of food.

Katya called out for Alina but got no response. Upon entering her bedroom, she found her sister sprawled out across the bed, passed out cold, wreaking of alcohol and smoke.

Shaking Alina for several minutes before arousing her from her lethally drunken state of mind, tears formed in her eyes as she realized the severity of her dear sister's problem. With Alina in no condition to engage in conversation, Katya simply helped her into her sleeping gown and tucked her under the beddings for the time being.

She had one hour before having to be home, when the boys' grandparents would deliver them back to her. They occasionally spent an afternoon with Nicholas' parents when Bjorn was in school.

Ridding the premises of its full ashtrays along with any sign of alcohol usage, was her first priority followed by picking up piles of messes strewn across the furnishings and floors. Once the home was recognizable again, Katya placed Katarina, the youngest, into the stroller and held Asa's hand for the short walk to her own home.

Their mother's problem was not a topic of conversation for the little ones. Katya would do all she could to help the girls while seeking assistance for their mother. Writing a note, she explained she had brought the children home with her. She would keep the children with her until Alina came by to pick them up! Completely sober!!!

With both of their husbands out at sea, making a living for their families, Katya was torn and confused about how to correctly handle the dire situation. Had Lorraine still been living in Sweden, Katya would have placed a call to her looking for answers to the predicament. Katya could not afford to place an overseas call on their minimal income. So, she quickly sent the letter to Lorraine with a prayer she could advise her as to what her next move should be.

Understandably saddened and fearful of Alina's overall health in her weakened and addicted state of mind, Lorraine discussed the matter with Fame after dinner that evening. Having worked with many children of alcoholics in Sweden, Lorraine's eyes had long ago been opened to the everyday challenges the young and innocent were forced to endure. In their desperation to be loved and nurtured, those children did anything to please an alcoholic parent in their younger years. Too embarrassed to speak up about the matter to anyone outside the home was the norm. Not only that, but society was very intolerant of the abusive or neglectful behavior displayed within the homes of those families. Once word got out about the family's dysfunction, parents would prevent their own children from associating with the unfortunate children of the alcoholics.

Lorraine and Fame immediately began frequent prayers for Alina's lost and broken family. Deciding the cost of an overseas phone call could be absorbed into their next month's expenses, Lorraine did exactly that, placing a call to Katya the following day. Upon hearing Lorraine's voice, the frustration from carrying the problem alone surfaced. Sending her children into their bedroom to keep occupied for a short time, Katya released the heavy weight she'd been carrying alone, into Lorraine's lap. Lorraine was very familiar with Katya's needs as well as Alina's. Not only had they prayed for Alina, but they'd prayed for Katya and her family as well.

Katya listened carefully as Lorraine provided her with crucial information. Information that might assist her in this dilemma. Alina had not subsided in her drinking habits whatsoever. She didn't care about herself, her family, or her life in any way. She felt she had been cursed since birth and she was of no value to the world. Lorraine explained to Katya this was the typical frame of mind of a severe alcoholic. The life-threatening effects of the poisonous alcohol in their systems constantly served as a vicious reminder of their failures in life, causing them to lose all inhibitions. They didn't understand why anybody would care if they drank or not, or if they lived or died. Many believed the world was a much better place when in an alcohol induced frame of mind. Laughter came easily, responsibilities were shunned, they even boasted of successful endeavors under the influence. Sadly, life became easier to cope with in an altered frame of mind.

Sober people can only vaguely grasp the intense depth and insecurity of an alcoholic. The same applies to the chemically addicted. As long as there are methods available to alter their frame of mind, addicts will continue using them. Lorraine was fully aware of the almost non-existent services available to alcoholics at that time in the world. The first resource Lorraine recommended to Katya was her pastor. Perhaps he could shed more light on the situation for her.

Katya thanked Lorraine repeatedly before ending their conversation. At least she had learned of one direction to take. Just as importantly, she had been allowed to release her pain and frustration with someone who loved Alina equally as much as herself. Both sisters spent precious time asking the Lord for His ever-loving guidance and wisdom in rendering help to their loved one.

Courage Times Three. A Novel

* * * * *

Spring once again ushered itself into Minnesota. Mother Nature still tossed in a few cold and snowy days in April, especially for those residing in the northern tier of Minnesota. Madeleine and Hal had postponed their honeymoon to the French Riviera a few months earlier. Now the time had arrived to travel abroad.

Madeleine was as excited as a young child, speaking of her familiarity with her homeland and all it had to offer, especially in the Spring. Tanning themselves on the hot sandy beaches of the Mediterranean in midsummer had lost its appeal. Spring blossoms in Paris and the Riviera were what they most looked forward to with great enthusiasm.

Thinking ahead, Madeleine drew up a plan to introduce Hal to the beautiful and seductive city of Paris. Not only was it the capital city, it was also the city she had resided in for several years before and after the wars. Hal, of course, was well aware of Madeleine's past, as she'd so confidently shared with him. Yet, the chance to personally reveal a glimpse of her past, while partaking together in the pleasant scents Spring offered, completely exhilarated her. Her life-saving ability to create a safe haven for herself, in her mind, was a treasure.

Madeleine believed she had been overstocked with the ability to tap into that wealth of resources to maintain her sanity following the death of her husband, Jon Paul. Maturity had given both Hal and Madeleine an understanding of the love they would continue to carry for their first love. Experience truly enables us to allow our new partner occasional visits to those memories, even sharing them, now and then, with one another. No jealousy could ever defy the current love they had come to know.

Lilly sometimes intensely avoided returning to the nightmarish experiences of the war. At times it relentlessly pushed its way into the forefront of her mind. Even with the children keeping her steadily occupied, she would find her mind slipping into yesteryear more often lately.

Valentin gently approached his wife one evening after the children had been bathed and put down for the night. Noticing her silent thoughts were becoming more frequent, he inquired if anything specific was bothering her. She seemed preoccupied lately, he'd said.

Lilly hesitated to share those thoughts at first, but soon realized if she refused to share them with her dearest Valentin, who would she share them with?

Struggling to find the right words, she hesitated. Why did she need to find the right words, she wondered. Were there really right words or wrong words? She supposed it was related to the overall confusion she was experiencing. Hadn't she been blessed with so much in her life now? So, why were those grueling times overtaking her mind now?

Once she began sharing those vivid recollections of torturous months and years, Valentin fully understood the intense depth of her wounds. He had often been astounded by her psychological stamina, leaving those memories behind her as she had throughout the years. She had virtually remained free of the haunting memories for so long. Hearing him mention his own struggles to keep those daunting times in the past somehow eased her concerns that she might be mentally or emotionally regressing.

Vowing to set up an appointment soon with their pastor, for possible counseling, Lilly set her mind to ease. Feeling she was losing some of her passion for her faith in God, also held some significance. She hoped Christian counseling would be the solution to overcoming the heinous thoughts continuing to invade her mind.

*****

Thankful for a smooth landing on the tarmac that sunny afternoon, Madeleine released a relieved sigh. After double checking their baggage, making sure they were, indeed, their own, the couple made their way through the crowd of busy travelers.

Madeleine's playful behavior began to surface instantly at the sight of the city. Intent on enjoying every moment of their delayed honeymoon, she stopped, momentarily, to spin around in circles on her toes. Stretching her arms out to the city, she announced, *Ahhh, gay Paris*!! Hal adoringly reached out to his lovely bride, embracing her childlike behavior. *Oh Maddy, how fortunate I am to have you as my beautiful wife!* Smiling at his words of affection, Madeleine suggested they hail a taxi to deliver them to their hotel.

Centrally located in the heart of the city, they were greeted by the concierge of the well established Hotel Concorde Saint Lazare. As with all prestigious guests, the concierge assumed full responsibility for their check-in and baggage. After receiving a quick history of the hotel, including the many amenities offered, the travel-weary, yet enthusiastic bride and groom comfortably settled themselves into their suite. A large sterling silver bowl, filled with various fruits, and an exquisite bottle of Dom Perignon, chilling in an ice filled silver bucket, awaited them in their luxurious suite. Madeleine was sure to remove the bottle from the ice once it had reached the perfect temperature of 45 degrees, a well known fact shared by most Parisians.

Set high above the streets, the locality of their suite offered sweeping views of the charming city. Never had Hal felt more like royalty. He had never been privy to that kind of luxury. But it also was a lavish treat for Madeleine.

The magnificence of the suite was more than intoxicating. Furnished in high-backed Queen Ann chairs and tables designed of rich marble, the rooms were dressed in finely hand-painted vases, filled with red, white and yellow long-stemmed roses strategically placed throughout their expansive quarters. Fluffy, white lace beddings adorned an enormous bed, lavished with soft, inviting pillows in the bedroom area. Massive, beautifully framed oil paintings, providing a taste of delicate French gardens, hung stately upon the softly painted walls.

The restaurant, located within walking distance of their hotel, provided a welcomed opportunity to stretch their legs as they leisurely strolled the cobblestone streets. Dining that first evening in Paris, Madeleine and Hal savored every bite of the fine French cuisine they'd been advised to experience. Always a necessary accompaniment with dinner, the fine wine they enjoyed was expertly chosen by the lovely Madeleine.

Feeling the aftereffects of their journey the lovebirds returned to their hotel for a good night's sleep.

Standing on the terrace accompanying their suite, inspired by the nightly view of the city all aglow, they sent a sincere thank you to their Heavenly Father for providing their undeserving souls with such grandeur and beauty. With the charm of the city still enticing them, they closed the doors to the outside world, allowing themselves to fulfill each other's Godly created desires.

Four days had been reserved to tour the grand city before continuing their travels to the south of France. Neither of them wanted to waste a single moment, taking in all Paris had to offer.

Hal was so captured by the history, the beauty, and the sights of Paris he wondered if he'd ever want to leave the City Of Lights. They partook in a visit to the Moulin Rouge, the oldest cabaret in Paris, a cruise on the scenic Seine River, providing them outstanding views of the Eiffel Tower, and a palace tour of Versailles, just to name a few.

Madeleine was especially anxious to show Hal the previously owned estate and vineyards once belonging to Aunt Melanie. She, herself, was curious to see it as well. She wondered if the new owners had made any changes to the existing structure or landscaping.

A sigh of relief welcomed Madeleine when she found the property entirely unchanged. Melanie would be pleased as well. She just knew it. From there they continued on to Reims where she found a stylishly structured new home in place of her previous residence. It pleased her to see the property occupied and the vineyards full of life once again. Memories flooded her mind of joyful times with Jon Paul and Lilly. It certainly seemed like another person had lived those memories, not herself.

Hal recalled the story of Valentin and Lilly finding nothing more than a heap of brick and debris in the location of her previous home. Looking at Madeleine, he could see the memories drifting through her mind. Allowing her the necessary time to reach back into her earlier life was important. Hal was very thankful for being allowed the opportunity to peek into her past. It would serve as a bonding tool now, and in the future.

Before departing for the south of France, Madeleine made an attempt to learn of her brother's whereabouts. It didn't take long to reach the authorities in Cologne, Germany. The news she received saddened her, as they conveyed to her his loss of life during the second world war. Oh, how she wished she'd been allowed the opportunity to know him as an adult. Now, she must put closure to that distant part of her life.

Enthusiastic anticipation abounded as they neared the city of Marseilles, opting for a scenic train ride to deliver them to their cozy seaside Villa on the Riviera. Rolling hills, covered in fields of lavender, provided pleasurable views throughout Provence. Madeleine assured Hal the sights he would encounter in Nice, St. Tropez, Monaco, Monte Carlo and more would take his breath away. It would prove to be a honeymoon unlike anything Harold had ever known.

Madeleine couldn't wait to run out unto the sandy beaches. She loved squishing her toes in the warm, sun-baked sand that ran for miles along the coastline. The warm sea breezes in her face stimulated a renewed energy in her.

Arriving at the address of their beachside villa, Hal generously tipped the taxi driver after carrying their bags to the door. Hearing him whistle at the magnificence of it all, Madeleine couldn't wait to enlighten Hal with the list of upcoming sights they would enjoy over the next few weeks. She knew his first encounter with this impressive vacationland would be total astonishment.

Madeleine handed the door key to Hal. Before she knew it, he unlocked the door, then whipped her into the air, carrying her over the threshold. Hal couldn't remember ever feeling this romantic. Madeleine was swept away by his charm and gentlemanly behavior. There they were, both near the fifty year mark in age, behaving like young lovers. The truth was, they felt every bit as young as that. Only now, they were a whole lot wiser.

Tidying up the villa would wait. First to come was a dinner of delicious Mediterranean cuisine. Beforehand, sliding open the windows and pulling back the window dressings would allow the fresh sea breezes to air out the stuffy rooms.

Proceeding their meal they walked a short distance to purchase fresh coffee beans and a few other necessary staples. Major shopping at the market would wait until tomorrow. Following a full and busy day they needed to relax and unwind on the beach for the evening. Madeleine exited the bedroom quarters wearing a chic one-piece swimsuit consisting of bright colors in yellows, greens, reds, and blues. A matching sarong, a traditional garment of Malayan archipelago, wrapped and tied itself around her waist. Her wide-brimmed, flamboyant hat loosely hugged her delicate facial features.

Deep mahogany colored hair hung lazily, giving the wind full freedom to have its way with her.

Hal had quickly changed into his flashy colored Bermuda shorts and a stark white tank top. Placed upon his head was a straight-rimmed, straw hat accented with a fashionable pair of sunglasses. Having worked hard physical labor throughout his lifetime, Hal had established a strong and muscular physique. Still maintaining his masculine structure in his early fifties pleased Madeleine immensely. Both smiled at the other's appearances.

It was fun sporting a new style and having a change of life this way. This wasn't how they would present themselves on the lake in Minnesota. This was their Mediterranean look, they'd decided.

A large canvas bag, filled with French fashion magazines, several leaflets highlighting the hot spots in the area, and a bottle of wine, hung from her shoulder. Handing two delicately designed wine glasses to Hal, Madeleine instructed her admiring husband to use caution while carrying them to the beach. Lightweight sandals protected their feet as they crossed the unpaved roadway to the sandy beach, directly across from their Villa. Once reaching the sand, Madeleine kicked off her sandals, once again enjoying the feel of the fine, warm sand between her toes.

Lying there on the beach, this couple, these two souls, who thought they would never love again, marveled at their good fortune … at how amazingly unique and pleasing this mature love was. After a few relaxing hours the lovebirds stood, soaking in the brilliant colors of the sunset in the western skies. Within a few mere moments, it dropped out of sight, offering a day of warmth to those on the other side of the world. The night could not have ended on a sweeter note. Tomorrow would offer a host of sights to pleasure in.

The fun began as the train carried Madeleine and Hal through quaint towns and tranquil villages scattered throughout Provence. Nice was the second largest city in France, providing panoramic views from nearby Mt. Boron. A tour of the famous Promenade des Anglais impressed Hal immensely. Cannes provided festivals galore. Traveling along the coastline to Golfe-Juan where Napoleon landed in 1815 gave one a strong sense of historical value.

Between travels, the couple enjoyed barefooted walks alongside the shoreline, seeking out exotic seashells and uniquely shaped driftwood. The weather on the Mediterranean, in early May, was none less than perfect. Both began sporting tan bodies before long, merely from spending the majority of their time outdoors. Jumbo shrimp was readily available at reasonable prices. Grilling was a favorite way of preparing dinner for themselves on their own private promenade. Madeleine, once again, filled it with plants and flowers galore, just as she had in New York City and on the lake in Minnesota.

Several days were spent touring the changing of the guard at Monte Carlo's palace and viewing the spectacular structures of many aged cathedrals. The numerous quaint towns provided fashionable boutiques and terrace cafés for their shopping and dining pleasures.

A striking scenery, in which the red rocks of the Esterel met the blue of the sea, aroused even the locals each day. Notre Dame de la Garde, along with other unique, architecturally dated structures continued to impress them both.

Their final rendezvous included stops in the lazy, coastal villages of St. Maxime, St. Raphael and the Golden Cornice. The impressive coastline featured dramatically sweeping views of the White Cliffs of Colanque de Cassis, offering Madeleine and Hal breathtaking photos.

What a magnificent way to end their four week honeymoon in the south of France. Realizing they could return, at any time, to these many wonders of the world, all located within such a close proximity, gave them a pleasing sense of warmth. Endless snapshots had been taken by both, as well as by total strangers, who were more than happy to forever capture the apparent love and admiration for one another they had.

Madeleine held her breath momentarily as the plane ascended into the skies, returning them back to U.S. soil. The next trip would most definitely include Lilly, Valentin and the grandbabies. Madeleine was more than pleased with her decision to sell the Paris property, in favor of buying the seaside villa. Years of pleasure would provide endless memories throughout the upcoming years. Now, the Thuringers would concentrate on building their garage and landscaping the yard of their serene lake cottage in Eveleth, Minnesota.

Chapter Twenty-One

Lorraine and Fame kept frequent communications going with Katya. Against her younger sister's advice, Lorraine decided against directly contacting Alina, fearing her retaliation against Katya for spreading word of her drinking problem would add fuel to the fire. The torture a caregiver often endures in such a strenuous situation, can leave them feeling helpless and disillusioned themselves. Katya spoke to her clergyman, as Lorraine had advised. He did provide her an outlet for releasing her pent up emotions, which she was grateful for. She remained vigilant in her mission to convince Alina to visit her pastor, but to no avail.

Asa and Katarina, the deprived, young daughters of Alina and Axel Johannson, were growing more and more dependent on Katya's love and affection. While pinching every penny she could to provide all five children with a daily meal, Alina did little more than spend her limited allowance on liquor.

Katya confided in her husband, Nicholas, of Alina's uncontrollable problem, making him swear not to tell Alex for awhile. She was sure she could bring Alina around to recognizing the damage she was inflicting on herself and her family. They had been so very close throughout their entire lives. Even though Alina had taken a bold stand against Christianity, Katya basically assumed that was the nature of her ways.

Nicholas, being a strong Christian throughout his life, was adamant about attending church faithfully. He believed living a Christian life was very important, insisting on raising their children in the same manner. Axel was raised a Lutheran, the same as Nicholas had been. Once he'd reached his teen years, however, he had taken a path leading him to drinking and troubles with the law at times.

When Nicholas found work as a commercial fisherman out on the Baltic Sea, he grasped at the opportunity to get his longtime friend, Axel, out on the sea, where trouble was few and far between. It had worked well for the young man, keeping him on the straight and narrow most of the time. Hoping to convince his friend to regain his Christianity, Nicholas would take time on a quiet evening at sea, to reacquaint him with Bible passages they had learned as boys.

Late May was approaching, ending another year of schooling and teaching for the younger Thuringer couple. While looking forward to a summer filled with fun activities in Duluth, they had even started looking for a home to purchase in the port city. Summer also meant they could see more of their precious little nieces on Long Lake.

Shortly after Hal and Madeleine returned from their one month honeymoon/vacation, the young couple was invited to spend a weekend in the guest bedroom of the cottage. The first evening, Madeleine presented a vast collection of photographs she had developed herself in her darkroom. Oohs and aahs were heard throughout the room as they viewed the many photos. All looked forward to spending time there someday too.

Fame and Valentin lent a hand erecting the garage while Lorraine assisted Lilly in the household chores and non-stop diaper changes. The twins, Rhonda and Robin, were still quite helpless at the ages of 5 months. Yet, they grew cuter and cuter every day.

Tia was growing into quite a mother's helper, running little errands and entertaining her baby sisters. She had greatly missed her Grandma and Grandpa "T" while away overseas. And when Lorraine walked in the door, Tia squealed with excitement calling out, *Auntie Wain, Auntie Wain* ... surely, several nicknames have been adopted from the mouths of babes in countless families. She had developed a close bond to the younger Thuringer couple as well. Not only was Grandpa "T" wrapped around her finger, Uncle Fame and her daddy were just the same.

With no commitments following the school year's end, Fame and Lorraine stayed at the lake until the garage project was completed.

Brother James and Nicole had driven down from International Falls on the weekend as well. Excitement overtook everyone when it was announced they would be marrying in late August. The

Thuringers had another celebration to look forward to that summer. Asking his brother to be his best man, Fame was proud to accept. All shared a common admiration for Nicole, knowing she would make an exceptional mother and wife.

Fame and Lorraine informed the group of their plans to purchase a home sometime before the new school year began. A pleasant weekend was had by all grilling outdoors and letting their hair down while boating, swimming and skiing.

Returning to Duluth, Fame and Lorraine started discussing their options for a new home. It should be a two or three bedroom with the hopes of one day finishing the basement into usable living quarters. Perhaps a recreation room for use through the colder months of the year would be wise. Both wanted the home to include a fireplace for chilly winter nights and a bathtub sizable enough for Fame's six foot body.

Showers were not a common commodity at that time. People of Finnish ancestry often built outdoor saunas, mostly in the rural areas. The tradition was to steam up the room to such an intensity, it would open the pores of the skin, releasing bacteria and germs, while at the same time opening the sinus passages. Once the body became nearly intolerant of the heat, a quick jump into the lake or a snow bank took quick care of things. Reentering the sauna house, they'd suds up, then pour water over themselves to rinse before completing their bathing. Those Finnish people have hearty bodies, without a doubt.

Chapter Twenty-Two

Fame hoped to find a home with some acreage on the outskirts of the city, allowing them more privacy than city folk. They had saved enough money for a down payment on an already existing home. Perhaps one day they would build new when better established.

Fame returned from the news stand with a current copy of the Sunday Duluth News and Tribune. Sitting at the kitchen table, they opened it to the classified section. Spreading it out for both to scan, they began pointing out the homes of specific interest.

As Lorraine responded to the whistling tea pot, the phone rang. Asking Fame to take the call, she prepared two steaming hot cups of tea to sip as they browsed the ads. Picking up the receiver, Fame said his hello. On the other end of the line, the operator inquired if the receiving party would accept an overseas collect call from Mrs. Nicholas Osterholm in Sweden.

Fame instantly motioned to Lorraine to come to the phone. Accepting the collect call, he put Lorraine on the line. Instant panic set in as Lorraine heard the sobbing cries of her sister Katya. It had to be news of Alina! What else could it be?

Desperate sobs were all Lorraine could hear. Asking Katya to calm herself while she explained the situation was of no consequence. Finally, in desperation, Lorraine yelled Katya's name into the mouthpiece of the phone.

Lorraine Nicholas and Axel - Nicholas and Axel are lost at sea. They were due to arrive home yesterday, but there has been no sign of them. The officials are still out scouring the waters, but they have little hope of their survival.

Sobbing uncontrollably, Katya unsuccessfully tried to maintain some sense of sound mind. Both Lorraine and Fame held the phone to their ears. Shock and dismay overtook them in a few single moments.

Katya, did they run into bad weather while out? asked Lorraine. *Yes, a storm advisory was issued. Normally they would dock further North if they were close enough to land. They just don't know the last general location of the fishing vessel, but no word has been received for over 24 hours. I know something is wrong Lorraine. I can feel it in my bones!*

Katya's continuous cries tore Lorraine into shreds. Handing the phone to Fame, she covered her face with a handkerchief, releasing a flood of tears. Fame gently spoke to his sister-in-law, doing his best to assure her there was still hope, and they would pray for the lives of their husbands. He promised to place a return call within approximately eight hours.

Katya begged them to call, regardless of the time differences. She knew her worries would rob her of any sleep that night. Setting down the receiver, Fame took Lorraine into his arms as she shed even more tears for her younger sisters. They had already lost their parents and a brother in their young lifetimes. Lorraine didn't know if they could take another severe blow like this.

Once Lorraine settled down, Fame placed a long distance call to his father and Madeleine, informing them of the tragic news. Next, Lorraine made the difficult call to brother Valentin. Extremely disturbed by the horrifying news, he stated he certainly would accompany Lorraine to Sweden. She assured him they would be able to handle the situation themselves and emphasized the need for him to keep the home fires burning.

Instructing her to keep them updated on the situation, he hung up the phone and cried like a child on Lilly's shoulder. It was the first time Lilly had ever heard her husband weep so intensely out of sorrow.

Madeleine offered to call Greta and Emma in Paris, as they, too, must be notified of the nightmarish situation confronting their sisters.

Whatever would the women do, if both their husbands were lost at sea? Alina would surely lose whatever remaining strength she had, and Katya likely wouldn't be able to help her sister now, let alone keep herself from breaking down. Lorraine knew both sisters were in an extremely precarious situation. She had no alternative other than to catch the first flight to Sweden before possibly losing another sibling, or even two.

Being a Sunday, Lorraine was unable to make any travel arrangements until morning. Fame surely wouldn't even consider sending Lorraine off on her own. Immediately assuring her that he, too, would make the trip, they knew it would mean spending most of their savings for a down payment on their house. No matter the cost, there was nothing they wouldn't do for family in a time of crisis.

Packing traveling bags and bathing that night afforded them the necessary time to reach the Minneapolis/St. Paul airport early the following day.

At 10 o'clock pm that Sunday night a call was placed to Katya with hope she had received promising news. Sadly, the desperate situation remained unchanged. Katya informed Lorraine she had brought Alina and the children home there with her, keeping Alina in sight at all times. It was clear she was on the brink of breaking. Lorraine could well recognize the shaky and fearful circumstances her younger sisters were facing. With extreme hesitancy, a promise to call again in the morning was shared with Katya. Lorraine could only pray that now their Lord would take the girls into His arms, preventing any harm from coming to either of them.

Fame served Lorraine a warm glass of milk to ease her tension before attempting to get a few hours of rest. They, too, would be robbed of a good night's sleep on this heartbreaking night. Nobody in the Thuringer or Baranowsky families in Minnesota, or the Moreau or Bonnet families in Paris, would sleep well.

Anxious thoughts and worries prevented Lorraine from sleeping a wink. At some point, she simply started speaking about the hell they had lived through after losing their parents. The burden of carrying those ugly memories alone had finally reached an end. Fame knew she would, one day, find it necessary to release those pent up thoughts. That time had arrived.

Lorraine knew nothing of what happened to the two rapists once the train reached the Baltic Sea. Aware that he could never leave the girls alone and deserted, the kind gentleman who had protected Alina and Katya waited with them in the darkened corner of the rail car. After the sheep were unloaded the car door remained open, which was a blessing in itself. He'd wondered what he would ever do if they locked them in.

Unfamiliar with their Polish language, he motioned to the girls to remain in the railcar until he returned. Lorraine was in much need of a woman's touch, possibly even doctoring. Yet, with the war at hand he must be diligent in his discretion.

The city they arrived in sat on the northernmost border of the Baltic Sea, very near the Russian border. The port was called Gdansk. It was the hometown the kind man had been raised in. After what seemed to be an eternity, he arrived on foot with two men and a woman.

The woman took Alina and Katya into her care while one of the men carried Lorraine to a nearby home. There, the girls were cared for and fed what little the poor peasants had to offer. Still, it was a Godsend to the young girls. An unknowing amount of time had lapsed since their arrival in the port city before Lorraine regained some sense of awareness. As she began to comprehend her surroundings, Alina and Katya clung to her every move. Surviving her ordeal seemed almost a curse to her. On the other hand, however, she was fully aware now of her baby sisters' enormous need for her survival. The kindly woman who had so lovingly nursed Lorraine back to health placed a holy rosary into Lorraine's hands, something meaning more to her than any other inanimate object in life. Before long the three youngest Baranowsky girls were placed into a large trunk and sent away to a better hiding place, they were told. Lorraine's tears fell unto her pillow as she continued sharing the details with Fame.

The better part of a day had passed before arriving at a new destination. Lorraine had prayed over and over throughout that day. Visions of their deaths raced through her mind. Still so very weak, undeniably broken from the rape, she lacked the ability to nurture her younger sisters just yet. She supposed she'd remained in a state of shock for some time afterward, as her recollections of the ugly incident were extremely vague.

Soon they found themselves being removed from the large vessel unto land. Stuffed inside the trunk felt like being entombed in a casket. Lilly trembled fiercely as she relived those horrifying hours. Fame assured her it wasn't necessary to continue if it was too difficult. He, himself, found it necessary to keep his tears from hitting her face as she laid in his arms. Her words were nearly impossible to tolerate without fierce anger surfacing. Yet, she must release this additional pent up burden in order to move forward now that they would be reconnecting with a part of her former life once again. He also would better understand how much the girls stood to lose once again. Both sisters had every right in the world to break down without the proper support so desperately needed.

Hearing mostly women's voices just outside of the trunk gave some sense of relief to the three girls. As the latch was opened and the lid lifted, they found themselves in the presence of nuns clothed in their habits and gowns. Never had Lorraine been more relieved than she was at that moment. One of the nuns offered her hand to Lorraine to assist her in getting out. Two other nuns lifted Katya and Alina into their arms. Immediately they were whisked away into a room with a large wooden table and a few large wooden chairs. With no windows, Lorraine was unable to determine anything of their whereabouts. She assumed they were in a convent or monastery of some sort.

Again, the nuns spoke in unfamiliar language. Frightened beyond words, silence was their only response as they sensed the nuns questioning them. Just as swiftly as they'd been escorted into the barren, lifeless room the nuns departed, shutting and locking the door behind them. Lorraine didn't know how many times she had begged God to take their lives. To spare them any further agony and pain. Over and over she wondered what they had ever done to deserve such pain and heartache.

Snapping her out of deep thought, a woman appearing to be in charge escorted two priests into the room. The girls sat trembling while the three spoke in hushed voices, occasionally pointing out one or the other. Lorraine thought it best to say something, rather than nothing, inquiring as to their whereabouts. Immediately silence filled the room as awareness of the girls spoken dialect was recognized.

This was not the reception she'd hoped for when initially seeing the nuns.

Where was simply a small bit of compassion in these people of God? She'd at least expected some type of nurturing care or concern where none was shown. A few hours later the girls were led into another room where three cots were set up. Upon each cot was a small pillow and a single blanket. Lorraine explained to Fame how she used hand gestures indicating a need to empty their bladders.

Darkness had set in outdoors though no awareness of day or night could be recognized in the cold, windowless vacancy of the room. Led down dark damp corridors they finally reached a door leading to the outside of the monastery. Little to nothing could be seen other than a pathway leading to an outhouse of sorts. Sister Ezmerelda held a dimly lit lantern to guide them along. Each girl held on tightly to the hands of one another until acknowledging their whereabouts, welcoming much relief after their day's journey. Immediately after returning to their sleeping quarters, a few rations of bread, soup and water was shared between them. Never did the girls recall being more hungry. *I knew then, we just might survive after all.*

Twice during that night, first Katya, then Alina, awoke in screams of fright. Nightmares! Nobody came to their rescue. Nobody heard or understood their pain. Only then did she fully realize they were on their own in the world and the sooner she accepted that, the better off they would be.

The following morning they pounded on the door in need of the bathroom once again. Eventually a bucket was brought into the room as the nun indicated they should use it to relieve themselves. Later they were fed meager bits of bread and water, yet remained locked in the room alone, afraid and abhorred by the cold treatment from the nuns.

Endless days were spent in the room alone, wondering where they were and if they would ever see their brothers or sisters again.

One day an elderly nun entered the room carrying paper and two pencils that she pulled out from beneath her robe. Also, a pail of cold water along with soap and a wiping cloth were shared with them. Gently, the nun tried to warm the soaped up cold cloth before wiping the dirty faces and hands of the younger girls. She allowed Lorraine to take care of her own needs, which suited her well.

One day the kindly nun, named Lena, began drawing pictures on the paper to teach the girls some of her language. She also took each of them into her embrace, cradling them for several minutes. It was the first sign of affection they had been offered since arriving several days earlier.

From that day on, the girls received daily visits from Lena, giving them some sense of nurturing and love. Although the feeling of abandonment would remain in them for several years, at last they had someone who cared.

Eventually they were moved off the Island of Bornholm onto the mainland of Sweden. There, they were placed in an orphanage for homeless children, but they weren't alone. Lena remained with them for the next two years until her death. By that time the girls had become familiarized with the orphanage and had somewhat adjusted to their new environment and lives.

By the age of seventeen Lorraine had learned much about caring for the children at the shelter. With the departure of an employee, she inquired about filling the position herself. They were happy to employ her while she remained living there. She knew it was a great opportunity to save what funds she could. Funds they would need to enter into the outside world once sent out on their own.

Another three full years would be spent living in the dark, lifeless shelter before at last leaving it together. Yet, they had come to know and love some of the long term caregivers at the orphanage. Grateful for a roof over their heads, a cot to sleep on and enough food to sustain them, each girl had learned to appreciate what they had. Numerous obstacles confronted them, day and night, month upon month, as they struggled to remain afloat for another two years on their own.

Lorraine briefed Fame in on the meeting of the girls with two young men working at the fishery where they, too, were employed on a part time basis. Lorraine continued to care for the children at the shelter until the girls married, providing them with the care and love they so deserved.

World War II had come to an end. Life was beginning to see improvements in many socio-economic areas. Following her sisters' weddings she was offered a job in Stockholm working in much improved conditions with far better pay. Seizing the opportunity, Lorraine moved herself into a small but quaint apartment. Confident of her baby sisters welfare now, having good hard-working husbands who would likely remain employed as fishermen in the Baltic for some time to come, Lorraine moved on with her life. She missed them horribly in the beginning but threw herself into her work avoiding the vacant solitude and emptiness.

And, not long afterward, I met and married the man of my dreams ... she spoke softly, tenderly into her loving husband's ear.

The two lay, side by side, Fame holding his beautiful wife in his arms, wanting never to let her go. Wanting never for her to hurt again in her life if he had anything to say about it. All he could do was love her to the best of his ability. There wasn't anything he wouldn't do for her. And now, he must do everything possible to bring goodness and happiness into her sisters' lives as well.

With only a few hours of rest, the two arose in the early morning hours, placing yet another call to Katya. She informed them the search for the missing vessel had been called off, assuming the worst, that the ship and crew had been lost at sea in the storm.

Through a barrage of tears, Lorraine informed her sister of their plans to leave immediately for the international airport in the Twin Cities. They hoped to arrive at her home within twenty-four hours. Katya couldn't thank her enough for coming to their aide. Lorraine assured her nothing could prevent them from flying out on the next available flight.

Madeleine and Hal had taken on the responsibility of making the travel arrangements for them as they drove to the airport. Placing a collect call from a phone booth upon their arrival, they received their flight instructions from Madeleine. Only a short two-hour wait was necessary before a flight would carry them to New York City. From there they would board another international flight carrying them to the capitol city of Stockholm, Sweden. A rental car or a train would be their last means of transport to complete their journey. Both were fortunate to receive a restful five hour nap on the flight.

*****

When critical times demand us to physically and mentally function on overload, we somehow have the amazing ability to carry on. The Lord certainly knew what He was doing when he created us. Our bodies and brains were remarkably created to sustain gruelingly long hours, often under intense pressure. Lorraine was very familiar with that ability, knowing plenty of divine sustainability would be required over the next several days.

The midnight hour approached as they neared the girls' homes. Lorraine reminded herself to keep a hold on her emotions, enabling her to assist her sisters at this time. Fame was more than willing to take over the care of the children for awhile.

Upon reaching Katya's home they stepped out of the automobile, stretching their legs in the darkness of the cool, damp night. Lights remained burning within the small, dreary looking home. Lack of money played a factor in the appearance of the barren yard and unpainted house. Nowhere did flowers or neatly trimmed bushes dress the mundane landscape. Evidence of a fairly poor existence was commonplace throughout the neighborhoods of the seaside fishing village. Fame and Lorraine hoped one day these young, devastated families would enjoy a life offering a few more simple pleasures.

Knocking on their door, they awaited a response. With no answer, they tried the door knob. Finding it unlocked, they quietly entered the home on tiptoes. Inside, they found sleeping bodies sprawled throughout the living room. All were finally getting a bit of much needed sleep.

Lorraine had napped a few more hours while Fame drove the distance from Stockholm. Assuring her husband she would be fine, Lorraine sent him to the back seat of the car, with a blanket, to sneak in a few hours of sleep himself.

Seating herself at the kitchen table, her eyes gazed upon various photos scattered about. Having experienced plenty of hardship in her younger years had toughened her up, but she didn't know what she would do if she lost her dear Fame so early in life. Who would care for her sisters' fatherless children and the husbandless wives? Neither girls had any advanced education that would offer the wages needed to sustain the costs of raising a family.

Lorraine frequently dabbed at tear laden eyes while viewing photographs. Katya had evidently been quite camera happy, filling a few scrapbooks with pictures. Pictures of her own family as well as Alina's. She would be forever thankful that she had, in fact, caught numerous warm and loving memories of the children with their fathers. It would be their strongest means of identifying with their past lives. They hadn't been afforded the luxury of time with their dads they would like to have had. The men often spent endless days and weeks earning a living away from home, leaving little time to connect with their respective family.

Hearing light footsteps crossing the floor behind her, Lorraine turned just as Katya entered the kitchen. Words were not necessary as they tightly embraced one another. They succumbed to a huge sense of relief, angst, heartache and shear closeness in those overwhelming moments. Having shed so many tears already, one would think there were none left to be shed. That was not the case however.

The crying soon awakened Alina from her light sleep. Jumping from the floor, she ran into the arms of her sister Lorraine. Trying their best to control their weepiness, the three younger Baranowsky sisters remained wrapped in each other's embrace as Lorraine prayed for God's strength over the upcoming days. Even Alina held strong to her sister's hands, finishing the prayer with her own "Amen".

Lorraine knew there was hope for her dear sister, Alina, after all. They did not yet know of her vow. From the moment she'd received word of her missing husband, she swore never to consume another drop of alcohol. With God's assistance, faith, hope and trust would provide the necessary tools to overcome the destructive addiction.

For the next few hours, they filled Lorraine in on a few of the details from the past five days. Most often, victims of such severe pain rarely recall what takes place immediately following such a traumatic incident. Typically, special moments experienced with loved ones surface sometime in the future. Now, sharing these moments together bonded them once again.

After having their fill of caffeine, Lorraine opened the refrigerator door, finding next to nothing in it. Daylight slowly crept in the windows like an undesirable invasion. The girls recognized little difference between day and night. It was all a blur — one minute, one hour, one day. Time running rampantly from one moment to the next. here was little awareness of time's passing. Life was at a standstill.

They could physically feel themselves, so they assumed they were still with the living. But their minds were void, empty slates. Lorraine undeniably knew God was protecting them as he had so many times. Yes, their hearts had shattered into a million pieces but He would carry them in the palm of His hand forever. That is how much God loves us. She knew all of mankind received that innate gift from birth. Sadly, many in life never recognize their blessings, however.

These young children would never have the privilege of knowing their fathers. At their young ages time had a way of erasing the past in a short period of time. The younger we are the sooner the memories flee our minds.

Knocking lightly upon the door Fame entered the house, embracing everyone. The children awoke one by one. Sleepy hugs were exchanged among all. Katya accompanied Fame to the bank to do a money exchange. They then drove to the market where he purchased a substantial amount of groceries for the refrigerator and cupboards. Lorraine had started preparing a huge breakfast before their return. Smiling faces of hungry children anxiously awaited the scrumptious-smelling meal. Lorraine insisted Katya and Alina do their best to eat as well. They would need something to sustain their strength and energy in the day ahead.

Once tummies were full Fame loaded the children into the car and off to the beach they went for a full day of sunshine and play. The women would complete the necessary arrangements in quiet solitude. In two short days, a memorial would be held for the lost fisherman aboard the sunken vessel. A total of twelve men had perished in the treacherous storm.

Katya's telephone rang shortly after Fame's departure with the children. It was a call from Valentin and Lilly inquiring of the Thuringer's arrival and the welfare of his young sisters. The girls took turns chatting for a few brief moments with Valentin. Lorraine then listened to his suggestions regarding the future well-being of their family. Both agreed the best direction to take was a move to the US. That would allow the older siblings a chance to care for them until the time arrived when they could care for themselves.

Lorraine was thinking along those same lines, having discussed it extensively with Fame the previous night. Valentin informed Lorraine of Madeleine and Hal's offer to cover the relocating costs of both families to the US. Madeleine certainly was making unselfish and generous choices in how she used her inheritance from Aunt Melanie. In what better way could she use her expansive bank account than this?

Upon disconnecting the long distance call, Lorraine prompted the girls to be seated on the sofa. While she was on the phone with Valentin, the sprawling beddings had been removed by the girls, making order of the disheveled room. Lorraine suggested they allow daylight into the room, lifting the blinds that likely hadn't been lifted in days. Seating herself between the girls on the sofa, she affectionately wrapped her arms around them, briefing them in on their hopes to relocate them to the US.

They were initially stupefied by her words. *Move all of us across the Atlantic to a country we have little-to-no knowledge of? What would we do? We don't even know how to speak the English language.*

Lorraine soothed their anxious emotions with kind words of assurance. Having Fame, Valentin, Lilly, Madeleine, Hal and herself at their beckoned call, their needs would be quite satisfied. Lorraine explained many emigrants were still relocating to the melting pot of the world from Europe and elsewhere. She also pointed out her affiliation with other Swedish natives, who, naturally, still spoke in their native tongues on occasion. A guarantee life would be much improved for them in Minnesota gave them reason to smile for the first time in several days. The girls and their children would receive excellent educations through the public school systems. Life in the U.S. offered unlimited opportunities.

Katya and Alina fully agreed with Lorraine's suggestion. Amid hugs and tears, joy and relief assuredly appeased the two sisters. They wondered how they would ever be able to repay everyone for their generosity? Lorraine reminded them of God's unending provisions in times of need. All they needed to do was simply love and trust in Him, in good times and in bad. Alina was just beginning to embrace the power and truth in those words.

The ladies walked the short distance to Alina's home to begin the daunting task of packing her husband's personal belongings. Most items would be given to Alex' parents and siblings. Naturally, Alina would keep some items. Assisting her through every moment of the heart-wrenching task was eminent. Katya tackled the chore of gathering the children's items. Lorraine tenderly encouraged them to keep some memorabilia as reminders of their life in Sweden. Once Fame returned with the automobile, sturdy crates were purchased for packing, that could withstand the long distance move.

The following day proved to be another long but productive one. Keeping her sisters busy aided in alleviating their invasive thoughts of the upcoming memorial service. Again, Fame removed the burden of childcare from the women for the second day. However, the youngest two were sent to the homes of their grandparents. The previous day had proven to be a bit more demanding than he had anticipated. Nevertheless, he was unquestionably a Godsend. A picnic lunch was prepared for their enjoyment outdoors in the warmth of the early June sun.

The young mothers, along with Lorraine, set aside everybody's best attire for the memorial services. The challenging task of bidding their final farewell to their husbands, fathers and brothers-in-law sat in the forefront of their minds. Valentin called again to boost the morale of his sisters, re-assuring them of everyone's love and their upcoming, positive futures.

A twelve gun salute, each representing one of the twelve crewmembers, marked the end of a moving memorial. One saving grace, agreed upon by both Fame and Lorraine, was the young ages of the children. Their ability to rapidly bounce back, adjusting to a new land, new faces and a new life would be an asset, including the tender ages of the widowed women.

Chapter Twenty-Three

Everyone marveled at the experience of flying in a huge jetliner. Especially Katya's oldest son, Bjorn. When flying low enough to recognize characteristics of the earth below, he would marvel at the visions. Bjorn was the one Katya most worried about. At the age of 6, he had spent the most time with his dad. Bjorn asked difficult questions aimed at the close proximity between himself and his daddy when they flew into the heavens on the big jet. *Mommy? Are we closer to heaven now where daddy is? Yes, Bjorn, I certainly believe we may be.*

But when he inquired about possibly seeing his daddy out the window, being as close to Heaven as they were, tears formed in Katya's eyes. Fame quickly interceded on his mother's behalf, changing the sensitive subject to an uplifting one.

Traveling by plane denied the rambunctious children the opportunity to wear off energy within the tightly enclosed walls. All were thankful for the four hour delay in New York City, providing a chance to tire themselves out. The final flight to Minnesota proved to be much easier with all five children napping. For this they were most grateful.

Reaching Minneapolis gave the adults a sense of relief. The group of nine filled the car entirely, sitting on one another's lap throughout the four hour drive from the airport to their Duluth home. Lorraine and Fame agreed on keeping the families together for companionship and support. The others, from Long Lake, would drive down to greet the weary travelers the following day, after all received a good night's sleep.

Lorraine had already made it her top priority to teach the English language to her sisters, and possibly Bjorn, over the summer. Bjorn was the only one needing to be placed in school that September. The younger children quickly picked up on the new language over time. Remaining together, in Fame and Lorraine's two bedroom rental home, avoided any problems stemming from a lack of communications at first. Two roll-away beds were placed in the living room, while low seated cots were placed in the bedroom along with the full sized bed.

Valentin drove Lilly and the girls to Duluth separately. Madeleine and Hal had their vehicle loaded down with gifts, treats and balloons galore as part of the welcoming committee. Everyone understood the feelings of despair from losing those so close. They also shared the awkwardness of becoming citizens in an unknown country. Not many years had passed since they, too, left their native homelands for the U.S. So, with wide-open hearts they embraced the seven new family members most passionately.

The children, accompanied by Katya, were playing ball in the back yard when their guests arrived the following morning. One by one, Valentin, Lilly, Madeleine and Harold entered the house with armloads of children and goodies. Immediately Alina alerted the family out back of their arriving family. Katya held the youngest, little Katarina, in her arms as the other children hid behind the skirts of their mother and Aunt.

Valentin understood the slightly shy behavior he'd expected from his younger sisters. After all, they had seen nothing of their older brother for so many years. Still, nothing could have prevented them from sharing long warm embraces. Kissing the tops of their heads, Valentin held both girls close, trying his best not to cry. His emotions finally got the better of him though. He knew the others would never view him as being weak for it. Once his tears started, the entire room followed suit. All of the men removed clean hanky's from their pockets while the women searched purses for their own.

Two separate conversations soon developed as both Fame and Lorraine translated greetings in between. No words were needed as Madeleine and Hal presented each child with a welcoming gift. The joy of giving and receiving needed no translation. Gifts were also affectionately bestowed upon Alina and Katya from all. The children frolicked in the large bouquet of balloons that were dispersed throughout the living room. A large pan of lasagna had been baked the previous evening by Hal. He had more than a few delicious recipes to share with the family after raising Fame and Jim by himself for so many years. In no time the young children lost all inhibitions they'd initially held, only remotely aware of the language barrier. Loads of hugs and smiles were shared among all. A new toy had been purchased by Madeleine and Harold for each of the children, including Tia.

The twins, Rhonda and Robin, had reached the age where they could keep well occupied on a blanket with a few rattles and stuffed animals. The young cousins spent endless hours playing with the babies. Together, they would become one of the closest knit families anyone could hope to be blessed with.

* * * * *

Their first summer in Minnesota proved to be challenging and rewarding for the Swedish families. The widowed mothers kept their late husband's families in Sweden abreast of their new lives in the United States. They had promised to always keep open communications with them from across the miles. Learning English was, of course, expected of everyone. However, the mothers of the children emphatically insisted they remain knowledgeable of their native Swedish language as well. That way they could keep continued communications with their paternal families.

Alina and Katya quickly became Americanized, as did the children. They especially enjoyed summer cook outs and water activities on Long Lake throughout the summers.

Much to their dismay, Lorraine was never able to become pregnant. It didn't take long for the loving couple to adopt children however. Within a few years they had adopted two infant girls. Tessa Lynn and Tiffany Sheri. They continued to be active in their nieces and nephews lives as well. Bjorn was proving to be an expert alpine skier. Fame had always enjoyed the sport, introducing Bjorn to it from a young age.

Late August arrived in the blink of an eye. James and Nicole had been busy planning their late summer wedding. Following a heart-warming ceremony under beautiful skies the reception was held indoors for the evening, avoiding the mosquitoes. Hal was proud of his youngest son. He had turned a somewhat fading business into a flourishing one with the hardware store he managed in International

Falls. Fame, too, was proud of his younger brother, proud of the good and caring man he had become.

The following Spring, James received an offer to manage a combination lumber yard and hardware store in Glendale, Arizona. The pay was more than he'd ever hoped for and the climate was very agreeable to both. Within three short months of their relocating, the young couple found themselves expecting their first child. Nicole's due date was March 15th. That winter flew by for them. Even Nicole felt outstandingly well throughout her entire pregnancy. As expected, they delivered a healthy baby girl, Abbigail Faith Thuringer. Another child would follow two years later, a precious and healthy baby boy, Owen Michael Thuringer.

In 1960 Lilly gave birth one more time to another baby girl, Barbara Lorraine. Valentin joked he was doomed to be surrounded by the female gender for his entire life. That was their final attempt at producing a boy. However, he was granted numerous opportunities to take his three nephews, Bjorn, Christian and Hans out into the great outdoors.

A keen eye, unlimited patience and a disciplined mastery of bow and rifle taught the boys to respect themselves and others in life. Many lifelong skills were acquired from those Godly encounters within the vast wilderness of northeastern Minnesota.

Valentin and Lilly could not have loved their four beautiful daughters more. As they grew, Tia became a highly skilled swimmer, enabling her to serve as a life guard at the Eveleth Beach on Ely Lake each summer.

Setting an example for her younger sisters, she went on to take top honors in swimming, placing first in regional's and state three years in a row. Placing second in nationals in her senior year, she was later approached by a scout seeking Olympic-qualifying athletes to compete in the next summer games to be held in three years. This would involve relentless and grueling practices to bring her to the top of her game. Grandma and Grandpa "T", along with Lilly and Valentin, continually encouraged Tia to go for the Gold.

Rarely did her parents miss a competition throughout the years. If they couldn't be there, then her grandparents or aunts and uncles would be there cheering her on. Tia had gained the speed and endurance necessary to hopefully qualify her for a chance to compete against worldwide swimmers internationally.

Her dream was truly realized when she placed in the earlier competitions in Sapporo, Japan. The years she had spent driving herself to the point of exhaustion, time and again, had finally paid off. Tia Lee Baranowsky went on to receive the Silver Medal that year. That didn't quite cut it for her though.

Four years later, she placed again, allowing her the opportunity to compete for the Gold once more. The Summer Olympics were held in Canada that year. Her parents, sisters and Grandma and Grandpa "T" were there in person to witness her success, out-swimming the competition by 8 full seconds, a record swim. It was a proud day for the US. Even more so for her family and the city of Eveleth, Minnesota.

Rhonda excelled at playing the piano, performing frequently at high school plays, nursing homes or an occasional banquet. Her constant commitment to help the less fortunate led her to acquire a nursing degree. Many years were spent teaching Sunday School and serving God, as well as assisting those in poor health. She married an electrician and moved to Minneapolis where she and her husband, Richard Domire, raised two wonderful children. Although Rhonda was committed to helping others in need, she knew her priorities and always placed her immediate family, as well as extended family, first. The Domires were outstanding parents, involving themselves in their children's sports, and in all activities throughout their years at home. To this day Rhonda is involved in the Multiple Sclerosis bikathon, which stretches a distance of 150 miles from Duluth, MN to Blaine, MN in a short two-day event. They are also anxiously awaiting the arrival of their first grandchild.

Robin married her high school sweetheart, Frank Fondsie, raising two highly motivated daughters, Penny and Kristen. Receiving her education later in life, she eventually became a high school English teacher. After the birth of her second daughter, Kristen, she became very active at the gym, demanding nothing less than perfection from herself. She also found God in her own personal way, becoming an avid reader of Christian literature and self-help books. She now teaches classes at her local YMCA and cares for her young granddaughter, Emily, whenever she is needed.

Barbara married at the age of twenty-two to another electrician by the name of Craig Masters. She became a special needs instructor at the High School in Virginia, MN. She and Craig adopted three children after she, too, was unable to bear more children beyond her first child, Charity Joan. They traveled to Columbia, South America, returning with sibling orphans, approximately aged eight and ten years, named Theresa and Joseph. Later they adopted another infant boy, Nathan, from the immediate area. They raised their family along with breeding precious house dogs. They remain living in rural Virginia where they have a strawberry farm.

Katya continued living with Lorraine and Fame for five years after arriving in the US. With Bjorn being a few years older than his brothers, she waited until Christian and Hans reached school age before enrolling at UMD to further her education. That is where she met and eventually married her husband, Brent Hascall. They resided in Duluth throughout their lifetime, having only one additional child, a daughter, Taryn Skye, who was spoiled by most but teased persistently by her big brothers.

Bjorn had also excelled in the winter sport of alpine skiing. He, too, surpassed the expectations of his coaches, peers and family. Placing twice in national competitions earned him the right to participate in the Olympics as well. Seeing his closest cousin take the Silver gave him cause to strive his very hardest to compete internationally as well. Nearly four years later the winter Olympics were held in Austria. The traveling distance and hotel accommodations were too much of a financial burden for Katya and Brent at that time, preventing them from watching their son compete in person.

One of their sons wouldn't receive those athletic abilities. Hans had developed a severe case of what doctors suspected was influenza. However, months passed with little improvement in his health. Eventually, he began to retreat from society, losing his ability to walk, continually suffering from twitching, pain, fatigue and flu-like symptoms. He was finally diagnosed with Multiple Sclerosis after two years. There was no known cause or cure for the ailment at that time. Illness had robbed him of the fun and opportunities healthy people were afforded.

The winter Olympics had begun in Austria. Bjorn smiled brightly when approached by two elderly people at the competitions. Believing they were fans, he prepared to give them his autograph. Immediately upon hearing the woman's voice however, spoken in his native Swedish tongue, he wondered if it could possibly be true.

Placing her hand upon the side of his face she gently asked, *How are you my dear grandson?* With ecstatic jubilee, he embraced the loving, elderly couple who had been physically absent from his life since he was a young boy. Never had he dreamed they would travel to Austria to cheer him on. He couldn't recall, ever before, seeing eyes shine with such unrelenting pride. That was the final boost Bjorn needed to send him soaring into first place, winning the Gold for the USA.

Following the awards ceremony, Bjorn's grandparents followed him to his hotel room, where he placed a collect call to his mother, Katya and step-father, Bryan. After congratulations and praises galore, Bjorn put his grandmother on the telephone. Katya, Bryan, Christian, Hans and Taryn were excited beyond belief when hearing the news of Bjorn's grandparents' journey to the competitions in Austria.

That appearance convinced Bjorn a trip to Sweden was necessary. The following year he traveled to Stockholm where his grandparents were currently living. A full month was spent hearing various stories of his and his father's pasts. Becoming acquainted with loads of extended family members was enormously gratifying, filling a somewhat empty void in his life.

Hans went on to become a pilot for Northwest Airlines, which was headquartered in Minneapolis/St. Paul. He remains single to this day, enjoying his freedom as a bachelor. Gifted with good looks and an enjoyable career, he dates women from around the world. Katya knew, one day, he would settle down and raise a family. He had a good heart and a love of children.

Christian even learned how to keep himself afloat by exercising his upper body as much as possible. He worked at the University of Duluth in the Special Ed department, assisting younger college-aged handicapped students.

Alina and her two daughters, Asa and Katarina, moved to Long Lake after six months of residing with Lorraine and Fame. Valentin and Lilly had finished off the basement, dividing it into three bedrooms and a recreation room. Soon Valentin found himself living within the confines of an entirely dominated female household. He didn't think he would ever be able to keep up with the many demands of six children and two adult females. He had to admit, he learned a great deal about having patience. He also developed a trickster personality, finding ways to overtake the bathroom on the rare occasions it would open up. After a time, Lilly became more than familiar with his somewhat warped sense of humor. A shake of the head and a hidden smirk on her face told him she enjoyed his upbeat personality.

Eventually Alina married as well. His name was Devin Armstrong, an accountant in Hoyt Lakes, Minnesota for the Erie Mining Company. Alina gave birth twice again to two boys, Klayten Jeffrey Lane and Landen Mathew Lee. When the last of the children entered high school, Alina was educated to become a counselor for alcoholics and drug addicts. She had long before returned to her Christian roots, avoiding the temptation of alcohol for the rest of her life.

Their daughter, Katarina, went on to become a successful attorney, later entering into politics. Today she is a Senator representing the state of Arizona. Their other three children live locally. Klayten is employed as a police officer, volunteering to assist the crew in the fire department when necessary. Landen is a coach and spiritual leader of teens at a Lutheran Church. Asa is a busy homemaker, married to a miner. She has a keen interest in horticulture. Endless hours are spent, during the spring, summer and fall, bringing greenery and flowers to life in their spacious yard.

Valentin's older sisters, Greta and Emma raised their families in Paris. A few family gatherings took place in the US and one in Marseilles, France. Madeleine and Hal traveled yearly to the French Riviera, frequently re-visiting the sights they'd encountered on their one month honeymoon.

Grandpa Hal, the kiddies pal, passed away in his sleep while in the south of France. Madeleine had learned much in life. Being saddened immensely by the loss of her husband was expected. Yet, she thanked the Lord for a long and prosperous life. She had been blessed with two kind and loving men in her lifetime, along with her precious Lilly and numerous grandchildren. She couldn't have asked for a more understanding and loving son-in-law.

Madeleine transferred the property to Lilly and Valentin following Hal's death. Only six months later, she, too, suffered a severe heart attack, disabling her for another six months before passing on.

Life for Lilly would never be the same after her dear mother suffered the heart attack. Lilly immediately became her caregiver. The demands placed on her, twenty four hours a day, seven days a week was physically and emotionally draining.

For six months Lilly agonized over her mother. It was a time to reach deep into the pockets of her Christianity for strength and endurance. Not only for her mother, but herself as well. The heartache of slowly watching her fade away into the arms of death was grueling. There wasn't anything Lilly wouldn't do for the brave and courageous woman she'd had the privilege of calling "Mama" for so many years.

Undoubtedly, there were numerous available and willing hands to aid in her care. Madeleine had won the love of many throughout her lifetime. In her younger years she sometimes felt cheated out of a larger family with Jon Paul. The good Lord knew of all she would receive one day however.

Never had she imagined having such a large crew of grandchildren and great-grandchildren. Until the day of her heart attack, Madeleine DeMornais-Thuringer kept a close watch on her well being, keeping physically fit and always sporting the latest trends in fashion. Her strength, love, care and concern for others played a huge role in molding the character of her many grandchildren. She had immediately taken in the children of Valentin's widowed sisters, treating them as her very own throughout the years.

Alina and Katya were forever indebted to the lovely Madeleine for her extreme generosity in their time of need. They'd spent years showering her with flowers, homemade gifts, French pastries and hats. Madeleine never lost her love for hats. Hal even had to build cabinets from floor to ceiling in one corner of the garage to house them all.

Fame and Lorraine's adopted daughters, Tessa and Tiffany, graduated with honors from the University of Arizona. Both girls found the desert climate much more appealing than the bitter cold winters of Minnesota. When needing to breath the cold air, or get out on the ski hills from time to time, they simply drove 120 miles north to Flagstaff where a full weekend was spent at the Snow Bowl ski resort.

Lorraine and Fame joined Valentin and Lilly on more than one holiday vacation to Marseilles, France. Valentin retired from the US Steel plant in Virginia, Minnesota after thirty years of devotion as an electrician. With their children raised and their young families steadily on the go, Lilly and Valentin started traveling. Lilly always wanted to see more of the country.

The newest method of transportation in the United States for retirees was a motor home. Providing them with all their needs while on wheels was a fantastic way to tour the states. The Thuringer cottage on Long Lake had been used as a guest cabin for the many children and grandchildren following Madeleine's death. Wishing to avoid the costs and maintenance of a large home, Valentin and Lilly sold the original homestead and kept the cottage for their summer stays.

Each winter provided a new destination for them, spending most of the coldest months in a warm climate. Earlier in life, Valentin had taken a severe fall on the ice of the lake. Going down hard, he'd hit his knee caps severely, rendering countless nights of pain and sleep loss. Occasionally the doctors would drain the fluid build-up on the knees, releasing the pressure for him. Knee surgery was just beginning to enter the medical world and he wasn't trusting of any surgeons.

Valentin continued suffering with the pain each winter, until they began spending time in the warmth of the south. He and Lilly took endless photos during their travels. Sights like Mt. Rushmore and the Badlands in South Dakota, the stunning Cascades and Teton mountain ranges in the northwest, Yellowstone National Park, Old Faithful, Zion National Park, and the Joshua forests were just some of the many beautiful sights they appreciated. Lilly was always captivated by the beautiful rushing waterfalls the northwest offered. The west coast of the Pacific captured breathtaking sunsets and sandy beaches. Disneyland, Sea World and Rodeo Drive in Hollywood were fun tourist attractions offering numerous memories to the retired couple.

Having lived in New York City for two years during their twenties provided them enough scenic tours of the Northeastern states. Knowing their curiosity wouldn't be satisfied until seeing it for themselves, they began their yearly winter trips to the southeast of the United States. Those sights included The Ozarks of Missouri, the bluegrass of Kentucky and Tennessee, the patriotic historical buildings and statues in Washington D.C., and endless coastlines along the Gulf of Mexico and the Atlantic, which wrapped themselves around the sunshine state of Florida.

Florida beckoned them back to its sunshine and warm oceanic breezes for a few winters. The couple took up the sport of golf which occupied much of their time. After a few years, however, Valentin's knee pain intensified.

One of the other areas of the country they had thoroughly enjoyed was the desert southwest, namely Phoenix, AZ. When passing through they had the opportunity to visit with Hal's son, James, and his family. Also, Lorraine and Fame's daughters, Tessa and Tiffany remained living in the valley of the sun.

It was the following winter in Phoenix when they decided to sell the motor home, instead purchasing a year-round two bedroom condominium in a retirement area called Sun City. The first thing Hal did was receive knee surgery. Just one knee was operated on at a time, allowing him the use of his non-surgical knee while on crutches.

The desert southwest proved to be a Godsend for them. They soon learned vast amounts of retirees from the northern plains of the Midwest shared the same exact thoughts as themselves. To live summers in the north and winters in the southwest. It didn't take long for them to develop an abundance of friends from their golf clubhouses, churches and neighborhoods. There was even a gathering of folks from the Midwest who congregated together once a winter to enjoy various ethnic foods, games and conversations throughout a weekend. The Baranowsky's became actively involved in the preparations of those weekend festivities.

Lilly developed cataracts shortly after moving to the southwest. She was placed in the well-established hands of top notch Ophthalmologic surgeons who removed the cataracts, providing much improved vision.

One highlight of choosing the Valley of the Sun for their winter retreat was having James' and Nicole's families, as well as Tessa and Tiffany nearby. Frequent meals and holidays were shared with family. Lorraine and Fame also started spending winters there. However, they located themselves closer to their daughters in the easternmost section of the valley, Apache Junction.

Courage Times Three. A Novel

A good seventy mile stretch expanded the metropolis from one corner to the other. Snowbirds galore invaded the city throughout the winter months. Even small golf carts were seen traveling the roads of Sun City, driven by happy-go-lucky retirees.

Oftentimes the subject of conversation among the retirees regarded their past lives. It never seized to amaze Valentin and Lilly just how many commonalities they shared with many elderly folks. Once they met a couple who lived just 300 miles away from their home on Long Lake. After lengthy chatter they learned this couple shared another commonality with them.

A retired surgeon, Dr. Dietrich and his wife, Elsie, had moved to the United States from Germany at precisely the same time as themselves, in 1951, although they exceeded the Baranowsky's in age by a generation. Rather than settling in New York City, they found permanent residence in the state of Massachusetts. It was there the doctor attended Harvard University, receiving his basic formal schooling before moving onward. Afterward he was accepted at the Mayo Clinic in Rochester, Minnesota, where he established his residency, remaining there throughout his doctoring years.

Something kept nudging Lilly in the back of her mind about his name. She inquired as to what ship they had traveled on from Europe to the United States. As it turned out, it wasn't the same ship they had traveled on, but another. Still, something kept giving her cause to continue her inquiries into their past.

The name seemed somewhat familiar and he appeared to have something oddly in common with her. She simply could not put her finger on it. As they pursued Valentin and Lilly's past lives in France, they learned from Lilly she had been raised in Reims. That knowledge pleased Dr. Dietrich immensely. He explained he'd lived near the French border in Germany as a young boy, but that he'd lost his parents to an illness at the age of six years old. He was taken in by a kindly uncle for just one year until he was sent to live with another childless couple in Bonn, Germany.

Dr. Dietrich continued to tell the story of his upbringing and how he and his wife came to meet and marry.

Following his story, Lilly had an inclination something important had not yet been revealed. She couldn't understand why she seemed so pressed to delve further into his past. She asked why he had been so pleased when learning of her living in Reims.

At first he waved it off as having no significance, yet something prompted him to reveal more information. It seemed he and his older sister had been separated from one another after their parents' untimely deaths. Lilly, knowing how millions of individuals had been torn apart from their families during the wars, at first listened with mild interest. When he spoke his sister's name, Madeleine, shivers went up her spine instantly. Lilly looked at Valentin with unbelieving, bewildered eyes.

She knew her next question might possibly reveal what she suspected to be the uncanny truth. *Do you have any knowledge as to where your sister was sent?*

Why yes! She was sent to live with our Aunt Melanie in Paris. We also had an Aunt Chantelle in the city of Reims, France.

Goose bumps covered Lilly from head to toe. She nervously squirmed in her chair, uncrossing her legs before standing up, straight as an arrow. Breaking into an instant sweat, Lilly began fanning herself with a piece of paper from her bag. Valentin wore a look of astonishment and disbelief as his wife continued to probe into the doctor's younger years.

The elderly couple immediately sensed the discomfort and confusion they'd caused Lilly and Valentin. *Are you quite alright Mrs. Baranowsky? Did I say something to upset you my dear*

Lilly knew this could not be possible. Yet, why had she felt so compelled to make her inquiries? One last question remained.

Did you begin sending letters to her in Reims, some years after your separation, in hopes of re-connecting with her? Lilly's voiced quivered.

With that question, Dr. Gus Dietrich's back stiffened, his mouth gaping in astonishment. Extremely confused, he asked *How did you know that? And why would you ask that? Who are you?*

Lilly placed a hand to her neck, rubbing, trying to prevent her throat from closing up, cutting off her breathing. Hot tears welled up in her eyes, stinging them, as the heat within her body escalated, spiraling upward like a vine choking her. Her mind rampantly began to spin.

It quite simply could not be possible. *Did you live in Cologne as a young boy with your parents?* When he responded with an emphatic "Yes", her suspicions were confirmed.

Lilly was unable to speak clearly as she struggled to release the words of her mother's long past secret. It had only been a short five years since Madeleine Dietrich DeMornais Thuringer had discovered the letters, sharing the disheartening news with them about her brother Gustav.

The doctor and his wife were stupefied by the astounding words rapidly flowing from Lilly's mouth. Each word sliced through him, like a razor sharp knife, while she revealed how Madeleine had been denied the opportunity to read his letters and of how Aunt Melanie had secretly hidden them. Not until several years later had she discovered the letters, along with a letter of apology from Aunt Melanie.

Their Aunt had intentionally kept the siblings apart for a lifetime due to jealousy and an unconscionable sense of obligation to her husband and their so-called high ranking social stature.

The truth unveiled itself like a spider's web unraveling. She explained how her mother had searched for Gustav later in life and how she'd been informed he'd died in the first world war. It seemed he'd escaped from Germany to Sweden, faking his death for the Gestapo, leaving behind no trace of his past, just as Valentin had done.

Gustav Dietrich could not believe the traumatic story that was unfolding, moment by moment, before him. He immediately inquired about his long-lost, but never forgotten sister, Madeleine. Grievously, Lilly shared the despairing news of her mother's death some years earlier. Bewilderment overtook him as he realized he had lived only a few hundred miles away from his only sibling for so many years. Their hearts went out to him with grave sorrow for the loss of his sister's love he'd missed out on over the years.

*****

Life hadn't ended for everybody however. It dawned on the good doctor Lilly was the very daughter of his lost sister. Although Gus Dietrich was doing very well for himself, physically, at eighty one years of age, his knees nearly gave way as he stood to softly embrace his dear white-haired niece, Lilly May DeMornais Baranowsky.

How is it God can create such gracious and astonishing events in life that are nothing less than miraculous? Why is it, even His strongest believers remain shocked and awe-inspired by His never-ending miracles, even though they have known so many in their lives?

Do we believe that divine intervention occurs only in others' lives? Do we think only believers are granted these miracles? Weren't they able to track down Valentin's sisters in Sweden? Did Lorraine just happen to meet her future husband in Sweden who would return her to her brother in America? Didn't God direct even Valentin and Lilly to each other, in their most desperate moments of life, to fall in love?

Yes! The answers to all of the above questions are an emphatic "Yes". God performs thousands upon thousands of miracles daily, the majority of them overlooked or unrecognized as the divine intervention of their Almighty Father in Heaven.

From that point onward Gus Dietrich and his wife spent numerous hours becoming acquainted with his niece and other family members. Lilly May, as well, relished in the joy of welcoming additional family into her life. They were exceedingly grateful for Madeleine's photographic abilities which, to Uncle Gustav's delight, provided endless photos of her family and self. How proud Madeleine would be of her little brother, a revered and highly qualified doctor at the world-renowned Mayo Clinic.

A sense of sadness often accompanied their conversations, however; the sadness that Madeleine wasn't there in the flesh to share in the laughter and hugs. Still, they knew, with every sense of their being, her spirit was a mere breath away. Perhaps she had a hand in leading them to each other. This, they would never truly know until reaching the other end of the rainbow themselves. The eternal resting place called Heaven!!!

* * * * *

Before age overtook them, Lilly and Valentin wished to see France once again. One Spring they departed Sun City early, traveling to the French Riviera before returning to Long Lake. They flew directly into Paris which was the normal routine from the U.S.

Courage Times Three. A Novel

This time, instead of going directly to Marseilles, Valentin and Lilly chose to return to Reims, to her old neighborhood. Aunt Chantelle had passed on several years earlier, leaving her vineyards and estate to another generation of DeMornais'. Before leaving Paris, however, Lilly did some research. She hadn't seen some dear old friends for many years and hoped to possibly locate them. To her delight and amazement, it took little time to track them down.

Lilly spent quality time in Reims revisiting her past. After breathing in the new life that had been reborn in the quaint town, she and Valentin boarded the train that would carry them to the Baltic Sea.

As the train pulled into the city, Lilly became restless and anxious. Valentin had seen this look on his wife's face more than once in their lives together. Taking her by the hand, he once again instructed her to look into his eyes, soothingly calming her nerves. Whatever would Lilly have done without her precious Valentin at her side? She knew a repeat of history was occurring exactly as it had once before. Memories flooded her mind as she touched base with the pain of so many years past. She had never expected those emotions to surface so profoundly after a lifetime of change.

He still had the ability to calm her emotions, just as he had back then, only now they were white haired and wearing bifocals.

Chapter Twenty-Four

De-boarding the train, Lilly instantly caught the eyes of her dear old friends, Jacque and Delores Pariseau, the wonderful friends who'd housed and fed them for a few months following the end of the second war.

Not only did tears spill from the eyes of the women, but from the men's eyes just the same Life in northern France in the mid 1940's was pure living hell. Seeing each other in person again ignited a slight bit of pain for all, recapturing those difficult times.

Jacque Pariseau drove the foursome to their newer home on the opposite side of the city from where they had lived during the war. A few communications had been shared between them in the earlier years, but there was much catching up to do.

Unfortunately, the Pariseau's three children had moved away from Calais when reaching adulthood. Still, they were warmed by the numerous photos of three generations displayed throughout the rooms. Stories of their lives were intertwined, sharing much commonality despite the distance and differing circumstances they had all experienced.

The Baranowsky's shared two fun filled days with the endearing couple. It was a much welcomed visit, instilling a renewed attitude toward Calais and the outlying areas that had held them captive for so long.

On their second and final day in Calais the Pariseaus drove their guests the short distance to Lille where the Void du Norde newspaper offices still remained. Although the building was new and production had grown immensely, it triggered many memories, good and not so good, for both Lilly and Valentin.

A lovely outdoor terrace café, located directly across the street from the offices, provided a delightful lunch for all. While enjoying the stimulating conversation, two gentlemen approached them with a newspaper. Both greeted the Pariseaus asking if they could join the foursome.

Seating himself next to Lilly, one nodded a hello, gently requesting her hand to place a friendly kiss upon it. Lilly so enjoyed the gentlemanly gestures offered by many French men. As he intentionally removed the empty plate of food from the table in front of her, a confused and irritated look planted itself square in the middle of her face.

Turning away from the man she looked, first, at Valentin then at the Pariseaus. In place of her plate he set down a newspaper. Lilly looked strangely at him again until her eyes were drawn to some highlighted print on the newspaper. In bold neon pink she read the names of the editor and assistant editor's names. Jerome Roux and Lucas Bernard.

Lilly couldn't believe her eyes. There, sitting right next to her, were the dear friends who'd nearly lost their lives while underground for five years in the hell hole of the Pariseau basement.

Lilly didn't know if her heart would hold out another minute. All were at a loss for words just then. She stood, as did Jerome and Lucas, embracing one another with engaging sincerity. The three held on for several minutes. Never had a single word of their existence reached her since leaving them in the hands of the elderly Pariseau couple so many years ago. When the Pariseaus had passed away years earlier, the hopes of finding her two underground mates had vanished. Only recently had Jacque learned of the editor's names and who they were.

When Lilly and Valentin contacted the Pariseaus two days earlier, Jacque mentioned their names to Delores. Putting the pieces of the puzzle together, they contacted Jerome and Lucas, informing them of the return visit of Lilly and Valentin Baranowsky.

An odd sense of completion embraced Lilly. Now, none of them would go to their graves wondering about their long past friends, their brothers and sister, who had survived the hell of war together.

Lilly thanked the Pariseaus repeatedly for giving her one of the best gifts she had ever received. Nobody was in a hurry to leave the table that afternoon as they shared their life histories together.

Both men had gone on to marry and raise families. They'd moved away from the difficult memories Lille had held for them for several years. Living separate lives with some distance between them hadn't hampered the frequent phone calls, visits, and family friendships they'd shared.

When Jerome was offered the lead position at the Void du Norde Newspaper, he relocated his family to Lille. Not long afterward, he found himself in need of a devoted employee to assist him. No other man could fill that need more than his dearest friend, Lucas Bernard. In no time the gentlemen found themselves living in harmony on the coast of the Baltic Sea.

Names, addresses and telephone numbers were exchanged among all as hugs were shared before catching the train that would, again, carry them to the Riviera.

The topic of conversation on the train was undoubtedly the blessed event that had just taken place. Lilly or Valentin could never well explain the sense of Godliness surrounding them each time they encountered divine intervention as such. Too often thoughts are invaded by the high demands we place on ourselves and those society places on us. To many it's a cut-throat world, each man or woman for themselves.

Every soul seated together at the terrace café that day was fully aware of the need to do for others in this sometimes cruel and ruthless world. They would always be thankful for their faith.

A night had been spent at the home of Greta Moreau, Valentin's elderly sister in Paris, when they'd initially arrived. They looked forward to spending time with her again when she could get down to the seaside villa to join them. Greta's husband, had died just two years earlier. Never having been one to sit idly, she poured herself into her work, rarely taking time to enjoy life's leisurely pleasures. Her children, Rene` and Andre, lived in Paris but rarely saw much of their mother any more.

Emma and her husband Anton, would be joining them in a week for a few days of shared relaxation and family conversations. Their daughter, Anastasie, had entered the field of fashion. Still struggling to make a name for herself, she had acquired much of the same drive her mother had.

Their oldest, Dominique, was a tour train conductor, a job he absolutely loved. Never did he have frumpy or disillusioned travelers aboard his train. The magnificent sights he delivered them to were second to none.

Unlike Greta's family, Emma and Anton's children and grandchildren often spent quality time together. Emma believed that Greta, being the oldest, had simply never learned how to slow down due to her many responsibilities in early life. Those circumstances created a fiercely driven woman. Emma often pitied her dear sister Greta.

The train carried them through the Springtime lavender fields in Provence. What a sight to behold! Fields of lavender as far as the eye could see. But even more impressive, was the scent of lavender filling the air for miles. The fresh and soothing aroma created a sense of calm among all travelers.

Lilly and Valentin felt just as Madeleine and Hal had during their stay in Marseilles, honeymooners each and every day. They, too, enjoyed the Mediterranean best in the Spring. Minnesota's autumn season took top rank when it came to the colorful beauty and splendor she displayed each year, however.

Once Emma and Anton arrived at the villa, they feasted on freshly grilled jumbo shrimp, Valentin using the special recipe shared with him by Madeleine and Hal. While Valentin headed up the grill duties, Lilly prepared some of her favorite French cuisine. Marinated vegetables with a tarragon vinaigrette and mixed olive tapenade were served as appetizers. Accompanying the delicately seasoned, grilled shrimp were mouth-watering salmon fillets and shrimp pate on crostini. Two excellent bottles of perfectly chilled wine were served by Anton with the delectable dinner.

Ah, life was grand! How blessed Lilly felt her life had been throughout the years. She'd been bestowed with a warm and loving husband and four beautiful children, all doing well in their daily lives. She truly believed if she hadn't been forced to live through those horrible years in her teens, she would never have become the caring and nurturing mother and wife she had been throughout the years. Certainly she'd made her mistakes as all parents do. But on the whole, she could truly look back with a pleasing smile.

Madeleine had suffered in her very young years, keeping the pain and embarrassment hidden from everyone other than Harold Thuringer. Lilly never had and never would learn of the hardships her mother lived with daily for ten long years.

Lorraine carried the weight of being raped and ruined for any other man at the innocent age of thirteen. It took years, along with the right man to trust with the truth, before she could release the pain of the atrocious rapes. When her inability to become impregnated was obvious, she suspected the savagery and brutality of the occurrence had ruined her. After all, she hadn't even entered puberty yet.

What outstanding courage these three women displayed throughout their lives, regardless of their appalling existences in their early lives. The courage to leave the past behind, to move forward in becoming kind and loving mothers — warm and affectionate wives, and most importantly, being proud and successful human beings. All of their good deeds were treasures they were storing up for themselves in heaven.

Each woman held those deep, dark secrets almost entirely to themselves throughout life. Never did they use their childhood pain to excuse them for being any less of a person than they were. They were conquerors of their own scars. They set inspiring examples for their children to be all they could be. Nobody wants a better life for their own young ones than their parents and grandparents. Valentin and Lilly returned to their cozy two bedroom cottage on Long Lake after enjoying a most wonderful time in France. Who would've ever known Valentin's family of seven siblings, separated so tragically from each other in their younger years, would come to know one another again in their adult lives. No distance, no mountains, no oceans could keep the Baranowsky family separated. Lilly knew she had married a quality man with strong morals and high scruples.

*****

Summer in Minnesota was long, cool, and damp. Days and weeks of overcast skies, emitting little more than fine sprays of damp cool mist, prevented most from enjoying the everyday outdoor activities they looked forward to each year.

Even the prematurely decaying leaves fell from the trees before displaying much of their colors. Valentin and Lilly decided an early departure would be good for them. They needed the everyday sunshine the Arizona skies provided. Lorraine and Fame agreed with the Baranowsky's to head southwest to the sunshine early.

Courage Times Three. A Novel

Plans were set to travel together, stopping along the way to enjoy the sights and attractions. A large gathering was planned at the home of the Thuringers in Duluth prior to leaving.

The spread of food and drinks were never ending. Everyone contributed favorite dishes making the occasion very festive. Marshmallow and wienie roasting, over an open fire, provided tasty treats and loads of fun for the children. Lilly reveled in her joy as she commented about God giving them such a large family. The times she had spent alone as an only child were often lonely without a sibling. He had certainly made up for it now. Following a long day and night, Lilly and Valentin packed their car and headed home to the cottage. Morning would come soon and they still had a few last minute details to attend to.

Their annual departure from Minnesota to the desert southwest was mid October. By then the beauty of the leaves in northern Minnesota had shed themselves, covering the ground with a blanket before freezing.

Oftentimes, Lorraine and Lilly would travel together during the day while the gentlemen carried on their own male conversations.

A substantial amount of chatter over recipes, the young ones, their hairdressers and the latest fashions would top the talk between the ladies. Rarely would they think about their early difficulties in life.

The guys, as usual, discussed the Minnesota Vikings and their biggest rival, the Green Bay Packers. Fishing, politics, scoreboard statistics, in many professional sports, dominated their conversations.

A stop in Oklahoma City for the night was the plan. They would take the easiest and quickest route on Interstate 35 from Minnesota to Oklahoma City. From there they would connect with Interstate 40, carrying them directly west to Flagstaff, Arizona. Then it was southbound on I-17, merely a short 120 miles, before they'd reach the Valley of the Sun.

Most of their days entailed approximately eight hours of driving. Frequent stops for stretches, gasoline, sightseeing and coffee were taken throughout their leisurely drive. All appreciated the terrain of the land changing vastly from one state to another. The rolling hills of Minnesota were left behind as they entered the cornfields of Iowa. There, endless miles of cornfields surrounded them in every direction. It certainly was the heartland of the USA. Des Moines offered them an easy route around the capitol city, which they much appreciated. Getting stuck in traffic in the midst of a metropolitan area wasn't their cup of tea, so to speak. Once entering the northwest corner of Missouri, they enjoyed beautifully treed terrain with scattered rivers. The wheat fields of Kansas, seen for miles on end from the tolled highways, always portrayed a sense of vastness. Convenient travel stops provided travelers with their needs. Oklahoma once again featured rolling hills and clean, modern rest area facilities for travelers.

Pulling into a hotel in Oklahoma City, the couples were ready to freshen themselves and find a suitable diner for their evening meal. Directly across the street sat a Village Inn. Not only would they enjoy dinner there, they would be provided a scrumptious breakfast the following morning as well.

Sleep came easily to them that night. All was well with the world and they'd left the cold winter to those who could more easily sustain it. All agreed to meet at 8am sharp at the Village Inn for their morning coffee and nourishment.

Upon entering the diner, apparent chaos and concerned looks confronted them. Confusing information was coming from the radio DJ. He wasn't sure what was happening. Somebody yelled for the radio to be turned louder. One man shouted for all to be silenced.

A plane just hit one of the towers of the World Trade Center in New York City. Utter silence overtook the diner as the DJ tried making sense of the catastrophic occurrence. Suddenly, they stated another plane had flown into the second of the twin towers.

A look of terror gripped each and every soul. What was happening? They didn't understand. Within minutes it was learned both planes were commercial passenger jets carrying hundreds of innocent victims and thousands were fleeing to escape eminent death.

Jaws dropped in horror! Tears began escaping the eyes of some. It hadn't been long since these Oklahoman's had experienced the shocking news of their very own Alfred P. Murrah Federal Building being bombed in 1995. Just six years earlier hundreds of innocent men, women and children had been recklessly and violently taken from their loved ones in a senseless and brutal bombing. The

Courage Times Three. A Novel

unforgettable pain of that horrifying day resounded in the hearts and minds of all.

Lilly squeezed Valentin's hand as the look of fear returned to her eyes, seemingly erasing every moment of time since her living hell had ended in 1945. At the same time, Lorraine stiffened with fear, nearly gasping for breath.

Although Lilly had shared small bits of information with Lorraine about her imprisoned underground years, neither woman understood the depth of the other's pain. The memories they'd strived enormously to push away, out of their minds forever, came into light instantly. Valentin and Fame both understood how and why these amazingly strong women were so fearful. They had heard threatening news over the radio before.

Lilly grabbed her purse, *We must get to a television We must see for ourselves what is happening. It will surely be on the televisions at the hotel.* The four of them scurried out of the restaurant, quickly running to the hotel lobby. There, they found a crowd of people standing and sitting in the lobby in front of the television.

Jaws dropped with every new development being released. The first twin tower collapsed entirely to the ground followed by the second tower's total collapse. Next, another commercial airliner flew directly into the Pentagon in Washington. Last to go down was the airliner in Pennsylvania, which had nearly been overtaken by the proud and brave American citizens on board. Thanks to their heroic bravery, the last planned attack on the White House in Washington D.C. was altered, going down in the fields of Pennsylvania, saving endless lives from sure death. Not a single soul could remove their eyes from the television broadcasts.

The inevitable was happening! America was being attacked!! But by whom? Intense and unrelenting disputes had been plaguing the US and the world for several years, brought on by more than one Mid-eastern country. Was this a retaliation? Hadn't the US been diligent in aiding those countries? Hadn't they been trying to bring peace and democracy to those less fortunate in the world who weren't afforded the same rights as those in the U.S.? As Americans, most knew little of the suffering and hardships faced by millions throughout the modern world.

For what seemed to be an eternity, planes filled with innocent victims, buildings filled with innocent lives unjustly sacrificed, covered the screens of every television set in our great nation. It was the first time America had ever been attacked on her own soil in history.

Valentin and Lilly thought about old friends they had left behind in New York City. Were any of them caught in the invasive and unwarranted attacks? Fame and Lorraine carried a cell phone with them at all times. Attempted phone calls to their families were without success. Throughout the country, throughout the world, land lines along with cell service were jammed on overload.

Every plane in the air over the United States was immediately instructed to land at the nearest airport. All planes ready to take off were grounded. Every officer of the law and every branch of the Armed Forces were put on high alert. Traffic throughout the entire country slowed to a near standstill as people listened in horror to the terror unfolding.

In a matter of minutes, the people of the United States, undoubtedly secure in the safety of the strongest nation in the world, were given reason to be fearful for their lives. Following four hours of shocking horror, both couples made a change of plans, deciding to travel with their own life partners on this tragic day. Eventually the children had been reached, assuring their parents of their safety. All but Hans. Hans was employed as a pilot for Northwest airlines. Nobody had reached him yet, but his flight schedule had been obtained by his parents. He, fortunately, wasn't anywhere near New York City. In fact, he had been scheduled to pilot a jumbo airliner to Las Vegas that morning, but was grounded before leaving the Minneapolis/St. Paul airport. Katya praised the Lord for her son's well being. For years following the catastrophic event, she would fear for him as a pilot.

The remainder of their journey to Phoenix was hampered severely by the tragedies. One could not, in all good conscience, enjoy freedom of life, the luxury we all take for granted. A sense of guilt overcame those trying to enjoy themselves throughout the next several days. It was the first time this expansive country, the melting pot of the world, had its freedoms and liberties jeopardized. People from every walk in life perished, buried in its aftermath.

A true sense of unison, as Americans, as free Americans, was adopted by all in a fashion unlike anything it had seen in its history. Every race, color, creed and gender gathered together, hand in hand,

Courage Times Three. A Novel

offering assistance to the needy, far outreaching the expectations of most. Millions of dollars were donated by scores of individuals, families, companies and even schoolchildren. Hundreds of policemen, firemen, even unqualified strangers, sacrificed their own lives in numerous attempts to save dying sisters and brothers hurt or trapped in debris.

The rate of crime came to a nearly complete stop. Americans opened their hearts and pocketbooks, donating all they could to those less fortunate than themselves. Every American felt a sense of invasion. The words "Not In My Life", fell through the cracks.

Once reaching Phoenix the couples departed to their own winter homes in opposite ends of the valley. An appreciation for life strongly embraced them before saying their temporary good-bye's. After what had just occurred on American soil, they were sure to be more appreciative of their everyday freedoms.

Chapter Twenty-Five

September 25th arrived quickly. The fifty-sixth wedding anniversary of Lilly and Valentin Baranowsky called for a celebration. The couple chose to quietly dine in that night, grilling their favorites on the outdoor grill. Nobody was invited to share in the special moment this year. Instead, solemn comfort welcomed them as they relished their many years of marriage together. Lilly would also be celebrating her 75th birthday on October 5th.

Why do you suppose God allowed us to survive back there in Lille, when so very many other's lives were taken, Valentin? Do you suppose it is just a matter of circumstance? Or do you believe God has every life planned out in advance for each of us? Do you suppose accidents and wars, illnesses and diseases, simply take life on a whim? Or has God planned life this way?

Valentin had no reply for Lilly. He wasn't sure he wanted to know himself. *Let that be known by none other than our Lord Himself, Lilly. If He wanted us to know that answer, He would allow it. Simple as that my dear ... Simple as that.*

I suppose you're right my love! Lilly softly replied with a far-away look in her eyes.

November 6th was a day to look forward to. Tessa Lynn Thuringer, the charming daughter of Lorraine and Fame, was to be married. Several members of the family had reservations to fly in for a long weekend of celebratory festivities. Katya, Bryan and Christian would stay in Lorraine and Fame's guest bedroom. The condominium provided the disabled access into the home and bathroom with ease. This had been an important detail when choosing their winter home. The van they drove could also accommodate their grandson's wheelchair.

Valentin and Lilly's guest bedroom would be filled along with their living room quarters. Most would be flying into Sky Harbor Airport on Thursday and a few on Friday. The wedding, taking place on Saturday afternoon, was planned outdoors, with a reception following on the same grounds.

Tessa's dearest sister, Tiffany Sheri, would be her maid of honor. Lilacs were her preferred choice of flowers, but with the wedding in November, it was impossible to fulfill her wish. In their place, an abundance of lavender would fill the air with the much desired fragrance.

Excitement grew with each passing hour on Friday and Saturday. Although Valentin and Lilly had witnessed a great amount of weddings over the years, including those of their children, this one in particular, aptly brought about memories of their own wedding in Paris.

The setting ironically held similarities to that of Aunt Melanie's courtyard. Ceramic statues of maidens were surrounded by lush greenery, creating an oasis of sorts in the midst of the desert.

Most immediate family members were arriving from out of state. As they arrived, Lilly became lost in thoughts of yesteryear. She recalled her own excitement when Aunt Chantelle and Valentin's sisters, Greta and Emma, arrived in Paris.

Warm sentiment engulfed Valentin and Lilly when Tessa first stepped out, walking down the path to exchange lifetime vows. The yards of satin that adorned her were amazingly reminiscent of her own wedding gown so many years ago. How could she expect anything less after witnessing the grand setting in which they'd chosen to exchange their vows.

This was, once again, God's reminder of their own blissful wedding day in late September of 1945. Lilly wondered if Valentin sensed the sameness of the weddings. As she was about to comment on it, he softly squeezed her hand while the minister inquired who would be giving this woman away.

Yes, Lilly! It is indeed very reminiscent of our own wedding. I loved you so much then, I didn't think any man could love a woman more than I loved you. And here we are, fifty-six years later, still in love. Only now, my love for you is tenfold

Tears formed in Lilly's eyes as she thanked God for the best treasure he had ever bestowed upon her. Not a single soul at the wedding had been present to witness their own perfect day in Paris, so very far in the past. Yet, it seemed like yesterday.

With the memories of September 11th still fresh in the minds of all, a special toast was made by Fame and Lorraine in remembrance of those who had perished on American soil that day. An appreciation of their previously assumed freedoms had been challenged, keeping it in the forefront of American's minds. Hopefully, forever. But we all know how pain fades over time. Sometimes it's for the best, and sometimes not. In this case, it is something that should remain solid in the mind of every American forever.

Tessa and her new husband were surprised with a round trip ticket to Paris by Valentin and Lilly for a wedding gift. It was well known by all the Baranowsky siblings and their children, the villa on the French Riviera was available for use at any time, thanks to the generosity of Madeleine DeMornais Thuringer.

* * * * *

A year after their wedding, Tessa and her husband Jeff, relocated out of state to Colorado Springs, Colorado. Another year later, Tiffany accepted a much sought after position in Paris in the fashion design world. She maintained an apartment in Surprise, Arizona near her grandparent's winter home.

Lilly and Tiffany spent endless hours discussing France. It warmed Lilly's heart that one of the children had, at least, frequent business dealing in Paris. It gave Lilly extreme pleasure listening to the stories of gay ole Paris and the fashion world. How her mother had adored fashion. Lilly had made it a point to take good care of Madeleine's vintage hats.

During the summer of 2004, Lilly had been outdoors watering her flowers. The summer was especially pleasant and she thrived on spending time with her many grandchildren and great-grandchildren. Since her mother's death, Lilly fondly paid special attention to the pots of flowers adorning her deck. How Madeleine loved to display a brilliance of colors in the warmer months. A longtime neighbor came walking up the driveway carrying what appeared to be letters. Yes, it was Bruce taking his daily walk. He'd kindly removed their mail as the carrier drove away, delivering it in person to Lilly.

Courage Times Three. A Novel

After a quick chat, Lilly sent him on foot in the direction of her husband, in the garage tinkering with something or another. Finding Valentin, they struck up a conversation about everything and anything. Lilly could overhear the hearty laughter echoing from inside.

Tomorrow Fame and Lorraine, along with several members of the family, would join them for the Independence Day celebration. Earlier in the morning, however, they would attend the parade followed by a massive town gathering on the Main Street. This was a holiday that attracted years of alma mater from Eveleth High School, a unique opportunity to reminisce with out-of-towners who were rarely seen anymore. Eveleth featured a clown band every year for as long as Valentin and Lilly could remember. A grand celebration highlighted by the band for hours following the parade was always enjoyed.

Everyone piled into their cars after their visits and headed to Long Lake to spend the day boating, water skiing, riding jet skis and swimming. This year, the sun shone brilliantly upon them throughout the day. Tired children struggled to stay awake, enjoying the fireworks display over the lake after dark. Tummies were filled with grilled burgers, bratwurst and hot dogs. Salads, fresh fruits and vegetables, along with scrumptious desserts remained available for munching throughout the day.

Dr. Gustav Dietrich and wife never missed a summer holiday on Long Lake after becoming acquainted with Lilly and Valentin years earlier. Another festive holiday was spent together by this close knit family. Lilly always missed her mother's presence as the years passed. Had it not been for her generosity on so many occasions, it was entirely possible they would not be sharing life together now as they were. Thoughts of her father, Jon Paul DeMornais, held a special place in her heart as well. Not only had she been blessed with an adoring father in her younger years, she'd also received the warmth and love of a stepfather from Harold Thuringer.

The summer provided the Baranowsky's with additional memories. Times spent with the great grandchildren were most enjoyed by the aging couple now. Seeing the characteristics and mannerisms of their own parents in the little ones, always amazed Lilly. And she had a keen eye for recognizing it. Valentin spent many hours competing in horseshoe games with neighbors, church friends, and others.

Late July and early August provided buckets of berries canned to bring to the southwest with them for the winter. With such pleasant weather conditions throughout the summer, they intended to remain in Minnesota until mid October.

September ushered in the most beautiful of seasons to them. The vast array of colors never ceased to impress all residents and travelers alike. Frequent drives to Lake Vermilion and Ely, Minnesota filled them with vastly tantalizing colors each autumn. Valentin had taken more than one fishing or hunting trip to the Boundary Waters Canoe Area, north of them. This was an area separating the U.S. from Canada, spanning a lengthy distance. A wildlife preserve, void of any boats or machinery with motors, provided endless hours of hunting and fishing. for men and women from around the country and Canada. Beautiful, untouched, vast lands of wildlife, rushing rapids, serene rivers and lakes accenting densely wooded countryside were enjoyed by those who chartered her waters and hiked her terrain. It is that special place, God's country, where man can touch base with his inner self, next to nature, allowing him to reach far into the depths of his soul.

Valentin had grown beyond the age of good enough health to pursue that adventure now, leaving it to younger generations of Baranowsky's to enjoy.

A casual season's-end boat ride on the waters of Long Lake enchanted the couple before needing to remove it from the water for the winter months. One side of the two-stall garage housed the boat, keeping it in tip-top shape for next year's use. Valentin spit shined the interior and exterior every autumn before tucking her away. The motor was filled with anti-freeze to endure the cold temperatures of winter, preventing any freeze damage it might sustain otherwise.

The drive to Arizona would once again be shared with Fame and Lorraine. They had all come to cherish this special time together each year, traveling to and returning from Arizona.

Lilly had a restless night's sleep on their last night in the cottage. Something didn't seem right. She couldn't put her finger on it though. For hours she tossed and turned, begging the nighttime to take her into a deep slumber.

With daylight approaching, Valentin awoke, rubbing his eyes to clear his vision. As he stretched and yawned he looked at Lilly to see if he had aroused her from her sleep. His inability to awaken her led him to get the coffee started himself, followed by a shower and shave. He would let her sleep a bit longer if she needed it. Usually Lilly was the first to rise and shine with the morning sun.

After dressing, Valentin added a dab of cologne to his shirt as he had done for years. It was time to awaken his lovely sleeping wife. Kissing her on the cheek, he softly whispered a "Good Morning" into her ear.

How many times had he awakened to her beautiful smile, her soft words of endearment, as she greeted him each morning? *It's time to rouse that body out of bed Mr. DuBois!* she would teasingly say. She knew that was always enough to get a reaction out of him. But this morning, she uttered no words. Valentin gave her a few moments to come to life. Returning to the bedroom, he once again attempted to awaken her.

Lilly, Lilly wake up! Finally Lilly began to stir. Her fluttering eyelids struggled to open. *There you are my dear wife. I thought for a moment you may not wake up.* Valentin patiently sat on the edge of the bed next to Lilly. We have a road trip ahead of us Mrs. Baranowsky.

Lilly put a smile on her face when seeing her loving husband at her bedside. Immediately Valentin noticed her smile only stretched across one side of her face. As she sat up, he observed an imbalance in her eyelids. One eye wasn't opening all the way. Lilly rubbed them,, trying to wipe away the night's slumber. Yet, the problem persisted. This concerned Valentin immensely.

As she opened her mouth to speak, the noises she uttered made no sense. Valentin then knew something was definitely wrong with his precious Lilly. Modern medicine had discovered, through advanced research and technologies, that the sooner a stroke victim received the proper care, the better the odds were of a complete recovery. He and Lilly had discussed this very scenario on a few occasions.

Valentin asked Lilly to remain seated on her bed for a short time. She was unaware of her symptoms as of yet. Not wanting to alarm her, but not wanting to take any chances either, Valentin thought it best to be forthright and honest.

Lilly my dear, it looks as though you may have had a mild stroke! Valentin had always been Lilly's rock. He didn't collapse under pressure. If anything, it strengthened him. But he knew time was of the essence.

Valentin wrapped Lilly's bathrobe around her, quickly tying the belt. He then slid her feet into her slippers before picking her up and carrying her out to their 2005 Chrysler 300. Gently placing her into the front seat, he reached over to secure her seatbelt in place. Scurrying around the vehicle he readied himself in his own belt, all the while keeping a close watch on any changes in Lilly's appearance.

For the most part, she had a splitting headache and seemed lethargic and confused. When trying to speak again, her words made little sense. Semi-scrambled words is how he heard it. This put more of a scare in Valentin than he'd expected. Pulling his cell phone from his pocket, he called "911" to notify them of his wife's emergency. It was agreed that two marked police cars would escort him through the city to the medical center. They would also notify the Emergency room of their approaching arrival.

Panic was rearing its ugly head in his direction. He knew he could not afford to lose his stamina just now. He pressed the #2 on the speed dial of his cell phone, a direct connection with Famous and Lorraine. Upon the second ring, Lorraine answered with a chipper voice. *Good morning my dear brother ... are you ready for a road trip?*

Valentin spoke softly and clearly into the phone. He didn't want to alarm Lilly, so he must be wise in his choice of words and tone of voice.

Lorraine, we are on our way to the Virginia Regional Medical Center. Lilly isn't doing well this morning. It would be much appreciated if the two of you could meet us in the Emergency Room as soon as possible. I'll be waiting for you. I'll fill you in on the details when you arrive. I love you! Then he closed the phone, replacing it into his pocket.

He could see the flashing red lights of the two police escorts in the distance as he rounded the corner of Highway 53. He wasn't planning on slowing down for a second so they'd best be prepared to jump in line alongside him he thought.

Courage Times Three. A Novel

These police officers had escorted more than one vehicle to the emergency room in their careers. As if having rehearsed it, they instantly fell into succession, one ahead of him and one behind, at a rapid rate of speed. He was pleased with his decision to notify the authorities. They were definitely safer this way, including other travelers on the roads.

He was smoothly escorted to the ER entrance where medical staff awaited them. Like clockwork, Lilly was placed onto a stretcher, with no time being wasted. Valentin ran alongside the stretcher, answering the barrage of questions being tossed his way to the best of his ability.

A flock of medical staff emerged through the doors to offer their assistance. It was explained to Valentin that the most common and challenging difficulty a stroke victim must deal with is loss of movement. He was told her complications could range from trouble doing normal activity, such as cooking and cleaning, to a total inability to walk. It appeared her stroke, at this time, seemed to be on the milder side, but they had numerous tests to run before they could confirm that. The most positive statement was that the situation wasn't hopeless and many therapies were now available to improve physical abilities.

Valentin felt pleased with the staff and their timely response to his precious Lilly's needs. Somebody was available to answer, to their best ability, his many questions. Following an exam and blood draws, Lilly was wheeled into the Imaging Department for an MRI scan.

Julie! Her name was Julie! Valentin's mother's name was Rosalie, but his father often referred to her as Julie. For some odd reason this placed him in a comfort zone he didn't quite understand. She was the caregiver who would perform Lilly's MRI.

Julie thoughtfully took the time to assure Valentin no pain was involved and the scanner was top-of-the-line. She explained most magnets in the local area were 1.5 teals, but the magnet strength of this machine doubled the strength of most. This meant they could achieve a more advanced assessment with higher quality, finer resolution than others. The best news was that it excelled at neurologic applications like brains and spinal cords, which is exactly what Lilly needed.

Valentin excused himself while Lilly was being tested. He walked straight out the door to place a call to Lorraine's cell phone. Just as the phone connection was made, his sister and husband pulled into the parking lot.

Lorraine was beside herself with worry. Her brother hadn't shared a single word with her of Lilly's specific medical situation, so she had no idea what to expect.

Valentin dug deep into his pant pocket for loose change. He desperately needed a cup of coffee. Not that he wasn't already wound up tight enough to explode in a moment. The flurry of excitement had taken its toll on him. He wasn't a youngster anymore and was definitely feeling it at the time.

He pushed the buttons on the coffee machine, indicating he would like cream added to it. While tending to his caffeine needs, he explained what had occurred from the time he'd tried to awaken her just a couple of hours earlier.

Valentin asked Lorraine and Fame to be seated for a short time while he returned to the imaging department to see Lilly again. He would be back with word as soon as possible. He wrapped his arms around Fame first, followed by a lengthier hug to his sister. If anybody knew how intense Valentin's love was for Lilly, it was this couple. So much of their lives had been spent together as adults. They assured Valentin all would be well. Their prayers hadn't gone to the wayside. Lorraine expressed the need to notify her brother's daughters, Tia, Rhonda, Robin and Barbara. Fame suggested they wait just a while longer until some results were received before placing those calls that could only instill panic. They knew Lilly was in good hands and all would be done for her now that could be.

The MRI results revealed precisely what they needed to know. Lilly had a cerebral aneurysm. The medical information the doctor was sharing with Valentin, Lorraine and Fame was mind boggling. The news was not good, yet consequently better than it could have been.

Due to the large size of the aneurysm their recommendation was to go into the brain to place a clip on the vessel and reroute the tiny vein in her brain. It was determined it likely was a familial or hereditary situation of which Lilly had no control over. If the surgeon waited to go in, the odds of it bursting beforehand increased by the hour.

Courage Times Three. A Novel

Lilly already began to normalize. On a positive note, the odds of her having received any permanent brain damage had been nearly 100% eliminated. Those odds could change momentarily, however, forever altering her future.

The decision was made, with Lilly's approval, allowing the doctors to go ahead with the surgery. Lorraine and Fame received permission to contact the girls immediately. Traveling plans were postponed until a later date. Life for the Baranowsky's was put on hold temporarily. Only one thing mattered right now and that was the care of Lilly May. Wife, mother, grandmother, great-grandmother, sister-in-law, niece, aunt and friend. Yes, Lilly was someone extraordinarily special to so very many people.

Surgery was scheduled for 3pm that very afternoon. Valentin hadn't left Lilly's side since she'd regained her mental abilities. He could see the fear in her eyes, all the while putting on a facade of his own to remove whatever fear from her he possibly could. When Lilly tried to discuss the necessary arrangements he would need to take in the event of her death, he flat-out refused to hear a single word of it.

Please hear me out Valentin Baranowsky. Any time surgery is performed there is a possibility it could take a negative turn.

Her words were futile in that he adamantly denied her any opportunity for open discussion. It wasn't as if they hadn't already dotted every "i" and crossed every "t" when it came to their living wills or final instructions in the event of either of their deaths. Valentin knew, with every breath, Lilly would survive this surgery, providing several upcoming years together.

Barbara was the first of Lilly's children to arrive at the medical center. Robin and Rhonda would have to make the drive from Minneapolis. Just a short drive of two-and-a-half hours would get them to their dear mother's side. All remained in steady prayer asking God to grant Lilly His grace, preventing the aneurysm from bursting before being surgically addressed.

All family members were contacted, asking for their prayers in Lilly's time of need. This strong Christian family knew the meaning of prayer. They also knew God's grace would be granted if it was ultimately of His choosing. They could only ask He allow Lilly to remain in their lives for some time too.

Chapter Twenty-Six

Good afternoon Lilly. It looks like we have to get a few things rearranged in you today. The mild mannered neurosurgeon smiled upon Lilly, taking her hand ever so gently. The entire staff had prepared her for the surgery in a timely and well rehearsed fashion. Lilly felt a sense of calm, knowing she was in such good hands.

Valentin led the family members, all fourteen of them, in prayer. They reverently requested God to guide the hand of the surgeon throughout Lilly's procedure. A profound acknowledgement was included in the prayer identifying God as the only one who knew Lilly's future at this time. They were putting her care in His hands entirely.

After what seemed to be an eternity in waiting for some word on her well being, the surgeon entered the lobby. Relentless inquisitions began emerging from the mouths of many. Valentin immediately stood. He searched the surgeons eyes in desperation to find a glimmer of hope in them. He didn't know if he was prepared to hear what was about to be said. With hands still folded in prayer, he listened intently.

Mr. Baranowsky, your wife, Lilly, withstood the surgery extremely well. We were able to close off the bleed successfully and re-route the vessel in her brain. She is a strong and healthy woman who should see many good years yet in her lifetime.

Hands flew into the air with shouts of joy and relief, thanking God for another of His many blessings. Valentin firmly shook the hand of the skilled surgeon, praising him relentlessly for his abilities in saving his wife's life. The surgeon briefed him in on the follow up care she would require, which was minimal in her case.

Valentin and his four daughters were allowed to see Lilly in the post surgical room for only a few short minutes. The pastor of their church had been notified by Katya as soon as they'd received word of Lilly's life-threatening circumstances. He, too, was allowed access upon the request of her family.

The constant flow of floral bouquets continued to arrive. Lilly's private room was filled with best regards and wishes for a speedy recovery from family, neighbors, sisters and brothers in Christ and other friends. If one hadn't known the intensity of her situation, they might have wondered why Lilly was even hospitalized.

Not a sign of a problem was evident. Lilly chattered away as though she hadn't a problem in the world. Valentin only left Lilly's side when he was instructed to leave at night. He would arrive back at the medical center before even being allowed to see her. He would use that time to inquire into her well being during night, seeing how she had faired.

My dearest Lilly! What a scare you gave me. My life simply could not go on without you my precious one. Valentin held Lilly's hand, kissing her face exactly the same way he had that first day in the underground newspaper office. Both his and Lilly's minds raced back to that date in time, a time when new love had just been realized.

How blessed we have been my dearest Valentin. If this had occurred even one day later, we would have been on the road and who knows what the outcome would have been.

Yes, yes indeed Lilly! We have been blessed. Valentin walked over to the window of Lilly's room as he heard the siren blaring, the paramedics delivering another patient in dire need of medical care. Another life, perhaps hanging by a string. He wondered who the unfortunate souls were that might possibly be losing their loved one, just as he had wondered a few days beforehand.

Lilly was released into the care of her loving husband just days after nearly losing her life, or the quality of life she had come to take for granted. Not that things would change much after this life-threatening occurrence for Lilly. Her heart was always in the right place. Never did she place her needs ahead of others. She would continue to eat wisely, get her proper exercise, and worship the Lord as she'd always done. One thing Lilly was definitely sure of, however, was that she wanted to spend every Spring in the French

Riviera from now on. A place where love had blossomed and re-blossomed for her mother and herself.

Lorraine and Famous had postponed their travels to the Valley of the Sun in Arizona until Lilly was fully able to sustain the drive. Another family gathering took place in the home of the Thuringers in Duluth before leaving. Precious home-made family gifts were bestowed upon Lilly and Valentin, the endearing and loving couple who had given so much guidance and care to the many youngsters.

Lilly and Valentin continued living happy and healthy lives for years to come. Lorraine and Famous were blessed with extremely good health as well, enabling them to travel not only the endless miles of countryside within North America, but in Europe as well.

God brought the Baranowsky's together at a time when merely having a few morsels of bread to sustain them was a daily struggle. He filled their lives with more joy and peace than they ever felt deserving of. Throughout their struggles and rewards in life, never did they fail to include Him in their day. Whether it be prayers of thanks, or requests for patience, guidance, wisdom, or anything they would need to carry them through.

Lorraine and Fame had joyfully been involved in the lives of her younger sisters and their families, as well as the raising of their adoptive daughters, Tessa and Tiffany. The bond that had formed between themselves and the Baranowsky's was impenetrable. Lorraine often looked back on her life, appreciating every opportunity she'd had, embracing all she'd been provided. God had known well ahead of time that two beautiful and needy children would cherish her love and mothering. She felt His warm embrace many times over, erasing any hurt and pain she'd been forced to endure in her younger years.

Madeleine DeMornais Thuringer provided unending opportunities for her own family and extended families. She found her true identity after losing her false sense of security in another human being, Jon Paul DeMornais. She came to recognize she needed to make God number one in her life. Only He could provide her with the infinite security that would carry her through life's tragedies.

This wisdom was passed on to the endless line of young ones, teaching them to embrace His love in order to fulfill their many needs. What more could one ask for, living in the land of milk and honey.

The courage and tenacity of these three strong women, Lilly, Madeleine and Lorraine, would positively impact endless others in life.

Today, and every day, we need to be reminded of the daily treasures we receive. Even if it's simply another day to witness the rising of the sun, one more time. Or the moon rising in the vast darkness of the skies, one more time. Most importantly, we need to be reminded of God's never ending love and the security He will never fail to provide. All we need do is believe. Just believe!

HOYT LAKES PUBLIC LIBRARY
206 KENNEDY MEMORIAL DRIVE
HOYT LAKES MN 55750

About The Author

Widowed at age 25, I was left to raise two young daughters alone. Withstanding other major tragedies at a young age taught me much about life. Raised a small town girl in northern Minnesota I escaped to new and exciting destinations for several years throughout my lifetime. A first time author, I've lived with chronic illnesses for nine years which developed from carbon monoxide poisoning, preventing me from providing a living for myself. I spent a generous amount of time while bedridden, creating this story. As often the story goes, when we hit bottom we might then turn to God. I was already a born-again Christian. However, the depth of my Christian walk grew tremendously, teaching me how to appreciate all I had in life. Jesus performed miracles in my life and I received the peace and joy that can only truly come from our Heavenly Father. I met and married a wonderful Christian man in 2011. We fill a void in each other's lives which is centered entirely on the Lord. God continues to provide us with His gentle love.

Made in the USA
Charleston, SC
28 October 2013